SCIENCE FICTION GEMS

Volume 4

JACK SHARKEY
and others

Edited by
GREGORY LUCE and LEANNE WRAY

ARMCHAIR FICTION
PO Box 4369, Medford, Oregon 97504

For more information about Armchair Books and products, visit our website at...

www.armchairfiction.com

Or email us at...

armchairfiction@yahoo.com

WHAT WOULD IT BE LIKE TO:

Have a computer decide not only your name, but what your life's vocation and social status should be?

Or…
Have a computer so advanced it is able to relay data directly to your senses, leaving nothing out—no room for doubt, no room for misunderstanding?

Or…
Witness the annihilation of an entire planet? To watch the destruction of a simple and symbiotic species due to Man's own cavalier egotism and his often unacknowledged ignorance?

This, my friend, is the book you are looking for! A barrage of yesteryear's greatest authors to entertain, challenge and enlighten the world of any Science Fiction fan—young or old.

TABLE OF CONTENTS

The Jupiter Weapon

By CHARLES L. FONTENAY

He was a living weapon of destruction—immeasurably powerful, utterly invulnerable. There was only one question: Was he human?

TRELLA feared she was in for trouble even before Motwick's head dropped forward on his arms in a drunken stupor. The two evil-looking men at the table nearby had been watching her surreptitiously, and now they shifted restlessly in their chairs.

Trella had not wanted to come to the Golden Satellite. It was a squalid saloon in the rougher section of Jupiter's View, the terrestrial dome-colony on Ganymede. Motwick, already, drunk, had insisted.

A woman could not possibly make her way through these streets alone to the better section of town, especially one clad in a silvery evening dress. Her only hope was that this place had a telephone. Perhaps she could call one of Motwick's friends; she had no one on Ganymede she could call a real friend herself.

Tentatively, she pushed her chair back from the table and arose. She had to brush close by the other table to get to the bar. As she did, the dark, slick-haired man reached out and grabbed her around the waist with a steely arm.

Trella swung with her whole body, and slapped him so hard he nearly fell from his chair. As she walked swiftly toward the bar, he leaped up to follow her.

There were only two other people in the Golden Satellite: the fat, mustached bartender and a short, square-built man at the bar. The latter swung around at the pistol-like report of her slap, and she saw that, though no more than four and a half feet tall, he was as heavily muscled as a lion.

His face was clean and open, with close-cropped blond hair and honest blue eyes. She ran to him.

"Help me!" she cried. "Please help me!"

He began to back away from her.

"I can't," he muttered in a deep voice. "I can't help you. I can't do anything."

5

The dark man was at her heels. In desperation, she dodged around the short man and took refuge behind him. Her protector was obviously unwilling, but the dark man, faced with his massiveness, took no chances. He stopped and shouted:

"Kregg!"

The other man at the table arose, ponderously, and lumbered toward them. He was immense, at least six and a half feet tall, with a brutal, vacant face.

Evading her attempts to stay behind him, the squat man began to move down the bar away from the approaching Kregg. The dark man moved in on Trella again as Kregg overtook his quarry and swung a huge fist like a sledgehammer.

Exactly what happened, Trella wasn't sure. She had the impression that Kregg's fist connected squarely with the short man's chin *before* he dodged to one side in a movement so fast it was a blur. But that couldn't have been, because the short man wasn't moved by that blow that would have felled a steer, and Kregg roared in pain, grabbing his injured fist.

"The bar!" yelled Kregg. "I hit the damn bar!"

At this juncture, the bartender took a hand. Leaning far over the bar, he swung a full bottle in a complete arc. It smashed on Kregg's head, splashing the floor with liquor, and Kregg sank stunned to his knees. The dark man, who had grabbed Trella's arm, released her and ran for the door.

Moving agilely around the end of the bar, the bartender stood over Kregg, holding the jagged-edged bottleneck in his hand menacingly.

"Get out!" rumbled the bartender. "I'll have no coppers raiding my place for the likes of you!"

Kregg stumbled to his feet and staggered out. Trella ran to the unconscious Motwick's side.

"That means you, too, lady," said the bartender beside her. "You and your boyfriend get out of here. You oughtn't to have come here in the first place."

"May I help you, Miss?" asked a deep, resonant voice behind her.

She straightened from her anxious examination of Motwick. The squat man was standing there, an apologetic look on his face.

She looked contemptuously at the massive muscles whose help had been denied her. Her arm ached where the dark man had grasped it.

The broad face before her was not unhandsome, and the blue eyes were disconcertingly direct, but she despised him for a coward.

"I'm sorry I couldn't fight those men for you, Miss, but I just couldn't," he said miserably, as though reading her thoughts. "But no one will bother you on the street if I'm with you."

"A lot of protection you'd be if they did!" she snapped. "But I'm desperate. You can carry him to the Stellar Hotel for me."

The gravity of Ganymede was hardly more than that of Earth's moon, but the way the man picked up the limp Motwick with one hand and tossed him over a shoulder was startling: as though he lifted a feather pillow. He followed Trella out the door of the Golden Satellite and fell in step beside her. Immediately she was grateful for his presence. The dimly lighted street was not crowded, but she didn't like the looks of the men she saw.

The transparent dome of Jupiter's View was faintly visible in the reflected night-lights of the colonial city, but the lights were overwhelmed by the giant, vari-colored disc of Jupiter itself, riding high in the sky.

"I'm Quest Mansard, Miss," said her companion. "I'm just in from Jupiter."

"I'm Trella Nuspar," she said, favoring him with a green-eyed glance. "You mean Io, don't you—or Moon Five?"

"No," he said, grinning at her. He had an engaging grin, with even white teeth. "I meant Jupiter."

"You're lying," she said flatly. "No one has ever landed on Jupiter. It would be impossible to blast off again."

"My parents landed on Jupiter, and I blasted off from it," he said soberly. "I was born there. Have you ever heard of Dr. Eriklund Mansard?"

"I certainly have," she said, her interest taking a sudden upward turn. "He developed the surgiscope, didn't he? But his ship was drawn into Jupiter and lost."

"It was drawn into Jupiter, but he landed it successfully," said Quest. "He and my mother lived on Jupiter until the oxygen equipment wore out at last. I was born and brought up there, and I was finally able to build a small rocket with a powerful enough drive to clear the planet."

She looked at him. He was short, half a head shorter than she, but broad and powerful as a man might be who had grown up in heavy gravity. He trod the street with a light, controlled step, seeming to deliberately hold himself down.

"If Dr. Mansard succeeded in landing on Jupiter, why didn't anyone ever hear from him again?" she demanded.

"Because," said Quest, "his radio was sabotaged, just as his ship's drive was."

"Jupiter strength," she murmured, looking him over coolly. "You wear Motwick on your shoulder like a scarf. But you couldn't bring yourself to help a woman against two thugs."

He flushed.

"I'm sorry," he said. "That's something I couldn't help."

"Why not?"

"I don't know. It's not that I'm afraid, but there's something in me that makes me back away from the prospect of fighting anyone."

Trella sighed. Cowardice was a state of mind. It was peculiarly inappropriate, but not unbelievable, that the strongest and most agile man on Ganymede should be a coward. Well, she thought with a rush of sympathy, he couldn't help being what he was.

They had reached the more brightly lighted section of the city now. Trella could get a cab from here, but the Stellar Hotel wasn't far. They walked on.

Trella had the desk clerk call a cab to deliver the unconscious Motwick to his home. She and Quest had a late sandwich in the coffee shop.

"I landed here only a week ago," he told her, his eyes frankly admiring her honey-colored hair and comely face. "I'm heading for Earth on the next spaceship."

"We'll be traveling companions, then," she said. "I'm going back on that ship, too."

For some reason she decided against telling him that the assignment on which she had come to the Jupiter system was to gather his own father's notebooks and take them back to Earth.

Motwick was an irresponsible playboy whom Trella had known briefly on Earth, and Trella was glad to dispense with his company for the remaining three weeks before the spaceship blasted off. She found herself enjoying the steadier companionship of Quest.

As a matter of fact, she found herself enjoying his companionship more than she intended to. She found herself falling in love with him.

Now this did not suit her at all. Trella had always liked her men tall and dark. She had determined that when she married it would be to a curly-haired six-footer.

She was not at all happy about being so strongly attracted to a man several inches shorter than she. She was particularly unhappy about feeling drawn to a man who was a coward.

The ship that they boarded on Moon Nine was one of the newer ships that could attain a hundred-mile-per-second velocity and take a hyperbolic path to Earth, but it would still require fifty-four days to make the trip. So Trella was delighted to find that the ship was the *Cometfire* and its skipper was her old friend, dark-eyed, curly-haired Jakdane Gille.

"Jakdane," she said, flirting with him with her eyes as in days gone by. "I need a chaperon this trip, and you're ideal for the job."

"I never thought of myself in quite that light, but maybe I'm getting old," he answered, laughing. "What's your trouble, Trella?"

"I'm in love with that huge chunk of man who came aboard with me, and I'm not sure I ought to be," she confessed. "I may need protection against myself till we get to Earth."

"If it's to keep you out of another fellow's clutches, I'm your man," agreed Jakdane heartily. "I always had a mind to save you for myself. I'll guarantee you won't have a moment alone with him the whole trip."

"You don't have to be that thorough about it," she protested hastily. "I want to get a little enjoyment out of being in love. But if I feel myself weakening too much, I'll holler for help."

The *Cometfire* swung around great Jupiter in an opening arc and plummeted ever more swiftly toward the tight circles of the inner planets. There were four crewmembers and three passengers aboard the ship's tiny personnel sphere, and Trella was thrown with Quest almost constantly. She enjoyed every minute of it.

She told him only that she was a messenger, sent out to Ganymede to pick up some important papers and take them back to Earth. She was tempted to tell him what the papers were. Her employer had impressed upon her that her mission was confidential, but surely Dom Blessing could not object to Dr. Mansard's son knowing about it. All these things had happened before she was born, and she did not know what Dom Blessing's relation to Dr. Mansard had been, but it must have been very close. She knew that Dr. Mansard had invented the surgiscope.

This was an instrument with a three-dimensional screen as its heart. The screen was a cubical frame in which an apparently solid image was built up of an object under an electron microscope.

The actual cutting instrument of the surgiscope was an ion stream. By operating a tool in the three-dimensional screen, corresponding movements were made by the ion stream on the object under the microscope. The principal was the same as that used in operation of remote control "hands" in atomic laboratories to handle hot material, and with the surgiscope very delicate operations could be performed at the cellular level.

Dr. Mansard and his wife had disappeared into the turbulent atmosphere of Jupiter just after his invention of the surgiscope, and it had been developed by Dom Blessing. Its success had built Spaceway Instruments, Incorporated, which Blessing headed.

Through all these years since Dr. Mansard's disappearance, Blessing had been searching the Jovian moons for a second, hidden laboratory of Dr. Mansard. When it was found at last, he sent Trella, his most trusted secretary, to Ganymede to bring back to him the notebooks found there.

Blessing would, of course, be happy to learn that a son of Dr. Mansard lived, and would see that he received his rightful share of the inheritance. Because of this, Trella was tempted to tell Quest the good news herself; but she decided against it. It was Blessing's privilege to do this his own way, and he might not appreciate her meddling.

At midtrip, Trella made a rueful confession to Jakdane.

"It seems I was taking unnecessary precautions when I asked you to be a chaperon," she said. "I kept waiting for Quest to do something, and when he didn't I told him I loved him."

"What did he say?"

"It's very peculiar," she said unhappily. "He said he *can't* love me. He said he wants to love me and he feels that he should, but there's something in him that refuses to permit it."

She expected Jakdane to salve her wounded feelings with a sympathetic pleasantry, but he did not. Instead, he just looked at her very thoughtfully and said no more about the matter.

He explained his attitude after Asrange ran amuck.

Asrange was the third passenger. He was a lean, saturnine individual who said little and kept to himself as much as possible. He was distantly polite in his relations with both crew and other passengers, and never showed the slightest spark of emotion...until the day Quest squirted coffee on him.

It was one of those accidents that can occur easily in space. The passengers and the two crewmen on that particular waking shift (including Jakdane) were eating lunch on the center-deck. Quest picked up his bulb of coffee, but inadvertently pressed it before he got it to his lips. The coffee squirted all over the front of Asrange's clean white tunic.

"I'm sorry!" exclaimed Quest in distress.

The man's eyes went wide and he snarled. So quickly it seemed impossible, he had unbuckled himself from his seat and hurled himself backward from the table with an incoherent cry. He seized the first object his hand touched—it happened to be a heavy wooden cane leaning against Jakdane's bunk—and propelled himself like a projectile at Quest.

Quest rose from the table in a sudden uncoiling of movement. He did not unbuckle his safety belt—he rose and it snapped like a string.

For a moment Trella thought he was going to meet Asrange's assault. But he fled in a long leap toward the companionway leading to the astrogation deck above. Landing feet-first in the middle of the table and rebounding, Asrange pursued with the stick upraised.

In his haste, Quest missed the companionway in his leap and was cornered against one of the bunks. Asrange descended on him like an avenging angel and, holding onto the bunk with one hand, rained savage blows on his head and shoulders with the heavy stick.

Quest made no effort to retaliate. He cowered under the attack, holding his hands in front of him as if to ward it off. In a moment, Jakdane and the other crewman had reached Asrange and pulled him off.

When they had Asrange in irons, Jakdane turned to Quest, who was now sitting unhappily at the table.

"Take it easy," he advised. "I'll wake the psychosurgeon and have him look you over. Just stay there."

Quest shook his head.

"Don't bother him," he said. "It's nothing but a few bruises."

"Bruises? Man, that club could have broken your skull! Or a couple of ribs, at the very least."

"I'm all right," insisted Quest; and when the skeptical Jakdane insisted on examining him carefully, he had to admit it. There was hardly a mark on him from the blows.

"If it didn't hurt you any more than that, why didn't you take that stick away from him?" demanded Jakdane. "You could have, easily."

"I couldn't," said Quest miserably, and turned his face away.

Later, alone with Trella on the control deck, Jakdane gave her some sober advice.

"If you think you're in love with Quest, forget it," he said.

"Why? Because he's a coward? I know that ought to make me despise him, but it doesn't any more."

"Not because he's a coward. Because he's an android!"

"What? Jakdane, you can't be serious!"

"I am. I say he's an android, an artificial imitation of a man. It all figures.

"Look, Trella, he said he was born on Jupiter. A human could stand the gravity of Jupiter, inside a dome or a ship, but what human could stand the rocket acceleration necessary to break free of Jupiter? Here's a man strong enough to break a spaceship safety belt just by getting up out of his chair against it, tough enough to take a beating with a heavy stick without being injured. How can you believe he's really human?"

Trella remembered the thug Kregg striking Quest in the face and then crying that he had injured his hand on the bar.

"But he said Dr. Mansard was his father," protested Trella.

"Robots and androids frequently look on their makers as their parents," said Jakdane. "Quest may not even know he's artificial. Do you know how Mansard died?"

"The oxygen equipment failed, Quest said."

"Yes. Do you know when?"

"No, Quest never did tell me, that I remember."

"He told me: a year before Quest made his rocket flight to Ganymede. If the oxygen equipment failed, how do you think *Quest* lived in the poisonous atmosphere of Jupiter, if he's human?"

Trella was silent.

"For the protection of humans, there are two psychological traits built into every robot and android," said Jakdane gently. "The first is that they can never, under any circumstances, attack a human being, even in self defense. The second is that, while they may understand sexual desire objectively, they can never experience it themselves.

"Those characteristics fit your man Quest to a T, Trella. There is no other explanation for him: he must be an android."

Trella did not want to believe Jakdane was right, but his reasoning was unassailable. Looking upon Quest as an android, many things were explained: his great strength, his short, broad build, his immunity to injury, his refusal to defend himself against a human, his inability to return Trella's love for him.

It was not inconceivable that she should have unknowingly fallen in love with an android. Humans could love androids, with real affection, even knowing that they were artificial. There were instances of android nursemaids who were virtually members of the families owning them.

She was glad now that she had not told Quest of her mission to Ganymede. He thought he was Dr. Mansard's son, but an android had no legal right of inheritance from his owner. She would leave it to Dom Blessing to decide what to do about Quest.

Thus she did not, as she had intended originally, speak to Quest about seeing him again after she had completed her assignment. Even if Jakdane was wrong and Quest was human—as now seemed unlikely—Quest had told her he could not love her. Her best course was to try to forget him.

Nor did Quest try to arrange with her for a later meeting.

"It has been pleasant knowing you, Trella," he said when they left the G-boat at White Sands. A faraway look came into his blue eyes, and he added: "I'm sorry things couldn't have been different, somehow."

"Let's don't be sorry for what we can't help," she said gently, taking his hand in farewell.

Trella took a fast plane from White Sands, and twenty-four hours later walked up the front steps of the familiar brownstone house on the outskirts of Washington.

Dom Blessing himself met her at the door, a stooped, graying man who peered at her over his spectacles.

"You have the papers, eh?" he said, spying the brief case. "Good, good. Come in and we'll see what we have, eh?"

She accompanied him through the bare, windowless anteroom which had always seemed to her such a strange feature of this luxurious house, and they entered the big living room. They sat before a fire in the old-fashioned fireplace and Blessing opened the brief case with trembling hands.

"There are things here," he said, his eyes sparkling as he glanced through the notebooks. "Yes, there are things here. We shall make something of these, Miss Trella, eh?"

"I'm glad they're something you can use, Mr. Blessing," she said. "There's something else I found on my trip, that I think I should tell you about."

She told him about Quest.

"He thinks he's the son of Dr. Mansard," she finished, "but apparently he is, without knowing it, an android Dr. Mansard built on Jupiter."

"He came back to Earth with you, eh?" asked Blessing intently.

"Yes. I'm afraid it's your decision whether to let him go on living as a man or to tell him he's an android and claim ownership as Dr. Mansard's heir."

Trella planned to spend a few days resting in her employer's spacious home, and then to take a short vacation before resuming her duties as his confidential secretary. The next morning when she came down from her room, a change had been made.

Two armed men were with Dom Blessing at breakfast and accompanied him wherever he went. She discovered that two more men with guns were stationed in the bare anteroom and a guard was stationed at every entrance to the house.

"Why all the protection?" she asked Blessing.

"A wealthy man must be careful," said Blessing cheerfully. "When we don't understand all the implications of new circumstances, we must be prepared for anything, eh?"

There was only one new circumstance Trella could think of. Without actually intending to, she exclaimed:

"You aren't afraid of Quest? Why, an android can't hurt a human!"

Blessing peered at her over his spectacles.

"And what if he isn't an android, eh? And if he is—what if old Mansard didn't build in the prohibition against harming humans that's required by law? What about that, eh?"

Trella was silent, shocked. There was something here she hadn't known about, hadn't even suspected. For some reason, Dom Blessing feared Dr. Eriklund Mansard...or his heir...or his mechanical servant.

She was sure that Blessing was wrong, that Quest, whether man or android, intended no harm to him. Surely, Quest would have said something of such bitterness during their long time together on Ganymede and aspace, since he did not know of Trella's connection with Blessing. But, since this was to be the atmosphere of Blessing's house she was glad that he decided to assign her to take the Mansard papers to the New York laboratory.

Quest came the day before she was scheduled to leave.

Trella was in the living room with Blessing, discussing the instructions she was to give to the laboratory officials in New York. The two bodyguards were with them. The other guards were at their posts.

Trella heard the doorbell ring.

The heavy oaken front door was kept locked now, and the guards in the anteroom examined callers through a tiny window.

Suddenly alarm bells rang all over the house. There was a terrific crash outside the room as the front door splintered. There were shouts and the sound of a shot.

"The steel doors!" cried Blessing, turning white. "Let's get out of here."

He and his bodyguards ran through the back of the house out of the garage.

Blessing, ahead of the rest, leaped into one of the cars and started the engine.

The door from the house shattered and Quest burst through. The two guards turned and fired together.

He could be hurt by bullets. He was staggered momentarily.

Then, in a blur of motion, he sprang forward and swept the guards aside with one hand with such force that they skidded across the floor and lay in an unconscious heap against the rear of the garage. Trella had opened the door of the car, but it was wrenched from her hand as Blessing stepped on the accelerator and it leaped into the driveway with spinning wheels.

Quest was after it, like a chunky deer, running faster than Trella had ever seen a man run before.

Blessing slowed for the turn at the end of the driveway and glanced back over his shoulder. Seeing Quest almost upon him, he slammed down the accelerator and twisted the wheel hard.

The car whipped into the street, careened, and rolled over and over, bringing up against a tree on the other side in a twisted tangle of wreckage.

With a horrified gasp, Trella ran down the driveway toward the smoking heap of metal. Quest was already beside it, probing it. As she reached his side, he lifted the torn body of Dom Blessing. Blessing was dead.

"I'm lucky," said Quest soberly. "I would have murdered him."

"But why, Quest? I knew he was afraid of you, but he didn't tell me why."

"It was conditioned into me," answered Quest. "I didn't know it until just now, when it ended, but my father conditioned me psychologically from my birth to the task of hunting down Dom Blessing and killing him. It was an unconscious drive in me that wouldn't release me until the task was finished.

"You see, Blessing was my father's assistant on Ganymede. Right after my father completed development of the surgiscope, he and my mother blasted off for Io. Blessing wanted the valuable rights to the surgiscope, and he sabotaged the ship's drive so it would fall into Jupiter.

"But my father was able to control it in the heavy atmosphere of Jupiter, and landed it successfully. I was born there, and he conditioned me to come to Earth and track down Blessing. I know now that it was part of the conditioning that I was unable to fight any other man until my task was finished: it might have gotten me in trouble and diverted me from that purpose."

More gently than Trella would have believed possible for his Jupiter-strong muscles, Quest took her in his arms.

"Now I can say I love you," he said. "That was part of the conditioning too: I couldn't love any woman until my job was done."

Trella disengaged herself.

"I'm sorry," she said. "Don't you know this, too, now: that you're not a man, but an android?"

He looked at her in astonishment, stunned by her words.

"What in space makes you think that?" he demanded.

"Why, Quest, it's obvious," she cried, tears in her eyes. "Everything about you...your build, suited for Jupiter's gravity...your strength...the fact that you were able to live in Jupiter's atmosphere after the oxygen equipment failed. I know you think Dr. Mansard was your father, but androids often believe that."

He grinned at her.

"I'm no android," he said confidently. "Do you forget my father was inventor of the surgiscope? He knew I'd have to grow up on Jupiter, and he operated on the genes before I was born. He altered my inherited characteristics to adapt me to the climate of Jupiter...even to being able to breathe a chlorine atmosphere as well as an oxygen atmosphere."

Trella looked at him. He was not badly hurt, any more than an elephant would have been, but his tunic was stained with red blood where the bullets had struck him. Normal android blood was green.

"How can you be sure?" she asked doubtfully.

"Androids are made," he answered with a laugh. "They don't grow up. And I remember my boyhood on Jupiter very well."

He took her in his arms again, and this time she did not resist. His lips were very human.

THE END

Martian Homecoming

By FRANK BELKNAP LONG
(author of "The Miniature Menace")

Through the veils of illusion, and waves of terrible remorse, they set out to slay the deadly creatures...

JIM MALDEN sat with his back to the metal wall of the shack, staring out gloomily into the driving rain. He was huge and hairy-chested, and he sat now with the light of a swollen fire reddening his flesh.

His wife threw another log into the fire and turned with an angry shrug. "Stop brooding, Jim," she complained. "We came to Mars of our own free will. There's nothing on Earth I miss. *Nothing, you hear?*"

"It's all right for you to talk," Jim said. "It don't take so much to make a woman happy. A woman never takes to craving things the way a man does."

"What things?" Mary Malden flared. "We've got a roof over our heads, haven't we? When you broke your hand and had to quit the ring you never talked that way. No, sir! You were mighty grateful for a chance to start over on Mars!"

"What did we get?" Jim grumbled. "A roof over our heads; sure. A settler's grant of five grand. But what else?"

"You dare to ask me that?" Mary raged. "The best years of my life I've given you, Jim Malden. I've slaved and denied myself and gone without—"

"Let's not quarrel, Mary," Jim said, wearily.

He stood up and ran trembling fingers over his calloused, misshapen right fist. He saw again the light-drenched stadium on Earth, his opponent sparring for an opening, the drifting faces of the crowd. He shut his eyes and the bright, splendid vision was gone.

The pinched, gray face of his wife stared at him out of the flickering firelight, her pupils questioning. She was thirty-four, but she looked fifty. Her hair straggled; her cheeks were sallow, and her lips were a tight, thin line.

A sudden tenderness and gratefulness came upon Jim Malden. He went up to her and patted her gently on the shoulder. "You're all right, old girl," he said. "Better get on with the supper now."

"You're a good man, Jim," Mary said, her eyes suddenly moist. "A fine figure of a man. You've been a good husband to me."

"Forget it," Jim said.

"It's the emptiness, the loneliness," Mary said. "I feel it too, Jim—especially at night. We've a colony here; we're all together, warm and friendly like we'd be in a little country town on Earth. But there's a difference too."

"Sure there is," Jim agreed. "The land isn't friendly; that's the big difference. It's just rock and sand, sand and more sand, blowing, drifting around. The canals are either dried up or filled with stagnant water. There's no good, clean moonlight or fresh running water."

Jim Malden forced a grin. "But there's nothing wrong with our neighbors, Mary. No man has a right to fret and complain when he's got a wife like you and good friends to stand by him. It's the folks who make a place, Mary."

"*Listen*," Mary said.

OUTSIDE THE shack there arose a shrill clamor. Running footsteps pattered along the quay and a child's terrified scream drowned out the distant boom of a warning rocket.

Jim rushed to the wall and took down a gun. He looked at his wife his face as grim as death. "You know what that is, Mary," he said. "Promise me you won't go outside."

"Jim, stay here with me," Mary pleaded, her lips white. "You don't have to go. Not this time. You've risked your life more often than the others."

"You mustn't talk that way," Jim said. "I can't shirk my duty."

"But you'll be killed, Jim. This time the dreams will kill you. You've a right to think of me. Oh, can't you see? You've been eating your heart out for Earth, for the old life. Your mind's far away, back on Earth with the cheering crowds. You've been longing for the ring again the way a young man longs for a woman."

"Now Mary—"

"You'll be trapped, Jim! Trapped and killed! It's a sickness with you now and you can't fight it. The Martian beast will get inside your mind and you'll see Earth again, you'll see the ring. You'll be sick and weak, but you won't know how sick."

"I've got to live with myself, Mary! I've got to do my share of the fighting!"

Jim took his wife firmly by the shoulder and drew her back into the warm room with its high-leaping fire. Avoiding her eyes, he walked quickly to the door and threw it open. He walked straight out into the darkness, his huge shoulders squared.

An icy wind lashed his face, tore at his clothes. Up from the dark canal drifted a shimmering cloud as sinister as the barren heart of midnight.

The Martian seemed all eyes. Vicious and furtive, it drifted straight past Jim and then drifted slowly back. Like a great, night-shadowed jellyfish it swirled along the stagnant tide, its eyes shifting about and lighting up its dark bulk.

Far down the village street a woman wailed in torment. She came slowly into view, tottering along the quay, moving like a somnambulist through the shadows. She wheeled suddenly, her face a livid mask of terror.

"Wait!" Jim shouted. "Get back!"

The woman continued to move forward, her hands pressed to her throat. She leapt with a despairing scream into the canal.

Jim heard the splash, saw the Martian sweep forward to wrap itself about her.

White-lipped, Jim raised his gun to his shoulder. As he took careful aim two tall figures emerged from shadows to stand at his side.

Instantly a warm sense of comradeship in danger swept over Jim. The man at his right was lean and sallow, with a gaunt, weather-beaten face. Jim recognized him. Grant Trask, a gentle, scholarly man who had spent his best years teaching school on Earth.

"Careful with your aim, Jim," Trask said. "It's sending out merciless cruel thoughts now—punishing thoughts. But soon it will be making us see the things we want most in life."

"That woman must have done something mighty horrible to throw herself into the canal at the first touch of its mind," Jim muttered.

"Not so horrible, Jim. Just something human she's been trying all these years to hide from herself. Martians can make the pangs of guilt and remorse seem intolerable."

The Martian was in motion again. It was coming closer, swirling up from the canal. Its eyes flashed, and shifted.

Jim blasted. Lightning forked from his gun, brightening the canal.

The Martian horror swirled back, quivered, and swept straight toward the three men like a devouring cloud. "Run for your life, Jim!" Trask shouted. "Run, run!"

Jim turned and ran along the quay. The quay was filling with frightened villagers swarming from their shacks. As another warning rocket boomed Jim halted abruptly, aware of a firm hand on his arm.

"It was a good try, Jim," Trask said.

Jim stared. Far in the distance a dark cloud faintly flecked with light was drifting desertward over the awakened village.

"We'll have to track it down now, Jim," Trask said. "It has the taste of people in its dark mind. It will come back and kill again."

GRANT TRASK knew more than Jim did about the Martians. His insatiable scholar's curiosity had taken him often to the towering ruins in the northeastern desert where a vanished humanoid race had built vast monuments beneath the stars.

Tremendous frescoes covered walls of crumbling stone, their pigments time-defying, gaudy with sun colors. Life on Mars had followed a strange evolutionary pattern. A primitive, amoebic form of intelligent life had survived the evolution of a humanoid race and the rich, exuberant growth of a humanoid culture.

The humanoids had been resourceful, creative, self-reliant; the amoebic life form parasitic and greedy. The amoebic life form, its powers of reproduction weakened by the slow drying up of the

Martian deserts, had preyed on the humanoids in their great stone cities.

Ever more insatiably it had drained the vital energies of the big-brained bipeds who resembled men. The lure it used was a psychic prod, inhuman, unnatural. It could make a man see the fulfillment of all his dreams in a blaze of glory. For thousands of years the humanoids, alone and in groups, driven and fearful, aspiring and maddened, had walked forward into the illusionary blaze of that deeper richer life—to be consumed utterly.

Most of the amoeba forms had succumbed to exhaustion and drought, but a few had lingered on, surviving the dying of the humanoid culture, sleeping for long ages in the desert wastes.

Now Earthmen, coming in rockets from Earth, had awakened them from their long slumber, filled them with a devouring hunger which nothing but death could slake.

The second man who had stood with Jim on the quayside came up, his face flushed with excitement. "No sense in making it a big party, Jim," he said. "We'll take care of it—just the three of us."

Dave Rawson was a big man with a shrewd, small, practical mind. When Martians threatened the village with their strange powers he was always in the forefront of the struggle.

Dave Rawson ran an inn. An innkeeper has to be popular and fearless; an innkeeper has to stand behind a wide bar with his sleeves rolled to his elbows—a jolly, fearless man.

But deep in his heart Dave Rawson was a blackguard. He cheated, lied and beat his wife; he liked to bully lesser colonists, the little men who came and went.

Jim stared into the man's deepset eyes and shrugged. "We'd better get started," he said.

The three men walked down the street and out of the village. Until the houses dwindled, the children followed them, admiring their air of fearlessness. The women watched from doorways with shining eyes. Some of the men made earnest efforts to join the party, but Grant Trask had a quiet, sure way of making his will prevail.

"Next time, George. You've done more than your share of tracking."

"Stay with your wife, Fred. She's ill and needs you."

BEYOND THE town the bleak Martian desert closed in like a flapping shroud. The wind howled and moaned, sending sandballs careening down steep slopes, filling the air with a continuous rustling.

Jim ploughed on with lowered head, dust stinging his nostrils, his gun jogging in the crook of his arm.

"I can't forget there were human beings on Mars once," Trask said. "Big-brained bipeds who walked erect. Builders and dreamers with brain pans as large as ours. They hurled a torch to us from a dead and buried past. They gave us the moral right to carryon the fight."

"We're men," Rawson grunted. "The Martians are crawling blobs of slime. That's enough for me."

"The Martians are as intelligent as we are," Trask said. "They can get inside our minds and make our secret thoughts real, three-dimensional. They can bring back Earth. They can offer men paradise, the forbidden fruit, the lost Eden. If men refuse to eat they can turn the human sense of guilt into a cruel, punishing reality. One way or another, all men, are vulnerable."

"Where do you think it went, Grant?" Jim asked.

"It will seek a deep hollow in the desert," Trask said. "It is sluggish now with death, fat like a grave worm with the life of that tortured woman."

Shadows leapt across the desert, purpled the rolling dunes. On the far horizon a cloud floated, assuming grotesque shapes.

Dawn was breaking over the desert when they found the Martian. It lay in a hundred foot hollow in the tumbled sand, sluggish with its feasting, its eighty eyes almost motionless in the chill light.

The three men descended into the hollow with their guns in readiness, their faces tight and strained. Trask was the calmest of the three. "Don't shoot until we're close," he warned. "We can't afford to miss this time."

Rawson said: "It's watching us. Its eyes—"

Rawson's speech congealed.

Rawson saw a light shine out from the beast. It was white and dazzling. The beast's eyes began to move, to shift about.

As Rawson stared the eyes melted and ran together and became a lake of fire.

"Dave, come back!" Trask shouted. "Dave, in the name of heaven—"

RAWSON WAS already running down into the hollow, his eyes bright with an eagerness such as he had never known. He tossed his gun aside, waved his arms. He ran faster.

Ahead of him the lake of fire brimmed with a rosy radiance. Out of it floated an immense translucent bubble. The bubble was not empty. Within it a woman stirred and opened sleepy eyes.

The woman reclined at full length, her arms extended in voluptuous appeal. She had green cat's eyes, and a mass of tumbled golden hair that encircled her pale face like a garland. Rubies scintillated against her fair skin.

The bubble with its tantalizing burden floated toward Rawson, and the woman looked out at him, and desire rained hot coals on his blood.

He fell to his knees and reached up with both arms as the bubble descended.

"Dave, *get up!* Get to your feet, man! You're looking at nothing, you're staring into vacancy!"

The hands on Dave's arm and shoulder were like steel bands. The hands of Grant Trask.

Rawson swung about with a curse, his eyes red-rimmed. "It's a lie! You want that woman for yourself. Get away from me or I'll kill you!"

"No, Dave," Trask pleaded. "It's an illusion; there's nothing there."

Rawson struck Trask in the face. He gritted his teeth and pivoted away from Trask on his knees. He saw blood run from Trask's mouth over his chin.

He was glad that he had hurt Trask. He could see the bubble again and the woman was still extending her arms toward him.

He got to his feet and staggered forward, his throat parched.

Trask bent and picked up his gun. He followed Rawson patiently, anxiously. He did not think of himself, of his own safety.

The savage blow that he had received meant nothing to him. Safe at home, in the village, he would have lain Rawson out cold.

But now Rawson was walking to his death, and had a claim on him. Friend or enemy; bully, sadist or coward—what did it matter? Rawson was a human being in deadly peril, a man in desperate need of help. Rawson shared with Trask a common humanity. They were both men, facing a threat that was alien to humanity.

JIM HAD seen the struggle and was advancing on the run, his gun raised. "Don't shoot, Jim!" Trask called. "He sees something we can't see! We've got to save him from himself!"

Jim nodded and lowered his gun.

But he still ran on.

Trask caught up with Rawson fifty feet from the Martian. He seized his arm and jerked him about.

"Listen to me, Rawson," he pleaded. "You're following a mirage. The beast has got inside your mind."

Rawson wrenched his arm free, his lips shaking. *"That's a lie. She's beautiful and I'll hold her in my arms if I die for it!* She's singing to me. Can't you hear her?"

"There's nothing but empty desert ahead of us, Dave."

"You want her for yourself. I've warned you before. Now—"

Rawson lurched suddenly. He grabbed Trask's wrist and twisted it viciously.

Rawson wrenched the gun from Trask's hand and gave him a shove. As Trask went reeling backward Rawson raised the gun to his shoulder and took careful aim.

Rawson fired, putting bullet after bullet into Trask, spinning him about and hurling him to the ground.

The desert sand spurted up about Trask sinking down in a red welter. Horror and pity looked for an instant out of Trask's glazing eyes. He fell forward upon his face, twisted convulsively; he lay still.

White with rage, Rawson crouched low as the sunlight threw a filmy haze between his reeling senses and the dead man.

He saw Jim coming toward him through the glare, armed and furious.

"Stay back. Jim!" Rawson warned. "Don't come any closer."

"I'm going to kill you, Rawson," Jim said. "You shot Trask down in cold blood. He was the best friend you'll ever have, and you shot him dead."

"Stay where you are, Jim! I warn you!"

Jim's face hardened.

He was about to squeeze the trigger of his gun when something in the desert between Rawson and the Martian stayed his hand. A flickering and a whirling, a deepening of the shadows which surrounded the Martian.

The shadows became vertical shafts of darkness in a matter of seconds. They converged and became a solid, moving wall closing in about Rawson.

Rawson turned with a startled cry.

The wall was circular and it swept in upon Rawson and embraced him from three sides. He was caught in a dark, circular trap, which loomed swiftly up above him in chill and dripping darkness.

The walls of a prison courtyard, the stones mottled and unyielding.

Rawson began to shake.

Far off in the dawn a bell tolled.

Rawson recoiled, his back to the wall of the courtyard, a convulsive horror in his stare.

A cold wind blew across the desert, stirring the sand at his feet. Around the edge of the wall came a procession of guards, walking slowly and two abreast.

The rising sun hid behind a cloud.

"*No, no, I don't want to die!*" Rawson screamed.

He dropped to his knees in pleading despair as the procession halted directly in front of him. A dark figure in the uniform of a prison warden spoke sharply.

"Get up! Must we help you to walk?"

Rawson cowered back against the wall, pleading, screaming.

Two guards stepped forward and took hold of him. They dragged him to his feet.

The walls of the prison swept away into chill, gray distances.

The electric chair loomed out of shadows, wrapped in a pale blue light.

Rawson was dragged screaming to the chair and strapped in.

Rawson shook his head in dazed horror and saw that he was walking straightforward into a blinding light. He was not condemned after all. His conscience had deceived him. He had murdered Trask, but the Justice of Earth could not touch him. On Mars—

The eyes of the Martian shifted about in the chill dawn as it moved forward to enfold Rawson. Its amoeba-like bulk flowed over him in hideous, greedy folds.

JIM STOOD motionless, his lips white, the gun still at his shoulder.

He had seen Rawson back away from him, and then rush straight toward the Martian with a scream of terror. He now saw Rawson disappear. He could only guess at the reason for the mad act. But now a great white glow came from the Martian. It swept toward Jim like the waves of an advancing sea. Out of the whiteness came voices, faces, a turbulent tide of moving, shouting people.

Jim sucked in his breath.

The great stadium loomed before him, bathed in dazzling light.

Jim looked down over himself. He saw a firm-fleshed torso, black tights, the legs of a younger man. Far off in the glow he saw the ring, a figure he knew standing in one corner waiting for him.

With a shout he moved forward between the crowds, pushing his way down the aisle, a surge of strength and pride mounting in him. His manager came toward him, slapped him soundly on the back.

"Jim, Jim lad. He's a pushover, Jim! The championship's in the bag, Jim! Go in there, son, and let him have it! Hear those cheers? They're all for you, Jim boy, all for you."

Light, excitement, joy, pride in a man's own strength. The crowds shouting, pushing; the bright, light-flooded ring; the great moment; the breathless hour of glory and triumph.

Jim stood very still, shaken, white, feeling the gun in his clasp, telling himself that he must not fail.

Even the rope, which rasped his palm as he climbed into the ring, seemed as real as the gun. But he was aware of the gun too, aware of a dim, dark stirring just beyond the splendid vision.

He was in the ring and he was not in the ring. He was two men at once. Beyond the glimmering stadium lights, beyond that white, steady blaze, luminous spots shifted about in a web of darkness.

The eyes of the Martian beast were trained upon him, with a devouring greediness.

Jim recoiled from the ringside, forcing his mind away from the referee, the big man in white tights facing him, the gleaming faces of the crowd.

His fingers tightened on the gun.

Jim blasted with a sudden, terrible concentration of all his faculties. He felt the gun leap in his clasp, saw the splendid vision dim and vanish.

The Martian desert came wavering back, wrapped in the chill light of dawn. Grayness, chillness, came sweeping back forty million miles from Earth.

The Martian beast shriveled in the searing blast. Its eyes opened, shut, puckered and ran hideously together on its shrinking bulk. Ten eyes became one, swelled to a hugely blinking orb filled with smoky light. Other eyes grew smaller, turned to blind lumps like gall blisters on terrestrial tree stumps.

The Martian became a black, oozing mass of charred jelly. It heaved and bubbled and ran in thin trickles over the sand. It became a thing of no real substance, a smudged residue like the jellyfish patterns cast up on the beaches of Earth by the resistless tides.

Most of the jellyfish gone, dried out by the sun. Just water, dissolving, running away, leaving only a faint, skeletal stain on the white and gleaming sand.

JIM WAS trembling when he turned. The desert had never seemed so chill. Before his eyes stretched only desolation, emptiness, a bleak and hostile land.

He started walking, vaguely aware that he was returning toward the village, but making no effort to follow a single trail.

His anger at fate had something in it of the burnt out land.

But then, miraculously, his despair ebbed a little. A man must carryon, he told himself grimly.

Soon the sun was a bright blaze in the distance and he could see the village, and the gleaming waters of the canal. He had never thought of the village as a part of himself before: It was curious, but he had never actually thought of the village as something he had helped to build.

Jim Malden, realist. Neither too good nor too bad. Just a stubborn fighter, liking his neighbors, liking kids and the rain on his face, and the good morning smell of frying bacon. Dogged, stubborn, wanting to do his part to make the Mars colony the kind of town a man could be proud of.

Jim entered the town and walked down the silent quayside in the dawn, his huge shoulders squared.

His shack had never seemed quite worth defending before. His wife and neighbors, sure—but not the shack itself. But now it wasn't just a tin-walled squatter's shack set down in a chill waste forty million miles from Earth.

It was—home.

Jim opened the door and went inside. His wife had thrown herself down on a sofa, fully clothed, and her face in the dawn light was haggard and worn.

Jim knelt beside the sofa and put his arms around her.

"Time for breakfast, Mary," he said.

Mary opened her eyes. "Jim!"

"I've come home, Mary. Thinking about Earth all the time, dreaming about Earth, was no good. I've come home to all the things a man never gets around to missing until he's lost them."

His wife stared at him with shining eyes.

"A man's home is wherever he's fought and struggled and really lived, Jim," she said. "Everybody changes. Everybody starts over every time the sun comes up. I knew you'd find that out someday, Jim. You've come home to Mars!"

Jim kissed her.

THE END

A Matter Of Protocol

By JACK SHARKEY

First Contact was always dangerous—but usually only to the man involved!

FROM space, the planet Viridian resembled a great green moss-covered tennis ball. When the spaceship had arrowed even closer to the lush jungle that was the surface of the 7000-mile sphere, there was still no visible break in the green cloak of the planet. Even when they dipped almost below their margin of safety—spaceships were poorly built for extended flight within the atmosphere—it took nearly a complete circuit of the planet before a triangle of emptiness was spotted. It was in the midst of the tangled canopy of treetops, themselves interwoven inextricably with coarse-leafed ropy vines that sprawled and coiled about the upthrust branches like underfed anacondas.

Into the center of this triangle the ship was lowered on sputtering blue pillars of crackling energy, to come to rest on the soft loamy earth.

A bare instant after setdown, crewmen exploded from the airlock and dashed into the jungle shadows with high-pressure tanks of gushing spume. Their job was to coat, cool and throttle the hungry fires trickling in bright orange fingers through the heat-blackened grasses. Higher in the trees, a few vines smoldered fitfully where the fires had brushed them, then hissed into smoky wet ash as their own glutinous sap smothered the urgent embers. But the fire was going out.

"Under control, sir," reported a returning crewman.

Lieutenant Jerry Norcriss emerged into the green gloaming that cloaked the base of the ship with a net of harlequin diamonds. Jerry nodded abstractedly as other crewmen laid a lightweight form-fitting couch alongside the tailfins near the airlock. On this couch Jerry reclined. Remaining crew members turned their firefighting gear over to companions and stood guard in a rough semicircle with loaded rifles, their backs to the figure on the couch, facing the jungle and whatever predatory dangers it might hold.

Ensign Bob Ryder, the technician who had the much softer job of simply controlling and coordinating any information relayed by Jerry, leaned out through the open circle in the hull.

"All set, sir," said the tech. Jerry nodded and settled a heavily wired helmet onto his head, while Bob made a hookup between the helmet and the power outlet that was concealed under a flap of metal on the tailfin.

Helmet secured, Jerry lay back upon the couch and closed his eyes. "Any time you're ready, Ensign."

Bob hurried back inside, found the panel he sought among the jumble of high-powered machinery there, and placed a spool of microtape on a spindle inside it.

He shut the panel and thumbed the button that started an impulse radiating from the tape into the jungle.

The impulse had been detected and taped by a roborocket, which had circled the planet for months before their arrival. It was one of the two Viridian species whose types were as yet uncatalogued by the Space Corps, in its vast files of alien life. Jerry's job, as a Space Zoologist, was to complete those files, planet by planet throughout the spreading wave of slowly colonized universe.

Bob made sure the tape was functioning. Then he clicked the switch that would stimulate the Contact center in Jerry's brain and release his mind into that of the taped alien for an immutable forty minutes.

Outside the ship, recumbent in the warm green-gold shadows, Jerry's consciousness was dwarfed for an instant by a white lightning-flash of energy. And then his body went limp as his mind sprang with thought-speed into Contact...

JERRY opened his eyes to a dizzying view of the dull brown jungle floor. He blinked a moment, then looked toward his feet. He saw two sets of thin knobby Vs, extending forward and partly around the tiny limb he stood upon, their chitinous surface shiny with the wetness of the jungle air.

Slowly working his jaws, he heard the extremely gentle "click" as they came together. The endoskeleton must exist all over his host's body.

After making certain it would not disturb his balance on the limb, he attempted bringing whatever on the alien passed for hands before his face.

Sometimes aliens had no hands, nor any comparable organisms. Then Jerry would have to soft-pedal the mental nagging of being "amputated," an unavoidable carryover from his subconscious "wrong-feeling" about armlessness.

But this time the effort moved up multi-jointed limbs, spindly as a cat's whiskers, terminating in a perpetually coiling soft prehensile tip. He tried feeling along his torso to determine its size and shape. But the wormlike tips were tactilely insensitive.

Hoping to deduce his shape from his shadow, he inched sideways along the limb on those inadequate-looking two-pronged feet toward a blob of yellow sunlight nearer the trunk.

The silhouette on the branch showed him a stubby cigar-shaped torso.

"I seem to be a semi-tentacled no-hop grasshopper," he mused to himself, vainly trying to turn his head on his neck. "Head, thorax and abdomen all one piece."

He tried flexing what would be, in a man, the region of the shoulderblades. He was rewarded by the appearance of long, narrow wings—two sets of them, like a dragonfly's—from beneath two flaps of chitin on his back.

He tried an experimental flapping. The pair of wings—white and stiff like starched tissue paper, not veinous as in Earth-insects—dissolved in a buzzing blur of motion. The limb fell away from under his tiny V-shaped feet. And then he was up above the blinding green blanket of jungle treetops, his shadow pacing his forward movement along the close-packed quilt of wide leaves below.

"I'd better be careful," thought Jerry. "There may be avian life here that considers my species the *piéce de resistance* of the pteroid set..."

Slowing his rapid wingbeat, he let himself drop down toward the nearest mattress-sized leaf. He folded his out-thrust feet in midair and dropped the last few inches to a cushiony rest.

A SLIGHT shimmer of dizziness gripped his mind.

Perhaps the "skull" of this creature was ill equipped to ward off the hot rays of the tropic sunlight. Lest his brain be fried in its own casing, Jerry scuttled along the velvet top of the leaf, and ducked quickly beneath its nearest overlapping companion. The wave of vertigo passed quickly, there in the deep shadow. Under the canopy of leaves Jerry crawled back to a limb near the top of the tree.

A few feet from where he stood, something moved.

Jerry turned that way. Another creature of the same species was balancing lightly on a green limb of wire-thickness, its gaze fixed steadily toward the jungle flooring, as Jerry's own had been on entering the alien body.

Watching out for predators? Or for victims?

He could, he knew, pull his consciousness back enough to let the creature's own consciousness carry it through its daily cycle of eating, avoiding destruction, and the manifold businesses of being an ambient creature, but he decided to keep control. It would be easier to figure out his host's ecological status in the planet's natural life-balance by observing the other one for awhile.

Jerry always felt more comfortable when he was in full control. You never knew when an alien might stupidly stumble into a fatality that any intelligent mind could easily have avoided.

Idly, as he watched his fellow creature down near the inner part of the branch, he wondered how much more time he would be in Contact. Subjectively he'd seemed to be enhosted for about ten minutes. But one of the drawbacks of Contact was the subjugation of personal time-sense to that of the host. Depending on the species he enhosted, the forty-minute Contact period could be an eternity, or the blink of an eye...

NOTHING further seemed to be occurring. Jerry reluctantly withdrew some of his control from the insect-mind to see what would happen.

Immediately it inched forward until it was in the same position it had been in when Jerry made Contact: V-shaped feet forward and slightly around the narrow branch, eyes fixed upon the brownish jungle floor, body motionless with folded wings. For awhile, Jerry tried "listening" to its mind, but received no readable thoughts. Only a sense of imminence... Of patience... Of waiting...

It didn't take long for Jerry to grow bored with this near-mindless outlook. He reassumed full control. Guiding the fragile feet carefully along the branch, he made his way to his fellow watcher, and tried out the creature's communication system. His mind strove to activate something on the order of a larynx; the insect's nervous system received this impulse, changed in inter-species translation, as a broad request for getting a message to its fellow. Its body responded by lifting the multi-jointed "arms" forward. It clapped the hard inner surfaces of the "wrists" together so fast that they blurred into invisibility as the wings had done.

A thin, ratchetty sound came forth from that hard-shell contact. The other insect looked up in annoyance, then returned its gaze to the ground again.

Aural conversation thus obviated, Jerry tried for physical attention getting. He reached out a vermiform forelimb-tip and tugged urgently at the other insect's nearest hind leg. An angry movement gave out the unmistakable pantomimic message: "For pete's sake, get off my back! I'm *busy!*" The other insect spread its thin double wings and went buzzing off a few trees away, then settled on a limb there and took up its earthward vigil once more.

"Well, they're not gregarious, that's for sure," said Jerry to himself. "I wish I knew what the hell we were waiting for."

He decided he was sick of ground watching, and turned his attention to his immediate vicinity. His gaze wandered along all the twists, juts and thrusts of branch and vine beneath the sunblocking leaves.

And all at once he realized he was staring at another of his kind. So still had its dull green-brown body been that he'd taken it for a ripple of bark along a branch.

Carefully, he looked further on. Beyond the small still figure he soon located another like it, and then another. Within a short space of time, he had found three dozen of the insects sitting silently around him in a spherical area barely ten feet in diameter.

ODDLY disconcerted, he once more spread his stiff white wings and fluttered away through the treetops, careful to avoid coming out in direct sunlight this time.

He flew until a resurgence of giddiness told him he was over-straining the creature's stamina. He dropped onto a limb and looked about once more. Within a very short time, he had spotted dozens more of the grasshopper-things. All were the same, sitting in camouflaged silence, steadily eyeing the ground.

"Damn," thought Jerry. "They don't seem interested in eating, mating or fighting. All they want to do is sit—sit and *wait*. But what are they waiting for?"

There was, of course, the possibility that he'd caught them in an off-period. If the species were nocturnal, then he wouldn't get any action from them till after sunset. That, he realized gloomily, meant a re-Contact later on. One way or another, he would have to determine the functions, capabilities and menace—if any—of the species with regard to the influx of colonists, who would come to Viridian only if his report pronounced it safe.

Once again, he let the insect's mind take over. Again that over-powering feeling of imminence...

He was irritated. It couldn't just be looking forward to nightfall! There were too many things tied in with the imminence feeling: the necessity for quiet, for motionlessness, for careful watching.

The more he thought on it, the more he had the distinct intuition that it would sit and stare at the soft, mulch-covered jungle floor, be it bright daylight or blackest gloom, waiting, and waiting, and waiting...

Then, suddenly, the slight feel of imminence became almost unbearable apprehension.

The change in intensity was due to a soft, cautious shuffling sound from down in the green-gold twilight. Something was coming through the jungle. Something that moved on careful feet along the springy, moist brown surface below the trees.

Far below, a shadow detached itself slowly from the deeper shadows of the trees, and a form began to emerge into the wan filtered sunlight. It—

An all-encompassing lance of silent white lightning. Contact was over...

Jerry sat up on the couch, angry. He pulled the helmet off his head as Bob Ryder leaned out the airlock once more. "How'd it go, sir?"

"Lousy. I'll have to re-establish. Didn't have time to Learn it sufficiently." A slight expression of disappointment on the tech's face made him add, "Don't tell me you have the other tape in place already?"

"Sorry," Bob said. "You usually do a complete Learning in one Contact."

"Oh—" Jerry shrugged and reached for the helmet again. "Never mind, I'll take on the second alien long as it's already set up. I may just have hit the first one in an off-period. The delay in re-Contact may be just what I need to catch it in action."

Settling the helmet snugly on his head once more, he leaned back onto the couch and waited. He heard the tech's feet clanking along the metal plates inside the ship, then the soft clang of an opening door in the power room, and—

Whiteness, writhing electric whiteness and cold silence. And he was in Contact.

DARKNESS, and musky warmth.

Then a slot of light appeared, a thin fuzzy line of yellow striped with spiky green. Jerry had time, in the brief flicker, to observe thick bearlike forelimbs holding up a squarish trapdoor fastened with cross-twigs for support. Then the powerful forepaws let the door drop back into place, and it was dark again.

He hadn't liked those forepaws. Though thick as and pawed like a bear's, they were devoid of hair. They had skin thin as a caterpillar's, a mottled pink with sick-looking areas of deathly white.

Skin like that would be a pushover to actinic rays for any long exposure. Probably the thing lived underground here, almost permanently. His eyes had detected a rude assortment of thick wooden limbs curving in and out at regular intervals in the vertical wall of soil that was the end of this tunnel, just below the trapdoor. Tree roots. But formed, by some odd natural quirk, into a utile ladder.

But why had the thing peered out, then dropped the door to wait? Did *every* species on this planet hang around expectantly and nothing else? And what was the waiting for?

Then he felt the urge within the creature, the urge to scurry up that ladder into the light. But there was, simultaneously, a counter-urge in the thing, telling it to *please* wait a *little* longer...

Jerry recognized the urge by quick anthropomorphosis. It was the goofy urge. The crazy urge. Like one gets on the brink of awesome heights, or on subway platforms as the train roars in: The impulsive urge to self-destruction, so swiftly frightening and so swiftly suppressed...

Yet, it had lifted and dropped that lid too briefly to have seen anything outside. Could it be *listening* for something? Carefully, he relinquished his control of the beast, fraction by fraction, to see what it would do.

It rose on tiptoe at once, and again lifted that earthen door.

It squinted at the profusion of green-yellow sunlight that stung its eyes. Then it rose on powerful hind limbs and clambered just high enough on that "ladder" to see over the grassy rim of the trapdoor-hole. Jerry then heard the soft shuffling sound that had re-alerted it, and saw the source.

Out on the matted brown jungle flooring, beneath the towering trees, another of the bear-things was moving forward from an open turf-door, emitting low, whimpering shorts as it inched along through the dappling yellow sunlight.

Obviously it was *following* that manic-destruction impulse that he just felt and managed to suppress. It must have been almost a hundred degrees out there. And the damned thing was *shivering*.

HERE and there, Jerry noticed suddenly, other half-opened trapdoors were framing other bear-things' heads. The air was taut with electric tension, the tension of a slow trigger-squeeze that moves millimeter by millimeter toward the instant explosion...

The soft shuffling sounds of the animal's movement jogged Jerry's memory then, and he knew it for the sound he had heard when enhosted in the grasshopper-thing. Was a bear-thing what they'd been waiting in the trees so silently for? And what would be the culmination of that vigil?

Then the bear-thing he was in Contact with hitched itself up another root-rung. Jerry saw the thing toward which the quaking creature was headed, in a hunched crawl, its whimpers more anguished by the moment.

Pendant in the green gloaming, about four feet above the spongy brown jungle floor, hung a thick yellow-gray gourd at the tip of a long vine. Its sides glittered stickily with condensed moisture that mingled with the effluvium of the gourd itself. The odor was both noisome and compelling, powerful as a bushel of rotting roses. It sickened as it lured, teased the nostrils as it cloyed within the lungs.

To this dangling obscenity the bear-thing moved. Its eyes were no longer afraid, but glazed and dulled by the strength of that musky lure. Its movements were fluid and trance-like.

It arose on sturdy hind limbs and struck at the gourd with a gentle paw, sending it jouncing to one side on its long green vine. As it bobbed back, the creature struck it off in the opposite direction with a sharper blow.

Jerry watched in fascination.

The gourd swung faster; the mottled pink-white alien creature swayed and wove its forelimbs and thick body in a ritual dance matching the tempo of the arcing gourd.

Then Jerry noted that the vine was unlike earth-vines, which parasitically employ treetops as their unwilling trellises. It is a limp extension of the tip of a tree branch itself. So were all the other vines in that green matting overhead.

A RIPPING sound yanked his gaze back to the dazed Creature and the gourd again.

A ragged tear had riven the side of the gourd. Tiny coils of green were dribbling out in batches, like watchsprings spilled from a paper bag. They struck with a bounce and wriggle on the resilient brown mulch. And then, as they straightened themselves, Jerry knew them for what they were: Miniature versions of the grasshopper-things, shaped precisely like the adults, but only a third as large.

The bear-thing's movements had gone from graceful fluidity to frenzy now. A loud whistle of fright escaped it as the last of the twitching green things flopped from its vegetable cocoon, whirred white wings to dry them and flew off.

And the lumbering creature had reason for its fright.

The instant the last coil of wiggly green life was a vanishing blur in the green shadows, a cloud of darker green descended upon the pink form of the beast from the trees.

The grasshopper-things were waiting no longer. Thousands swarmed on the writhing form, until the bear-thing was a lumpy green parody of itself.

As quickly as the cloud had plunged and clustered, it fell away. The earth was teeming with the flip-flopping forms of dying insects, white wings going dark brown and curling like cellophane in open flame. The bear-thing itself was no longer recognizable, its flesh a myriad egg-like white lumps. It swayed in agony for a moment, then toppled.

Instantly the other creatures—his host with them—were racing forward to the site of the encounter. Jerry felt his host's long gummy tongue flick out and snare one—just one—of the dead adult insects. It was ingested whole by a deft backflip of tongue to gullet. As his host turned tail and scurried for the tunnel once more, Jerry swiftly took control again, and halted it to observe any further developments.

EACH of the other things, after a one-insect gulp, was just vanishing back underground. The turf-tops were dropping neatly into almost undetectable place hiding the tunnels. The sunlight nipped at his pale flesh, but Jerry held off from a return to the underground sanctuary, still watching that lump-covered corpse on the earth. Then...

The vine, its burden gone, began to drip a thick ichor from its ragged end upon the dead animal beneath it.

And as the ichor touched upon a white lump, the lump would swell, wriggle, and change color. Jerry watched with awe as the color became a mottled pink, and the surface of the lumps cracked and shriveled away, and tiny forms plopped out onto the ground: miniature bear-things, tiny throats emitting eager mouse-squeaks of hunger.

They rushed upon the body in which they'd been so violently incubated and swiftly, systematically devoured it, blood, bone and sinew.

And when not even a memory of the dead beast was left upon the soil, the tiny pink-white things began to burrow downward into the ground. Soon there was nothing left in the area but a dried fragment of vine, a few loose mounds of soil and a vast silence.

"I'll be a monkey's uncle!" said Jerry...forgetting in his excitement that this phrase was nearly a concise parody of the Space Zoologists' final oath of duty, and kiddingly used as such by the older members of the group.

The whole damned planet was symbiotic! After witnessing those alien life-death rites, it didn't take him long to figure out the screwball connections between the species. Insects, once born of vine-gourds and fully grown, then propagated their species by a strange means: laying bear-eggs in a bear-thing and dying. And dying, eaten by the surviving bears, they turned to seeds which—left in the tunnels by the bear-things as droppings—in turn took root and became trees.

And the trees, under the onslaught of another bear-thing on a dangling pod, would produce new insects, then drip its ichor to fertilize the eggs in the newly dead bear-thing...

Jerry found his mind tangling as he attempted a better pinpointing of the plant-animal-insect relationship. A dead adult insect, plus a trip through a bear-thing's alimentary canal, produced a tree. A tree-pod, with the swatting stimulus of a bear-thing's paws, gave birth to new insects. And insect eggs in animal flesh, stimulated by the tree-ichor, gestated swiftly into young animals...

That meant, simply, that insect plus bear equals tree, tree plus bear equals insect, and insect plus tree equals bear. With three systems, each relied on the non-inclusive member for the breeding-ground. Insect-plus-ichor produced small animals in the animal flesh. Dead-insect-plus-bear produced tree *in* the tree-flesh (if one considered dead tree leaves and bark and such as the makeup of the soil.) Bear-swats-plus-tree produced insects... "Damn," said Jerry to himself, "but *not* in the insect-flesh. The thing won't round off..."

He tried again, thinking hard. In effect, the trees were parents to the insects, insects parents to the bears, and bears parents to the trees... Though in another sense, bear-flesh gave birth to new bears, digested insects gave birth (through the tree-medium) to new insects, and trees (through the insect-medium) gave birth to new trees...

Jerry's head spun pleasantly as he tried vainly to solve the confusion. Men of science, he realized, would spend decades trying to figure out which species were responsible for which. It made the ancient chicken-or-egg question beneath consideration. And a lot of diehard evolutionists were going to be bedded down with severe migraines when his report went into circulation...

A dazzle of silent lightning, and Contact was over.

"READY with that first tape again," Bob Ryder said as Jerry removed the Contact helmet and brushed his snow-white hair back from his tanned, youthful face. "Or do you want a breather first?"

Jerry shook his head. "I won't need to re-Contact that other species, Ensign. I got its life-relation ships from the second Contact."

"Really, sir?" said Bob. "That's pretty unusual, isn't it?"

"The whole damned planet's unusual," said Jerry, rising from his supine position and stretching luxuriously in the warm jungle air. "You'll see what I mean when you process the second tape."

Bob decided that Jerry—running pretty true to form for a Space Zoologist—wasn't in a particularly talkative mood, so he had to satisfy himself with waiting for the transcription of the Contact to get the details.

Later that day, an hour after takeoff, with Viridian already vanished behind them as the great ship plowed through hyper-space toward Earth and home, Bob finished reading the report. Then he went down the passageway to the wardroom for coffee. Jerry was seated there already. Bob, quickly filling a mug from the polished percolator, slid into a seat across the table from his superior and asked the question that had been bugging him since seeing the report.

"Sir—on that second Contact. Has it occurred to you that you'd relinquished control to the host *before* you saw that other creature move out and start swatting the gourd-thing?"

"You mean was I taking a chance on being destroyed in the host if the creature I was Contacting gave in to the urge to do the swatting?"

"Yes, sir," said Bob. "I mean, I know you can take control any time, if things get dangerous. But wasn't that cutting it kind of thin?"

Jerry shook his head and sipped his coffee. "Wrong urge, Ensign. You'll note I recognized it as the *goofy* urge, the impulse to die followed instantly by a violent surge of self-preservation. It wasn't the death-wish at all. Myself and the creatures who remained safely at the tunnel-mouths had a milder form of what was affecting the creature that *did* start swatting the gourd."

"Then what was the difference, sir? Why did that one particular creature get the full self-destruction urge and no other?"

Jerry wrinkled his face in thought. "I wish I didn't suspect the answer to that, Ensign. The only thing I hope it *isn't* is the thing I have the strongest inkling it *is*: Rotation. Something in their biology has set them up in a certain order for destruction. And that rite I saw performed was so unanimal, so formalized—"

Bob's eyes widened as he caught the inference. "You think they have an inbuilt protocol? That if one particular creature missed its cue, somehow, the designated subsequent creature would simply wait forever, never jumping its turn?"

"That's what I mean," nodded Jerry. "I hope I'm wrong."

"But the right creature made it," said Bob, blinking. "We can't have upset the ecology, can we?"

"Things develop fast on Viridian," mused Jerry. "If I figure the time-relationship between their egg-hatching rate and growth rate, those trees must mature in growth in about a month. And we managed to shrivel a half dozen vines with our rocket fires when we landed, and probably that many again when we blasted off..."

"We dropped CO_2 bombs after we cleared the trees," offered the tech, uneasily. "The fire was out in seconds."

"That wouldn't help an already-shriveled vine, though, now would it," sighed Jerry. "And if my hunch about protocol is correct—"

"The life-cycle would interrupt?" gasped the tech.

"We'll see," said Jerry. "It'll take us a month to get back, and there'll be another six months before the first wave of engineers is sent to begin the homesteads and industry sites. We'll see. Ensign."

IT took two months for the engineers to go out and return.

They hadn't landed. A few orbits about the planet had shown them nothing but a vast dead ball of dust and rotted vegetation, totally unfit for human habitation. They brought back photographs taken of the dead planet that no longer deserved the name it had rated in life.

But Jerry Norcriss, Space Zoologist, made it a special point to avoid looking at any of them.

THE END

Friends and Enemies

By FRITZ LIEBER

In a world blasted by super-bombs and run by super-thugs, Art vs. Science can be a deadly debate!

THE SUN hadn't quite risen but now that the five men were out from under the trees it already felt hot. Far ahead, off to the left of the road, the spires of New Angeles gleamed dusky blue against the departing night. The two unarmed men gazed back wistfully at the little town, dark and asleep under its moist leafy umbrellas. The one who was thin and had hair flecked with gray looked all intellect; the other, young and with a curly mop, looked all feeling.

The fat man barring their way back to town mopped his head. The two young men flanking him with shotgun and squirtgun hadn't started to sweat yet.

The fat man stuffed the big handkerchief back in his pocket, wiped his hands on his shirt, rested his wrists lightly on the pistols holstered either side his stomach, looked at the two unarmed men, indicated the hot road with a nod, and said, "There's your way, professors. Get going."

The thin man looked at the hand-smears on the fat man's shirt. "But you haven't even explained to me," he protested softly, "why I'm being turned out of Ozona College."

"Look here, Mr. Ellenby, I've tried to make it easy for you," the fat man said. "I'm doing it before the town wakes up. Would you rather be chased by a mob?"

"But why—?"

"Because we found out you weren't just a math teacher, Mr. Ellenby." The fat man's voice went hard. "You'd been a physicist once. *Nu*clear physicist."

The young man with the shotgun spat. Ellenby watched the spittle curl in the dust like a little brown worm. He shifted his gaze

43

to a dead eucalyptus leaf. "I'd like to talk to the College Board of regents," he said tonelessly.

"I'm the board of regents," the fat man told him. "Didn't you even know that?"

At this point the other unarmed man spoke up loudly. "But that doesn't explain my case. I've devoted my whole life to warning people against physicists and other scientists. How they'd smash us with their bombs. How they were destroying our minds with 3D and telefax and handies. How they were blaspheming against Nature, killing all imagination, crushing all beauty out of life..."

"I'd shut my mouth if I were you, Madson," the fat man said critically, "or at least lower my voice. When I mentioned a mob, I wasn't fooling. I saw them burn Cal Tech. In fact, I got a bit excited and helped."

The young man with the shotgun grinned.

"Cal Tech," Ellenby murmured, his eyes growing distant. "Cal Tech burns and Ozona stands."

"Ozona stands for the decencies of life," the fat man grated, "not alphabet bombs and pituitary gas. Its purpose is to save a town, not help kill a world."

"But why should I be driven out?" Madson persisted. "I'm just a poet singing the beauties of the simple life unmarred by science."

"Not simple enough for Ozona," the fat man snorted. "We happen to know, Mr. Poet Madson, that you've written some stories about free love. We don't want anyone telling Ozona girls it's all right to be careless."

"But those were just ideas, ideas in a story," Madson protested. "I wasn't advocating—"

"No difference," the fat man cut him short. "Talk to a woman about ideas and pretty soon she gets some." His voice became almost kindly. "Look here, if you wanted a woman without getting hitched to her, why didn't you go to shantytown?"

Madson squared his shoulders. "You've missed the whole point. I'd never do such a thing. I never have."

"Then you shouldn't have boasted," the fat man said. "And you shouldn't have fooled around with Councilman Classen's daughter."

At the name, Ellenby came out of his trance and looked sharply at Madson, who said indignantly, "I wasn't fooling around with Vera-Ellen, whatever her crazy father says. She came to my office because she has poetic ability and I wanted to encourage it."

"Yeah, so she'd encourage you," the fat man finished. "That girl's wild enough already, which I suppose is what you mean by poetic ability. And in this town, her father's word counts." He hitched up his belt. "And now, professors, it's time you started."

Madson and Ellenby looked at each other doubtfully. The young man with the squirtgun raised its acid-etched muzzle. The fat man looked hard at Madson and Ellenby. "I think I hear alarm clocks going off," he said quietly.

They watched the two men trudge a hundred yards, watched Ellenby shift the rolled-up towel under his elbow to the other side, watched Madson pause to thumb tobacco into a pipe and glance carelessly back, then shove the pipe in his pocket and go on hurriedly.

"Couple of pretty harmless coots, if you ask me," the young man with the shotgun observed.

"Sure," the fat man agreed, "but we got to remember peoples' feelings and keep Ozona straight. We don't like mobs or fear *or* girls gone wild."

The young man with the shotgun grinned. "That Vera-Ellen," he murmured, shaking his head.

"You better keep *your* mind off her too," the fat man said sourly. "She's wild enough without anybody to encourage her poetic ability or anything else. It's a good thing we gave those two their walking papers."

"They'll probably walk right into the arms of the Harvey gang," the young man with the squirtgun remarked, "especially if they try to short-cut."

"Pretty small pickings for Harvey, those two," the young man with the shotgun countered.

"Which won't please him at all."

The fat man shrugged. "Their own fault. If only they'd had sense enough to keep their mouths shut. Early in life."

"They don't seem to realize it's 1993," said the young man with the shotgun.

The fat man nodded. "Come on," he said, turning back toward the town and the coolness. "We've done our duty."

The young man with the squirtgun took a last look. "There they go, Art and Science," he observed with satisfaction. "Those two subjects always did make my head ache."

ON THE HOT ROAD Madson began to stride briskly. His nostrils flared. "Smell the morning air," he commanded. "It's good, good!"

Ellenby, matching his stride with longer if older legs, looked at him with mild wonder.

"Smell the hot sour grass," Madson continued. "It's things like this man was meant for, not machines and formulas. Look at the dew. Have you seen the dew in years? Look at it on that spiderweb!"

The physicist paused obediently to observe the softly twinkling strands. "Perfect catenaries," he murmured.

"What?"

"A kind of curve," Ellenby explained. "The locus of the focus of a parabola rolling on a straight line."

"Locus-focus hocus-pocus," Madson snorted. "Reducing the wonders of Nature to chalk marks. It's disgusting."

Suddenly each tiny drop of dew turned blood red. Ellenby turned his back on the spiderweb, whipped a crooked little brass tube from an inside pocket and squinted through it.

"What's that?" Madson asked.

"Spectroscope," Ellenby explained. "Early morning spectra of the sun are fascinating."

Madson huffed. "There you go. Analyzing. Tearing beauty apart. It's a disease." He paused. "Say, won't you hurt your eyes?"

Turning back, Ellenby shook his head. "I keep a smoked glass on it," he said. "I'm always hoping that some day I'll get a glimpse of an atomic bomb explosion."

"You mean to say you've missed all the dozens they dropped on this country? That's too bad."

"The ball of fire's quite fleeting. The opportunities haven't been as good as you think."

"But you're a physicist, aren't you? Don't you people have all sorts of lovely photographs to gloat over in your laboratories?"

"Atomic bomb spectra were never declassified," Ellenby told him wistfully. "At least not in my part of the project. I've never seen one."

"Well, you'll probably get your chance," Madson told him harshly. "If you've been reading your dirty telefax, you'll know the Hot Truce is coming to a boil. And the Angeles area will be a prime target." Ellenby nodded mutely.

They trudged on. The sun began to beat on their backs like an open fire. Ellenby turned up his collar. He watched his companion thoughtfully. Finally he said, "So you're the Madson who wrote those *Enemies of Science* stories about a world ruled by poets. It never occurred to me back at Ozona. And that non-fiction book about us—what was it called?"

"*Murderers of Imagination*," Madson growled. "And it would have been a good thing if you'd listened to my warnings instead of going on building machines and dissecting Nature and destroying all the lovely myths that make life worthwhile."

"Are you sure that Nature is so lovely and kind?" Ellenby ventured. Madson did not deign to answer.

They passed a crossroad leading, the battered sign said, one way to Palmdale, the other to San Bernardino. They were perhaps a hundred yards beyond it when Ellenby let go a little chuckle. "I have a confession to make. When I was very young I wrote an article about how children shouldn't be taught the Santa Claus myth or any similar fictions."

Madson laughed sardonically. "A perfect member of your dry-souled tribe. Worrying about Santa Claus, when all the while something very different was about to come flying down from over the North Pole and land on our housetops."

"We did try to warn people about the intercontinental missiles," Ellenby reminded him.

"Yes, without any success. The last two reindeer—Donner and Blitzen."

Ellenby nodded glumly, but he couldn't keep a smile off his face for long. "I wrote another article too—it was never published—about how poetry is completely pointless, how rhymes inevitably distort meanings, and so on."

Madson whirled on him with a peal of laughter. "So you even thought you were big enough to wreck poetry!" He jerked a limp, thinnish volume from his coat pocket. "You thought you could destroy this?"

Ellenby's expression changed. He reached for the book, but Madson held it away from him. Ellenby said, "That's Keats, isn't it?"

"How would you know?"

Ellenby hesitated. "Oh, I got to like some of his poetry, quite a while after I wrote the article." He paused again and looked squarely at Madson. "Also, Vera-Ellen was reading me some pieces out of that volume. I guess you'd loaned it to her."

"Vera-Ellen?" Madson's jaw dropped.

Ellenby nodded. "She had trouble with her geometry. Some conferences were necessary." He smiled. "We physicists aren't such a dry-souled tribe, you know.

Madson looked outraged. "Why, you're old enough to be her father!"

"Or her husband," Ellenby replied coolly. "Young women are often attracted to father images. But all that can't make any difference to us now."

"You're right," Madson said shortly. He shoved the poetry volume back in his pocket, flirted the sweat out of his eyes, and looked around with impatience. "Say, you're going to New Angeles, aren't you?" he asked, and when Ellenby nodded uncertainly, said, "Then let's cut across the fields. This road is taking us out of our way." And without waiting for a reply he jumped across the little ditch to the left of the road and into the yellowing wheat field. Ellenby watched him for a moment then hitched his rolled towel further up under his arm and followed.

IT WAS stifling in the field. The wheat seemed to paralyze any stray breezes. Their boots hissed against the dry stems. Far off they heard a lazy drumming. After a while they came to a wide, brimful irrigation ditch. They could see that some hundreds of feet ahead it was crossed by a little bridge. They followed the ditch.

Ellenby felt strangely giddy, as if he were looking at everything through a microscope. That may have been due to the tremendous size of the wheat, its spikes almost as big as corncobs, the spikelets bigger than kernels—rich orange stuff taut with flour. But then they came to a section marred by larger and larger splotches of a powdery purple blight.

The lazy drumming became louder. Ellenby was the first to see the low-swinging helicopter with its thick, trailing plume of greenish mist. He knocked Madson on the shoulder and both men started to run. Purple dust puffed. Once Ellenby stumbled and Madson stopped to jerk him to his feet. Still they would have escaped except that the copter swerved toward them. A moment later they were enveloped in sweet oily fumes.

Madson heard jeering laughter, glimpsed a grotesquely long-nosed face peering down from above. Then, through the cloud, Ellenby squeaked, "Don't breathe," and Madson felt himself dragged roughly into the ditch. The water closed over him with a splash.

Puffing and blowing, he came to his feet—the water hardly reached his waist—to find himself being dragged by Ellenby toward the bridge. It was all he could do to keep his footing on the muddy bottom. By the time he got breath enough to voice his indignation, Ellenby was saying, "That's far enough. The stuff's settling away from us. Now strip and scrub yourself."

Ellenby unrolled the towel he'd held tightly clutched to his side all the while, and produced a bar of soap. In response to Madson's question he explained, "That fungicide was probably TTTR or some other relative of the nerve-gas family. They are absorbed through the skin."

Seconds later Madson was scouring his head and chest. He hesitated at his trousers, muttering, "They'll probably have me for indecent exposure. Claim I was trying to start a nudist colony as well as a free-love cult." But Ellenby's warning had been a chilly one.

Ellenby soaped Madson's back and he in turn soaped the older man's ridgy one.

"I suppose that's why he had an elephant's nose," Madson mused.

"What?"

"Man in the copter," Madson ' explained. "Wearing a respirator."

Ellenby nodded and made them move nearer the bridge for a change of water.

They started to scrub their clothes, rinse and wring them, and lay them on the bank to dry. They watched the copter buzzing along in the distance, but it didn't seem inclined to come near again. Madson felt impelled to say, "You know, it's your chemist friends who have introduced that viciousness into the common man's spirit, giving him horrible poisons to use against Nature. Otherwise he wouldn't have tried to douse us with that stuff."

"He just acted like an ordinary farmer to me," Ellenby replied, scrubbing vigorously.

"Think we're safe?" Madson asked.

Ellenby shrugged. "We'll discover," he said briefly.

MADSON SHIVERED, but the rhythmic job was soothing. After a bit he began to feel almost playful. Lathering his shirt, he got some fine large bubbles, held them so he could see their colors flow in the sunlight.

"Tiny perfect worlds of every hue," he murmured. "Violet, blue, green, yellow, orange, red."

"And dead black," Ellenby added.

"You would say something like that," Madson grunted. "What did you think I was talking about?"

"Bubbles."

"Maybe some of your friends' poisons have black bubbles," Madson said bitingly. "But I was talking about these."

"So was I. Give me your pipe."

The authority in Ellenby's voice made Madson look around startledly, "Give me your pipe," Ellenby repeated firmly holding out his hand.

Madson fished it out of the pocket of the trousers he was about to wash and handed it over. Ellenby knocked out the soggy tobacco, swished it in the water a few times, and began to soap the inside of the bowl.

Madson started to object, but "You'd be washing it anyway," Ellenby assured him. "Now look here, Madson, I'm going to blow a bubble and I want you to watch. I want you to observe Nature for all you're worth. If poets and physicists have one thing in common it's that they're both supposed to be able to observe. Accurately."

He took a breath. "Now see, I'm going to hold the pipe mouth down and let the bubble hang from it, but with one side of the bowl tipped up a bit, so that the strain on the bubble's skin will be greatest on that side."

He blew a big bubble, held the pipe with one hand and pointed with a finger of the other. "There's the place to watch now. There!" The bubble burst.

"What was that?" Madson asked in a new voice. "It really was black for an instant, dull like soot."

"A bubble bursts because its skin gets thinner and thinner," Ellenby said. "When it gets thin enough it shows colors, as interference eliminates different wavelengths. With yellow eliminated it shows violet, and so on. But finally, just for a moment at the place where it's going to break, the skin becomes only one molecule thick. Such a mono-molecular layer absorbs all light, hence shows as dead black."

"Everything's got a black lining, eh?"

"Black can be beautiful. Here, I'll do it again."

Madson put his hand on Ellenby's shoulder to steady himself. They were standing hip-deep in water, their bodies still flecked with suds. Their heads were inches from the new bubble. As it burst a voice floated down to them.

"Is this the Ozona Faculty Kindergarten?"

They whirled around, simultaneously crouching in the water.

"Vera-Ellen, what are you doing here?" Madson demanded.

"Watching the kiddies play," the girl on the bridge replied, running a hand through her tousled violet hair. She looked down at her slacks and jacket. "Wish I'd brought my swim suit, though I gather it wouldn't be expected."

"Vera-Ellen!" Madson said apprehensively.

"It doesn't look very inviting down there, though," she mused. "Guess I'll wait for Aqua Heaven at New Angeles."

"You're going to New Angeles?" Ellenby put in. It is not easy to be conversationally brilliant while squatting chest deep in muddy water, acutely conscious of the absence of clothes.

Vera-Ellen nodded lazily, leaning on the railing. "Going to get me a city job. With its reduced faculty Ozona holds no more intellectual interest for me. Did you know math's going to be made part of the Home Ec department, Mr. Ellenby?"

"But how did you know that we—"

"Daughter of the man who got you run out of town ought to know what the old bully's up to. And if you're worrying that they'll come after me and find us together, I'll just head along by myself."

Madson and Ellenby both protested, though it is even harder to protest effectively than to be conversationally brilliant while squatting naked in coffee-colored water.

Vera-Ellen said, "All right, so quit playing and let's get on. You have to tell me all about New Angeles and the kind of jobs we'll get."

"But—?"

"Modest, eh? I'm afraid Pa wouldn't count it in your favor. But all right." She turned her back and sauntered to the other side of the bridge.

MADSON and Ellenby cautiously climbed out of the ditch, brushed the water from their skins, and wormed into their soggy clothes.

"We've got to persuade her to go back," Madson whispered.

"Vera-Ellen?" Ellenby replied and raised his eyebrows.

Madson groaned softly.

"Cheer up," Ellenby said. And he seemed in a cheerful humor himself when they climbed to the bridge. "Vera-Ellen," he said, "we've been having an argument as to whether man ruined Nature or Nature ruined man to start with."

"Is this a class, Mr. Ellenby?"

"Of sorts," he told her. Behind him Madson snorted, flipping his Keats to dry the pages. They started off together.

"Well," said Vera-Ellen, "I like Nature and I like...human beings. And I don't feel ruined at all. Where's the argument?"

"What about the bombs?" Madson demanded. "By man our physicist here means Technology. Whereas I mean—"

"Oh, the bombs," she said with a shrug. "What sort of job do you think I should get in New Angeles?"

"Well..." Madson began.

"Say, I'm getting hungry," she raced on, turning to Ellenby.

"So am I," he agreed.

They looked at the road ahead. A jagged hill now hid all but the tips of the spires of New Angeles. On the top of the hill was a tremendous house with sagging roofs of cracked tiles, stucco walls dark with rain stains and green with moss yet also showing cracks, and windows of age-blued glass, some splintered, flashing in the sun, which tempted Ellenby to whip out his spectroscope.

Curving down from the house came a weedy and balding expanse that had obviously once been a well-tended lawn. A few stalwart patches of thick grass held out tenaciously.

Pale-trunked eucalyptus trees towered behind the house and to either side of the road where it curved over the hill.

In a hollow at the foot of the one-time lawn, just where it met the road, something gleamed. As Madson, Ellenby and Vera-Ellen tramped forward, they saw it was an old automobile, one of the jet antiques that were the rage around 1970—in fact, a Lunar '69. Coming closer Ellenby realized that it had custom-built features, such as jet brakes and collision springs.

A man with an odd cap was poking a probe into the air intake, while in the back seat a woman was sitting, shadowed by a hat four feet across. At the sound of their footsteps the man whirled to his feet, quickly enough though unsteadily. He stared at them, wagging the probe. Just at that moment something that looked like an animated orange furpiece leaped from the tonneau.

"George!" the woman cried. "Widgie's got away."

The small flattish creature came on in undulating bounds. It was past the man in the cap before he could turn. It headed for Ellenby then changed direction. Madson made an impulsive dive for it, but it widened itself still more and sailed over him straight into Vera-Ellen's arms.

They walked toward the car. Widgie wriggled. Vera-Ellen stroked his ears. He seemed to be a flying fox of some sort. The man eyed them hostilely, raising the probe. Madson stared puzzledly at the cap. Out of his older knowledge Ellenby whispered an explanation: "Chauffeur."

The woman stood in the back seat, swaying slightly. She was wearing a white swim suit and dark teleglasses under her hat. At first she seemed a somewhat ravaged thirty. Then they began to see the rest of the wrinkles.

SHE RECEIVED Widgie from Vera-Ellen, shook him out and tucked him under her arm, where he hung limply, moving his tiny red eyes.

"Come in with me, my dear," she told Vera-Ellen. "George, put down that crazy pole. Pay no attention to George—he can't recognize gentlefolk when he sees them, especially when he's drunk. Gentlemen," she continued, waving graciously to Madson and Ellenby, "you have the thanks of Rickie Vickson." As she pronounced the name she surveyed them sharply. Her gaze settled on Ellenby. "You know me, don't you?"

"Certainly," he answered instantly. "You were my first—my favorite straight 3D star."

"Are you in 3D?" Vera-Ellen asked, a sudden gleam in her eyes.

"Was, my dear," Rickie said grandly. She ogled Ellenby through the fish-eye glasses. "Ah, straight 3D," she sighed. "Simple video-audio in depth—there was a great art-form." She began to sway again and they caught the reek of alcohol. "You know, gentlemen, it was handies that ruined my career. I had the looks and the voice, but I lacked the touch. Something in me shrank from the whole idea—be still, Widgie—and the girls with itchy fingers took over. But I'm talking too much about myself. It's hot and you wonderful gentlemen must be thirsty. Here, have a—"

The chauffeur glared at her as she reached fumblingly down into the tonneau. She caught the look and quailed slightly.

"—sandwich," she finished, coming up with a shiny can.

Madson accepted it from her, clicking the catch. The top popped four feet in the air, followed lazily by the uppermost sandwich, which he caught deftly. He handed the can to Ellenby, who served himself and handed it up to Vera-Ellen. Soon all three of them were munching.

"Miss Vickson," Vera-Ellen asked between mouthfuls, "do you think I could get a job in broadcast entertainment?"

Rickie looked at her sideways, leaning away to focus. "Not with that ghastly atom glow hair," she said. "Violet is old hat this year—it's either black, blonde or bald. But give me your hand, my, dear."

"Going to tell my fortune?"

"After a fashion." She held up Vera-Ellen's hand, squeezing and prodding it thoughtfully, as if she were testing the carcass of an alleged spring chicken. Then she nodded. "You'll do. Good strong hand, that's all that's needed, so you can really crunch the knuckles of the bohunks. They love it rough. Of course the technicians could step up the power when they broadcast your hand-squeeze, but the addicts don't feel it's the same thing." She looked sourly at her own delicate claws. "Yes, my dear, you'll have a chance in handies if you don't mind cuddling with two million dirty-minded bohunks every night and if Rickie Vickson's still got any entree at the studios." She made a face and dipped again into the tonneau, apparently to gulp something, for the chauffeur's glare was intensified.

"You're from New Angeles?" Madson asked politely when Rickie came up beaming.

"Old Angeles," she corrected. "My home's in a contaminated area. After 3D lighting I've never been afraid of hard radiations. But this time my psychic counselor told me—Widgie, I'm going to put you away in a nice little urn—that the bombs are going to miss New Angeles and fall on Old. That's why George is jetting me to the mountains. Others drink to still their fears. I do something about it—too."

"You mean you're going *away* from the studio?" Vera-Ellen demanded incredulously while Ellenby mumbled, "Bombs?" through a mouthful of sandwich.

"Of course," Rickie nodded. "Don't you know? Russia's touched a match to the Hot Truce. You charming gentlemen should keep up with these things."

"You see, I told you," Madson said to Ellenby. "One more victory for science."

"Miss Vickson, we better be getting on," the chauffeur interrupted, speaking for the first time. His voice was drunkenly thick. "We aren't out of the fusion fringe by a long shot and I don't like the looks of this place."

Rickie ignored him. Ellenby asked, "Was the news about Russia telefaxed?"

"Of course not." Rickie's smile was scornful. "They never tell the real truth these days. But they said to get out of our houses, and what else could that mean?"

"Miss Vickson, we better—" George began again.

"Quiet, George," Rickie ordered.

George groaned faintly, shrugged his shoulders, and reached out an arm to her without looking. Rickie handed him a red, limp plastic bottle. Just as he was putting it to his lips, he jerked as if stung, vaulted into the car, and began to stamp and punch at the controls.

With a mighty *pouf* the jet took hold. Ellenby skittered away from the hot blast. The Lunar '69 jumped forward.

THINGS hissed and snicked through the air. From nowhere, men began to appear. With a great lurch the car gained the road, roared toward the bridge. Vera-Ellen jumped up as if to get out, then was thrown back into the tonneau. Rickie lunged forward across the seat to save the red bottle. Her four-foot hat leaped upward, hesitated, and then spun off like a flying saucer.

A man rose from the wheat near the bridge. As the car jounced across it, he leveled a rapid-fire weapon. But just as he got it trained on the car, Rickie's hat landed on him. He went over backwards, firing at the sky.

Madson and Ellenby looked around in bewilderment. There must have been a dozen men. As they stared, another bunch came hurrying down the ruined lawn from the house on the hill.

The man by the bridge got up, went over to Rickie's hat and stamped on it.

Madson and Ellenby jumped as the sky-climbing missiles from his gun pattered down around them. When they looked around again, the men from the house on the hill were closing in.

Their leader was about five feet tall, but thick. His head had been formed in a bullet mold, his features looked drop-forged.

"I'm Harvey," he told them blankly. "What you got?"

Harvey's people wore everything from evening dress to shorts. There were even two women (who drifted toward Harvey) one in a gold kimono, the other in an off-the-bosom frock of filthy white lace. Everybody was armed.

"What you got?" Harvey repeated sharply. "I know you're loaded, I saw you talking with that rich-witch in the jet." He looked them over and grabbed at Madson's side pocket. "Books, huh?" he said like a hangman, dangling the Keats by a stray page. Then he turned to Ellenby. "Come on, Skinny," he said, "shell out."

When Ellenby hesitated, two of Harvey's men grabbed him, dumped him, and passed the contents of his pockets to their chief. When the spectroscope turned up, Harvey grinned. The eyes of his people twinkled in anticipation.

"Science gadget, huh?" he said. "Folks, there's been too much science in the world and too many words. Any minute now, more bombs are gonna fall. I do my humble bit to help 'em. I'm a great little junkman." He let the brass tube fall to the ground and lifted his foot. "Blow it a good-bye kiss, Skinny."

"Wait," Madson said abruptly, taking a step toward Harvey. "Don't do it." Then the poet's eyes grew wide and alarmed, as if he hadn't known he was going to say it.

Breaths sucked in around them. Harvey's turret head slowly turned toward Madson, its expression seemingly vacuous. "Why not?" Harvey whispered.

"Don't pay any attention to my friend," Ellenby interjected rapidly. "He just said that on account of me. Actually he hates science as much as you do. Don't—"

"Shaddup!" Harvey roared.

Then his voice instantly went low again. "Ain't nobody hates science more'n me, but ain't nobody tells me so. Shoulda kept your mouth shut, Skinny. Now there's gonna be more'n gadgets stomped, more'n books tore."

SILENCE CAME except for the faint sucks of breath, the faint scuffle of shoes on grit as Harvey's people slowly moved in. Ellenby stood helplessly, yet at the same time he felt a widening and intensification of his sensory powers. He was aware of the delicately lace-edged tree shadows cast from the hill ahead by the westering sun. At the other limit of his vision the copter no longer trailed its green caterpillar; for some reason it was buzzing closer along the road. At the same time he was conscious with a feverish clarity of the page by which Harvey dangled the Keats, and without reading the words he saw the lines:

Beauty is truth, truth beauty—that is all
Ye know on earth, and all ye need to know.

Suddenly the slowly advancing faces seemed to freeze and Ellenby was aware of something spectral and ominous about the yellowing sunlight and the whole acid-etched scene around him. It was something more than the physical threat to him and Madson— it was something that seemed to well up menacingly from the ground under his feet.

There was a sudden faint thunder and even as something inside Ellenby said, "That isn't it, that isn't what the sky's waiting for," he saw the chrome muzzle of the Lunar '69 bulleting toward them across the bridge with Vera-Ellen's violet mop above the wheel.

But even as the braking blasts gouted out redly from under the hood and the car crunched toward a stop in their midst, even as Harvey's people broke to either side and pistols popped with queerly toy-like reports, the thunder multiplied until it was impossible that the Lunar '69 was causing it, until it was like the thunder of a thousand invisible jets crushing the air around them. The sky shifted, rocked. The road shook. There came a shock that numbed Ellenby's feet and sent everyone around him reeling, and a pounding, smashing sound that made any remembered noise seem puny.

The Lunar '69, which had stopped a dozen feet from Ellenby, was pitching and tossing like a silver ship in a storm. Vera-Ellen was gripping the steering wheel with one hand and motioning to him frantically with the other. In the seat beyond her Rickie Vickson was jouncing as if in a merry-go-round chariot.

Ellenby lurched as a hand clutched his shoulder and a stag-gering Madson howled in his ear through the tumult, "Now you've got your rotten bombs!" Between him and the car Harvey's bullet head reared up and as suddenly dropped away. Looking down,

Ellenby saw that a chasm four feet wide had split the road between him and the car. Its walls were raw, smoking earth and rock. Down it Ellenby saw vanishing, in one frozen moment, Harvey and the Keats and the little brass spectroscope.

Then Ellenby realized he had grabbed Madson by the shoulder and thrown the two of them forward and shouted, "Jump!" For a moment the chasm gaped beneath them and a white little face stared upward. Then the chasm closed with a giant crunch and Ellenby's hand caught the side of the heaving car and he pitched into the back seat.

Through the diminishing thunder and shaking there came the toy roar of the car's jet and a new movement tipped him backward and he was looking toward the hill and it was getting bigger. He tried to put his feet down and felt something bulk under them. For a moment he thought it was Madson, but Madson was beside him on the seat, and then he saw it was George. He looked up and Rickie Vickson was watching him from where she was crouched in the front seat, her eyes without the teleglasses looking as foxy as Widgie's, whom she was holding close to her wrinkle-etched cheek.

"Vera-Ellen had to conk him," she explained, her gaze dipping to George. "The bum tried to betray us."

The pitching of the car had given way to a steady forward lunge. Ellenby nodded dully at Rickie and hitched himself around and looked back.

Harvey's people were scattering like ants through a dust cloud rising from the road.

The house on the hill still stood, though there were more and larger cracks in it and a nimbus of whiter dust around it.

By the bridge the copter had crashed and was flaming brightly. A tiny figure was running away from it.

ELLENBY'S face slowly lightened with understanding.

"We were on the San Andreas Rift," he said softly. "Madson, that wasn't the bombs at all. That wasn't Technology or Man." A smile trembled on his lips. "That was Nature. An earthquake."

Madson was the first to comment. "All right," he said, "it was Nature—Nature showing her disgust for Man."

"An idea like that is the sheerest animism," Ellenby reacted automatically. "Now if you try analyzing—"

"Analyzing," Madson snorted with a touch of the old fire. "You scientists are always—"

"Whoa, boys," Rickie Vickson interrupted. "If it hadn't been for that little quake to confuse things, Vera-Ellen couldn't have snatched you out no matter how pretty she tried. And I'm in no mood for arguments now. I'm not the arty type and all the science I know is what my psychic counselor tells me. Widgie, quit pounding your heart; it's all over now."

Ellenby touched her arm. "Do I understand," he asked, "that Vera-Ellen made you turn back just to save us?"

"Of course not," Rickie assured him. "Her father and his pals tried to stop us a couple of miles back. They'd been radioed by a farmer in a copter and had the road blocked. George wanted to hand you all over to Vera-Ellen's father, but we conked George—he's such a weakling—and got away. Picking you up was an afterthought."

Vera-Ellen flashed a wicked smile over her shoulder.

Ellenby realized he was feeling vastly contented. He started to lift his feet off George, then settled them more comfortably. He looked at the violet-topped new chauffeur handling the Lunar as if she'd never done anything else, and she picked that moment to flash him another half friendly, half insulting grin. He nudged Madson and said, "We'll continue our argument later—*all* our argument." Madson looked at him sharply and almost grinned too. Ellenby wondered idly what jobs they had for poets and physicists in 3D and handie studios.

Rickie Vickson's eyes widened. "Say," she said, "if they were just warning us about that little old earthquake, then Old Angeles isn't radioactive—I mean any *more* radioactive than it's ever been."

"Oh boy," Vera-Ellen crowed as the car topped the hill and the blue spires came back in sight, "New Angeles, here we come."

THE END

I, The Unspeakable

By Walt Sheldon

"What's in a name?" might be very dangerous to ask in certain societies, in which sticks and stones are also a big problem!

CHAPTER ONE

I FOUGHT to be awake. I was dreaming, but I think I must have blushed. I must have blushed in my sleep.

"Do it!" she said. *"Please do it! For me!"*

It was the voice that always came, low, intense, seductive, the sound of your hand on silk…and to a citizen of Northem, a conformist, it was shocking. I was a conformist then; I was still one that morning.

I awoke. The glowlight was on, slowly increasing. I was in my living machine in Center Four, where I belonged, and all the familiar things were about me, reality was back, but I was breathing very hard.

I lay on the pneumo a while before getting up. I looked at the chroner: 0703 hours, Day 17, Month IX, New Century Three. My morning nuro-tablets had already popped from the tube, and the timer had begun to boil an egg. The egg was there because the real food allotment had been increased last month. The balance of trade with Southem had just swung a decimal or two our way.

I rose finally, stepped to the mirror, switched it to positive and looked at myself. New wrinkles—or maybe just a deepening of the old ones. It was beginning to show; the past two years were leaving traces.

I hadn't worried about my appearance when I'd been with the Office of Weapons. There I'd been able to keep pretty much to myself, doing research on magnetic mechanics as applied to space drive. But other jobs, where you had to be among people, might be different. I needed every possible thing in my favor.

Yes, I still hoped for a job, even after two years. I still meant to keep on plugging, making the rounds.

I'd go out again today.

The timer clicked and my egg was ready. I swallowed the tablets and then took the egg to the table to savor it and make it last.

As I leaned forward to sit, the metal tag dangled from my neck, catching the glowlight. My identity tag.

Everything came back in a rush—

My name. The dream and *her* voice. And her suggestion.

Would I dare? Would I start out this very morning and take the risk, the terrible risk?

YOU remember renumbering. Two years ago. You remember how it was then; how everybody looked forward to his new designation, and how everybody made jokes about the way the letters came out, and how all the records were for a while fouled up beyond recognition.

The telecomics kidded renumbering. One went a little too far and they psycho-scanned him and then sent him to Marscol as a dangerous nonconform.

If you were disappointed with your new designation, you didn't complain. You didn't want a sudden visit from the Deacons during the night.

There had to be renumbering. We all understood that. With the population of Northem already past two billion, the old designation was too clumsy. Renumbering was efficient. It contributed to the good of Northem. It helped advance the warless struggle with Southem.

The equator is the boundary. I understand that once there was political difference and that the two superstates sprawled longitudinally not latitudinally, over the globe. Now they are pretty much the same. There is the truce, and they are both geared for war. They are both efficient states, as tightly controlled as an experiment with enzymes, as microsurgery, as the temper of a diplomat.

We were renumbered, then, in Northem. You know the system: everybody now has six digits and an additional prefix or suffix of four letters. Stateleader, for instance, has the designation AAAA-111/111. Now, to address somebody by calling off four letters is a little clumsy. We try to pronounce them when they are pronounceable. That is, no one says to Stateleader, "Good morning, A-A-A-A." They say, "Good morning, Aaaa."

Reading the last quote, I notice a curious effect. It says what I feel. Of course I didn't feel that way on that particular morning. I was still conformal; the last thing in my mind was that I would infract and be psycho-scanned.

Four letters then, and in many cases a pronounceable four-letter word.

A four letter word.

Yes, you suspect already. You know what a four-letter word can be.

Mine was.

It was unspeakable.

The slight weight on my forehead reminded me that I still wore my sleep-learner. I'd been studying administrative cybernetics, hoping to qualify in that field, although it was a poor substitute for a space drive expert. I removed the band and stepped across the room and turned off the oscillator. I went back to my egg and my bitter memories.

I will never forget the first day I received my new four letter combination and reported it to my chief, as required. I was unthinkably embarrassed. He didn't say anything. He just swallowed and choked and became crimson when he saw it. He didn't dare pass it to his secretarial engineer; he went to the administrative circuits and registered it himself.

I can't blame him for easing me out. He was trying to run an efficient organization, after all, and no doubt I upset its efficiency. My work was important—magnetic mechanics was the only way to handle quanta reaction, or the so-called non-energy drive, and was therefore the answer to feasible space travel beyond our present limit of Mars— and there were frequent inspection tours by Big Wheels and Very Important Persons.

Whenever anyone, especially a woman, asked my name, the embarrassment would become a crackling electric field all about us. The best tactic was just not to answer.

THE chief called me in one day. He looked haggard.

"Er—old man," he said, not quite able to bring himself to utter my name, "I'm going to have to switch you to another department. How would you like to work on nutrition kits? Very interesting work."

"Nutrition kits? *Me?* On nutrition kits?"

"Well, I—er—know it sounds unusual, but it justifies. I just had the cybs work it over in the light of present regulations, and it justifies."

Everything had to justify, of course. Every act in the monthly report had to be covered by regulations and cross-regulations. Of course there were so many regulations that if you just took the time to work it out, you could justify damn near anything. I knew what the chief was up to. Just to remove me from my post would have taken a year of applications and hearings and innumerable visits to the capital in Center One. But if I should infract—deliberately infract—it would enable the chief to let me go. The equivalent of resigning.

"I'll infract," I said. "Rather than go on nutrition kits, I'll infract."

He looked vastly relieved. "Uh—fine," he said. "I rather hoped you would."

It took a week or so. Then I was on Non-Productive status and issued an N/P book for my necessities. Very few luxury coupons in the N/P book. I didn't really mind at first. My new living machine was smaller, but basically comfortable, and since I was still a loyal member of the state and a verified conformist, I wouldn't starve.

But I didn't know what I was in for.

I went from bureau to bureau, office to office, department to department—any place where they, might use a space drive expert. A pattern began to emerge; the same story everywhere. When I mentioned my specialty they would look; delighted. When I handed them my tag and they saw my name, they would go into immediate polite confusion. As soon as they recovered they would say they'd call me if anything turned up…

A FEW weeks of this and I became a bit dazed.

And then there was the problem of everyday existence. You might say it's lucky to be an N/P for a while. I've heard people say that. Basic needs provided, worlds of leisure time; on the surface it sounds attractive.

But let me give you an example. Say it is monthly realfood day. You go to the store, your mouth already watering in anticipation. You take your place in line and wait for your package. The distributor takes your coupon book and is all ready to reach for your package— and then he sees the fatal letters N/P. Non-Producer. A drone, a drain upon the State. You can see his stare curdle. He scowls at the book again.

"Not sure this is in order. Better go to the end of the line. We'll check it later."

You know what happens before the end of the line reaches the counter. No more packages.

Well, I couldn't get myself off N/P status until I got a post, and with my name I *couldn't* get a post.

Nor could I change my name. You know what happens when you try to change something already on the records. The very idea of wanting change implies criticism of the State. Unthinkable behavior.

That was why this curious dream voice shocked me so. The thing that it suggested was quite as embarrassing as its non-standard, emotional, provocative tone.

Bear with me; I'm getting to the voice—to *her*—in a moment.

I want to tell you first about the loneliness, the terrible loneliness. I could hardly join group games at any of the rec centers. I could join no special interest clubs or even State Loyalty chapters. Although I dabbled with theoretical research in my own quarters, I could scarcely submit any findings for publication—not with my name attached. A pseudonym would have been non-regulation and illegal.

But there was the worst thing of all. I could not mate.

FUNNY, I hadn't thought about mating until it became impossible. I remember the first time, out of sheer idleness, I wandered into a Eugenic Center. I filled out my form very carefully and submitted it for analysis and assignment. The clerk saw my name, and did the usual double take. He coughed and swallowed and fidgeted.

He said, "Of course you understand that we must submit your application to the woman authorized to spend time in the mating booths with you, and that she has the right to refuse."

"Yes, I understand that."

"M'm," he said, and dismissed me with a nod.

I waited for a call in the next few weeks, still hoping, but I knew no woman would consent to meet a man with my name, let alone enter a mating booth with him.

The urge to reproduce myself became unbearable. I concocted all sorts of wild schemes.

I might infract socially and be classified a nonconform and sent to Marscol. I'd heard rumors that in that desolate land, on that desolate planet, both mingling and mating were rather disgustingly unrestricted. Casual mating would be terribly dangerous, of course, with all the wild irradiated genes from the atomic decade still around, but I felt I'd be willing to risk that. Well, almost...

About then I began to have these dreams. As I've told you, in the dream there was only this woman's seductive voice. The first time I heard it I awoke in a warm sweat and swore something had gone wrong with the sleep-learner. You never hear the actual words with this machine, of course; you simply absorb the concepts unconsciously. Still, it seemed an explanation. I checked thoroughly. Nothing wrong.

The next night I heard the woman's voice again.

"*Try it,*" she said. "*Do it. Start tomorrow to get your name changed. There will be a way. There must be a way. The rules are so mixed up that a clever man can do almost anything. Do it, please—for me.*"

SHE was not only trying to get me to commit nonconformity, but making heretical remarks besides. I awoke that time and half expected a Deacon to pop out of the tube and turn his electric club upon me.

And I heard the voice nearly every night.

It hammered away.

"*What if you do fail? Almost anything would be better than the miserable existence you're leading now!*"

One morning I even caught myself wondering just how I'd go about this idea of hers. Wondering what the first step might be.

She seemed to read my thoughts. That night she said, "*Consult the cybs in the Govpub office. If you look hard enough and long enough, you'll find a way.*"

Now, on this morning of the seventeenth day in the ninth month, better known as September, I ate my boiled egg very slowly and actually toyed with the idea. I thought of being on productive status again. I had almost lost my fanatical craving to be useful to the State, but I did want to be busy—desperately. I didn't want to be despised anymore. I didn't want to be lonely anymore. I wanted to reproduce myself.

I made my decision suddenly. Waves of emotion carried me along, I got up, crossed the room to the directory, and pushbuttoned to find the location of the nearest Govpub office.

I didn't know what would happen and almost didn't care.

CHAPTER TWO

LIKE most important places, the Govpub Office in Center Four was underground. I could have taken a tunnelcar more quickly, but it seemed pleasanter to travel topside. Or maybe I just wanted to put this off a bit. Think about it. Compose myself.

At the entrance to the Govpub warren there was a big director cyb, a plate with a speaker and switch. The sign on it said to switch it on and get close to the speaker and I did.

The cyb's mechanical voice—they never seem to get the "th" sounds right—said, "This is Branch Four of the Office of Government Publications. Say, 'Publications,' and/or, 'Information desired,' as thoroughly and concisely as possible. Use approved voice and standard phraseology."

Well, simple enough so far. I had always rather prided myself on my knack for approved voice, those flat, emotionless tones that indicate efficiency. And I would never forget how to speak Statese. I said, "Applicant desires all pertinent information relative assignment, change or amendment of State Serial designations, otherwise generally referred to as nomenclature."

There was a second's delay while the audio patterns tripped relays and brought the memory tubes in.

Then the cyb said, "Proceed to Numbering and Identity section. Consult alphabetical list and diagram on your left for location of same.

"Thanks," I said absent-mindedly.

I started to turn away and the cyb said, "Information on tanks is military information and classified. State authorization for—"

I switched it off.

NUMBERING and Identity wasn't hard to find. I took the shaft to the proper level and then it was only a walk of a few hundred yards through the glowlit corridors.

N. & I. turned out to be a big room, somewhat circular, very high ceilinged, with banks of cyb controls covering the upper walls.

Narrow passageways, like spokes, led off in several directions. There was an information desk in the center of the room.

I looked that way and my heart went into free fall.

There was a girl at the information desk. An exceptionally attractive girl. She was well within the limits of acceptable standard, and her features were even enough, and her hair a middle blonde—but she had something else. Hard to describe. It was a warmth, a buoyancy, a sense of life and intense animation. It didn't exactly show; it radiated. It seemed to sing out from her clear complexion, from her figure, which even a tunic could not hide, from everything about her.

And if I were to state my business, I would have to tell her my name.

I almost backed out right then. I stopped momentarily. And then common sense took hold and I realized that if I were to go through with this thing, here would be only the first of a long series of embarrassments and discomforts. It had to be done.

I walked up to the desk and the girl turned to face me, and I could have sworn that a faint smile crossed her lips. It was swift, like the shadow of a bird across one of the lawns in one of the great parks topside. Very non-standard. Yet I wasn't offended; if anything, I felt suddenly and disturbingly pleased.

"What information is desired?" she asked. Her voice was standard—or was it?

Again I had the feeling of restrained warmth.

I used colloquial. "I want to get the dope on State Serial designations, how they're assigned and so forth. Especially how they might be changed."

She put a handsteno on the desktop and said, "Name? Address? Post?"

I froze. I stood there and stared at her.

She looked up and said, "Well?"

"I—er—no post at present. N/P status."

Her fingers moved on the steno.

I gave her my address and she recorded that.

Then I paused again.

She said, "And your name?"

I took a deep breath and told her.

I didn't want to look into her eyes. I wanted to look away, but I couldn't find a decent excuse to. I saw her eyes become wide and noticed for the first time that they were a warm gray, almost a mouse color. I felt like laughing at that irrelevant observation, but more than that I felt like turning and running. I felt like climbing and dashing all over the walls like a frustrated cat and yelling at the top of my lungs. I felt like anything but standing there and looking stupid, meeting her stare—

SHE looked down quickly and recorded my name. It took her a little longer than necessary. In that time she recovered. Somewhat.

"All right," she said finally, "I'll make a search."

She turned to a row of buttons on a console in the center of the desk and began to press them in various combinations. A typer clicked away. She tore off a slip of paper, consulted it, and said, "Information desired is in Bank 29. Please follow me."

Well, following her was a pleasure, anyway. I could watch the movement of her hips and torso as she walked. She was not tall, but long-legged and extremely lithe. Graceful and rhythmic. Very, very feminine, almost beyond standard in that respect. I felt blood throb in my temples and was heartily ashamed of myself.

I would like to be in a mating booth with her, I thought, the full authorized twenty minutes. And I knew I was unconformist and the realization hardly scared me at all.

She led me down one of the long passageways.

A few moments later I said, "Don't you sometimes get—well, pretty lonely working here?" Personal talk at a time like this wasn't approved behavior, but I couldn't help it.

She answered hesitantly, but at least she answered. She said, "Not terribly. The cybs are company enough most of the time."

"You don't get many visitors, then."

"Not right here. N. & I. isn't a very popular section. Most people who come to Govpub spend their time researching in the ancient manuscript room. The—er—social habits of the pre-atomic civilization."

I laughed. I knew what she meant, all right. Pre-atomics and their ideas about free mating always fascinated people. I moved up beside her. "What's your name, by the way?"

"L-A-R-A 339/827."

I pronounced it. "Lara. Lah-rah. That's beautiful. Fits you, too."

SHE didn't answer; she kept her eyes straight ahead and I saw the faint spot of color on her check.

I had a sudden impulse to ask her to meet me after hours at one of the rec centers. If it had been my danger alone, I might have, but I couldn't very well ask her to risk discovery of a haphazard, unauthorized arrangement like that and the possibility of going to the psychoscan.

We came to a turn in the corridor and something happened; I'm not sure just how it happened. I keep telling myself that my movements were not actually deliberate. I was to the right of her. The turn was to the left. She turned quickly, and I didn't, so that I bumped into her, knocking her off balance. I grabbed her to keep her from falling.

For a moment we stood there, face to face, touching each other lightly. I held her by the arms. I felt the primitive warmth of her breath. Our eyes held together...proton...electron...I felt her tremble.

She broke from my grip suddenly and started off again.

After that she was very businesslike.

We came finally to the controls of Bank 2 and she stood before them and began to press button combinations. I watched her work; I watched her move. I had almost forgotten why I'd come here. The lights blinked on and off and the typers clacked softly as the machine sorted out information.

She had a long printed sheet from the roll presently. She frowned at it and turned to me. "You can take this along and study it," she said, "but I'm afraid what you have in mind may be—a little difficult."

She must have guessed what I had in mind. I said, "I didn't think it would be easy."

"It seems that the only agency authorized to change a State Serial under any circumstances is Opsych."

"Opsych?" You can't keep up with all these departments.

"The Office of Psychological Adjustment. They can change you if you go from a lower to higher E.A.C."

"I don't get it, exactly."

As she spoke I had the idea that there was sympathy in her voice. Just an overtone. "Well," she said, "as you know, the post a person is qualified to hold often depends largely on his Emotional Adjustment Category. Now if he improves and passes from, let us say, Grade 3 to

Grade 4, he will probably change his place of work. In order to protect him from any associative maladjustments developed under the old E.A.C., he is permitted a new number.

I groaned. "But I'm already in the highest E.A.C.!"

"It looks very uncertain then."

"Sometimes I think I'd be better off in the mines, or on Marscol—or—in the hell of the pre-atomics!"

She looked amused. "What did you say your E.A.C was?"

"Oh, all right. Sorry." I controlled myself and grinned. "I guess this whole thing has been just a little too much for me. Maybe my E.A.C's even gone down."

"That might be your chance then."

"How do you mean?"

"If you could get to the top man in Opsych and demonstrate that your number has inadvertently changed your E.A.C., he might be able to justify a change."

"By the State, he might!" I punched my palm. "Only how do I get to him?"

"I can find his location on the cyb here. Center One, the capital, for a guess. You'll have to get a travel permit to go there, of course. Just a moment."

She worked at the machine again, trying it on general data. The printed slip came out a moment later and she read it to me. Chief, Opsych, was in the capital all right. It didn't give the exact location of his office, but it did tell how to find the underground bay in Center One containing the Opsych offices.

We headed back through the passageway then and she kept well ahead of me. I couldn't keep my eyes from her walk, from the way she walked with everything below her shoulders. My blood was pounding at my temples again.

I tried to keep the conversation going. "Do you think it'll be hard to get a travel permit?"

"Not impossible. My guess is that you'll be at Travbur all day tomorrow, maybe even the next day. But you ought to be able to swing it if you hold out long enough."

I sighed. "I know. It's that way everywhere in Northem. Our motto ought to be, 'Why make it difficult when with just a little more effort you can make it impossible?'"

SHE started to laugh, and then, as she emerged from the passageway into the big circular room, she cut her laugh short.

A second later, as I came along, I saw why.

There were two Deacons by the central desk. They were burly and had that hard, pinched-face look and wore the usual black belts. Electric clubs hung from the belts. Spidery looking pistols were at their sides.

I didn't know whether these two had heard my crack or not. I know they kept looking at me.

Lara and I crossed the room silently, she back to her desk, I to the exit door. The Deacons' remote, disapproving eyes swung in azimuth, tracking us.

I walked out and wanted to turn and smile at Lara, and get into my smile something of the hope that someday, somewhere, I'd see her again—but of course I didn't dare.

CHAPTER THREE

I HAD the usual difficulties at Travbur the next day. I won't go into them, except to say that I was batted from office to office like a ping pong ball, and that, when I finally got my travel permit, I was made to feel that I had stolen an original Picasso from the State Museum.

I made it in a day. Just. I got my permit thirty seconds before closing time. I was to take the jetcopter to Center One at 0700 hours the following morning.

In my living machine that evening, I was much too excited to work at theoretical research as I usually did after a hard day of tramping around. I bathed, I paced a while, I sat and hummed nervously and got up and paced again. I turned on the telepuppets. There was a drama about the space pilots who fly the nonconformist prisoners to the forests and pulp-acetate plants on Mars. Seemed that the Southern political prisoners who are confined to the southern hemisphere of Mars, wanted to attack and conquer the north. The nonconformists, led by our pilot, came through for the State in the end. Corn is thicker than water. Standard.

There were, however, some good stereofilm shots of the limitless forests of Mars, and I wondered what it would be like to live there, in a green, fresh-smelling land. Pleasant, I supposed, if you could put up with the no doubt revolting morality of a prison planet.

And the drama seemed to point out that there was no more security for the nonconformists out there than for us here on Earth. Maybe somewhere in the universe, I thought, there would be peace for men. Somewhere beyond the solar system, perhaps, someday when we had the means to go there...

Yet instinct told me that wasn't the answer, either. I thought of a verse by an ancient pre-atomic poet named Hoffenstein. (People had unwieldy, random combinations of letters for names in those days.) The poem went:

> Wherever I go,
> *I* go too,
> And spoil everything.

That was it. The story of mankind.

I turned the glowlight down and lay on the pneumo after a while, but I didn't sleep for a long, long time.

Then, when I did sleep, when I had been sleeping, I heard the voice again. The low, seductive woman's voice—the startling, shocking voice out of my unconscious.

"*You have taken the first step,*" she said. "*You are on your way to freedom. Don't stop now. Don't sink back into the lifelessness of conformity. Go on...on and on. Keep struggling, for that is the only answer...*"

I DIDN'T exactly talk back, but in the queer way of the dream, I *thought* objections. I was in my thirties, at the midpoint of my life, and the whole of that life had been spent under the State. I knew no other way to act. Suppressing what little individuality I might have was, for me, a way of survival. I was chockfull of prescribed, stereotyped reactions, and I held onto them even when something within me told me what they were. This wasn't easy, this breaking away, not even this slight departure from the secure, camouflaged norm...

"*The woman, Lara, attracts you,*" said the voice.

I suppose at that point I twitched or rolled in my sleep. Yes, the voice was right, the woman Lara attracted me. So much that I ached with it.

"Take her. Find a way. When you succeed in changing your name, and know that you can do things, then find a way. There will be a way."

The idea at once thrilled and frightened me.

I woke writhing and in a sweat again.

It was morning.

I dressed and headed for the jetcopter stage and the ship for Center One.

The ship was comfortable and departed on time, a transport with seats for about twenty passengers. I sat near the tail and moodily busied myself watching the gaunt brown earth far below. Between Centers there was mostly desert, only occasional patches of green. Before the atomic decade, I had heard, nearly all the earth was green and teemed with life...birds, insects, animals, people, too. It was hard rock and sand now, with a few scrubs hanging on for life. The pre-atomics, who hadn't mastered synthesization, would have a hard time scratching existence from the earth today.

I tried to break the sad mood, and started to look around at some of the other passengers. That was when I first noticed the prisoners in the forward seats. Man and woman, they were, a youngish, rather nondescript couple, thin, very quiet. They were manacled and two Deacons sat across from them. The Deacons' backs were turned to me and I could see the prisoners' faces.

They had curious faces. Their eyes were indescribably sad, and yet their lips seemed to be ready to smile at any moment.

They were holding hands, not seeming to care about this vulgar emotional display.

I had the sudden crazy idea that Lara and I were sitting there, holding hands like that, nonconforming in the highest, and that we were wonderfully happy. Our eyes were sad too, but we were really happy, quietly happy, and that was why our lips stayed upon the brink of a smile.

I SIGHED. My mood was just as sad, if not sadder, than it had been before.

Later, in the rest room, I had a chance to talk to one of the Deacons guarding these two. I was washing my hands when he came in, and he nodded to me briefly and said, "Nice day for a flight."

He seemed pleasant enough, more than I would expect a Deacon to be. He was tall and blond and rather lithe; his shoulders sloped forward like a boxer's.

"Taking those prisoners to Center One?" I asked.

He nodded. "Yup. Habitual nonconforms. About as bad as they come."

"What did they do?"

He chuckled lasciviously. "Kept meeting each other in the rec centers. Didn't know they were being watched. We nabbed 'em topside after they'd gone out in the desert together."

"What happens to them now—Marscol?"

"They'd be lucky, brother, if that was only it. Oh, we'll ship 'em to Mars sooner or later, but first they got to be interviewed."

"You mean for reclassification?"

"No. Just interviewed. We do it routine with everybody we pick up now. Specially morals cases. That's how we crack down on other nonconforms. They got a regular organization, you know."

"They *have?*"

"Sure. They're all Southern spies. Trying to weaken us for an attack, that's all. I can spot 'em a mile away."

I frowned and cleared my throat a little. "Wouldn't you think that any spies would try to act as normal as possible and not call attention to themselves by infracting morally?"

He put a big finger on my chest. "Listen, you got no idea. I see these buzzards in operation all the time. I know what goes on."

"Of course. I'm sure you do." I kept the sarcasm out of my voice, but it was a struggle.

The finger tapped my chest, once to every word, it seemed. "We interview 'em all. Some of 'em, they really got nothing to tell us and the interview kind of breaks 'em. Know what I mean? But we got to do it. If we only get dope on other nonconforms from one out of ten, we figure we didn't waste our time."

"You mean these—interviews of yours are a form of *torture?*"

He gave me a hard eye and said, "We don't call it that, brother. We don't call it that."

"Of course," I said again, and went back to washing my hands.

I watched the prisoners for the rest of the flight. I couldn't stop watching them. And all this time I kept thinking of Lara, visualizing her, seeing her young figure and her light hair and her mouse-colored eyes, and not really knowing why.

I had the overpowering desire to spring forward and throttle the two Deacons and help the prisoners to escape. *Almost* overpowering. I didn't, naturally.

The jetcopter lowered toward the great green parks that cover the topside area of Center One. It was really refreshing to see them. I understood that the lucky residents of Center One were allowed to wander in these parks, and look at the growing things and the sky. Then, presently, the parks were out of sight again and we were settling on the concrete landing stage and I was back to reality.

THE first contact at the Office of Psychological Adjustment was, as usual, an information desk. There were people instead of cybs to greet you and I suppose that was because of the special complications of problems brought here. The cybs have their limits, after all.

A gray man with a gray eye and a face like a mimeographed bulletin looked at me and said, in approved voice and standard phraseology, "what information is desired?"

I told him.

His eyebrows rose, as if suddenly buoyant. *"Change your name? That's impossible."*

I quoted, verse and chapter, the regulation covering it. "H'm," he said. His eyebrows came down, cuddling into a scowl. "Well, that's highly unusual procedure. Better let me see your identity tag."

I gave that to him and he saw my N/P status, and then my unspeakable name, and his eyebrows went up again.

"Perhaps you'd better get this straightened out with General Administration first," he said. He scribbled a slip of paper, showing me how to get there.

The rat race was on.

I found General Administration. They sent me to Activity Control. Activity Control said they couldn't do a thing until I was registered. I went to Registration. Registration said oh, no, I shouldn't have been sent there—although they'd try to direct me to the proper office if I got an okay from Investigation and Security. I. & S. said the regulation I quoted had been amended and I would have to have the amendment first and I could find that in Records. Records sent me back to the first place to get a Search Permit.

And so on.

I kept at it doggedly. Toward the end of the day my legs ached and my head felt like a ball of granite. I had discovered that Opsych had nearly as many levels and tunnels and bays as Center Four in its entirety and I had taken the intercom cars when possible, but most of it had been walking. I tightened my jaw and pulled my stomach in. I'd get to see the Chief if it took me a year.

That was hyperbole, of course. No man could last a year walking those dim, monotonous, aseptic corridors. How can I describe the feeling? The corridors are the same wherever you go. The glowlight comes steadily, unblinkingly, from the walls. The color is a dead oyster white.

There is always the feeling of being lost—even when you know, or think you know, exactly where you are.

IT WAS near the end of the day and I was back at the information desk.

"You again," said the gray man with the gray eye.

"Records says I need a Search Permit. I have to find an amendment on the regulation covering my case."

"Why don't you just give up? You're causing us a great deal of trouble, you know. We have other work to do. Important work."

"So have I. I'm a magnetic mechanics expert. I could be working for the State right now if I could get a post. I can't get a post till my name's changed."

"That's ridiculous."

"I agree. But it's true just the same."

"Well, here's your Search Permit. But I still think you'd be wiser to forget it. And you'd save us a lot of fuss."

I leaned across the desk. "You could save the whole organization a lot of fuss if you'd direct me to the Chief's office. Then I could take my case up with him directly. I've been keeping my eye open for it, but I can't find it anywhere, and of course nobody'll direct me there, even if they know where it is."

He stared at me with mild horror. *"Go direct to the Chief's office? Without going through channels?"*

"Well, that's what I had in mind."

"Then you'd better get it out of your mind. That's pretty dangerous thinking. That's close to infraction."

"All right." I sighed. "I'll do it the hard way." I took the Search Permit and went back to Records. I was still searching for the amendment when closing time came.

I went back into the dim white corridors and found a foodmat, got some nuro-pills and reviewed the day. These workers here in Center One were experts at putting you off. They were much more skilful than the officials in Center Four. Maybe that was why they were in Center One. Maybe I never would wear them down.

That thought came along and formed a ball of ice right in the bottom of my stomach.

I had to think. I had to think and rest. Real air and a night breeze would help.

I found a shaft and went topside.

I started walking along a winding trail in the great park. The stars were out. They were diamonds, ground to dust, and thrown carelessly across the black velvet of the sky. The moon had not yet risen. There was a breeze, cool and light, and it brought temporary sanity. At least it helped me realize I was tired.

I came to a little brook, and, instead of crossing the footbridge, I turned and followed the brook upstream. It led through groves of trees and presently I found a little clearing where the bank sloped gently and was covered with soft moss. At the water's edge, the bank and a rock formation made a kind of overhanging ledge and I sat on this a while and stared at the water, liquid silver, tumbling below.

Finally I moved up the bank a little, wrapped my cloak around me and lay down. I looked at the stars. I wondered which one might be Mars. It was red, I'd heard, but I saw nothing like that. Probably it wasn't visible now. I got to thinking about Mars, and I got to thinking about the prison colony there, and then I got to thinking about the primitive life, and then free-mating.

That made me think of Lara, and her firm body and long, clean limbs and blonde hair and mouse-colored eyes.

I drifted off to sleep. Lara stayed with me; she stepped into my dream. It was a wonderful dream. Her voice, when she broke from standard, was thrilling and delicious. It was linked with the tumbling of the brook somehow. She was warm and vibrant in my arms. She was alive, so alive. She was all movement.

We were laughing together and...

I AWOKE to the sound of shooting.

The moon had risen and the broad glades were silver green and the trees were casting shadows. Voices were barking back and forth within the woods.

"Over that way!" called one.

"Cut 'em off! Cut 'em off!" yelled another.

A man and woman, both entirely naked, both speckled with wounds and bruises, all standard in questioning, stumbled into the clearing. Their eyes were wild, big for their faces. They were thin. They gasped for breath. They looked around them, rats in mazes, and then saw me.

They drew back.

"This way!" called a voice from the wood.

Another shot rang out.

I stared at the man and woman, still too surprised to know what to do or say.

They were the two prisoners I had seen in the jetcopter on my way to Center One.

CHAPTER FOUR

MAYBE I was not quite awake. Maybe I was not really bright, though everybody thinks of himself as bright, I suppose. Maybe it was everything that had happened since the renumbering. Maybe I was fed up and maybe something about the quiet woods called out: *Rebel! Rebel!*

I don't know.

I pointed to the brook, the overhanging bank, and said, "In there! Quick!"

They scuttled. They passed me and looked at me half-thankfully, half-fearfully.

The voices came nearer.

"Come on! This way! They can't get far!"

I wrapped myself in my cloak and sat down and pretended to be gazing at the stars.

A moment later three Deacons burst upon the clearing. I turned slowly, and stared at them, showing mild artificial surprise. Handsome, burly fellows. The one in the middle was a positive Apollo; I was sure that he waved his hair. He glared at me.

"You," he said.

"Me?"

"Yes, you. What are you doing here ?"

I said, "I'm sitting here."

"What for?"

"The night air. To study the stars. Get a change of scene." I shrugged.

Apollo stepped forward and held out his hand. "Your tag."

This was it. When he saw my four-letter name he'd really start working on me. I unsnapped the tag from my neckband and handed it to him.

He looked at it, but didn't change expression. The Deacons are well trained. He looked up again. "N/P, eh?"

"Yes."

"And you belong in Center Four."

"Yes."

"Explain."

I did. Or tried to. Things were roiling around inside me, keeping me from thinking clearly. Once, as I talked, I thought I heard movement under the bank, but the Deacons didn't seem to notice anything. I tried to tell them of my troubles.

There was no sympathy in their eyes.

Apollo said, "See anybody pass by here?"

"Pass by?" I hoped my look was innocent. "Who?"

"Two fugitives. Nonconforms. Escaped during interview. Got the force screen turned off somehow—must have had spies helping them. You didn't see them, eh?"

I shook my head. "I haven't seen anyone for several hours."

APOLLO and his two friends traded glances. The one on the right was bull-necked and redheaded; the one on the left had a neck and nose like a crane. It was the one on the left who suddenly smiled. Not a pleasant smile. He stepped up to Apollo and whispered something in his ear. Then Apollo smiled and turned to me again.

"You're *sure* you haven't seen anyone."

He knew something. I didn't know what, but it was too late to back out now. I said, "Of course I'm sure."

Apollo kept his eyes on me, hard, flat, stony, and held out his hand to the crane-like Deacon. "Your light," he said. The other handed it to him. Apollo flashed it on the ground. It came to rest upon unmistakable footprints in the soft moss. They led to the bank.

I could be certain of arrest and one of their little interviews now. I really had nothing to lose. Nothing that wasn't already lost—

"Run!" I shouted at the top of my lungs. "They're coming!"

There was a rustling under the bank.

I leaped at Apollo. I leaped hard, with my feet solid, pushing me forward. My shoulder hit him in the midriff. He went down. I scrambled over him and jammed my thumb into his shoulder. He screamed.

There was a buzzing sound and the smell of burned flesh, and a tenth of a second later I felt pain. One of the others had jammed his electric truncheon into the small of my back. It bored in, it burned, and I writhed and yelled. I couldn't help it. I rolled over.

Someone was kicking at me. I grabbed his leg and pulled him down and when he struck the ground I twisted. Another shape blurred toward me—Apollo, recovered and on his feet again. Then buzzing, burned flesh, and the pain this time in the back of my neck. My head swirled. I thrashed, trying to get away. Get away where? That made not much difference. Away, that was all.

The buzzing continued. It was through my flesh now and touching the spine. It would destroy the nerves in a moment. I would be dead—or even worse, a limp cripple, a rag doll.

The smell of roasted flesh and hair was a thick, choking, sickening fog of decay. I couldn't breathe. There was blackness, swirling and concentric, closing in.

I think one of them kicked me in the groin before I lost consciousness.

I couldn't be sure. I couldn't be sure of anything.

COMING out. Sound before sight and I heard the low voices. My eyes were already open. Nebulous shapes, now sharpening.

I was in a small room with gleaming metal walls and I was on my back on a sort of table. Three men were in the room with me, standing over me. Apollo...the bull-necked man...the man with the nose like a crane.

Apollo was smiling. Pour water over that smile and immediately a film of ice would form.

"A spy," said Apollo, looking into my open eyes. "Another damn spy."

I shook my head. Ridiculous, but that's what I did. The movement pulled at the wound in the back of my neck and sharp pain, starting there, shot through my whole body. I grimaced and groaned.

Apollo laughed, then suddenly brought his club hard across my face. My cheekbone seemed to make a crunching sound.

"A spy, a damned spy," said Apollo.

"We got a confession for you to sign," said the Crane.

Apollo said, "Shut up. Not yet. We got to interview him first."

"Look," I said, trying to lift my head, trying to rise upon my elbows, "call your chief. Call anybody like that. I can explain this whole thing. It's a long story—"

HE HIT me again across the other cheekbone.

Shall I describe the next timeless endless hour? All the details? I don't remember all of them, of course, just the moments of sharpest pain that lifted me from the daze. Just the sound of my own screaming at times, and the helpless dryness of my own throat, and the sounds that kept coming from it even when the vocal cords were numb.

Apollo and his pals had fun.

There were the electric clubs. They become so hot at the tip that they will burn through an inch of pine in a couple of seconds. They go even quicker through flesh. After a while the smoke of my own burning flesh was thick in the room, and we all choked a little on it.

They had more fun with their fists, though. They didn't burn me in the worst places. They saved them for their fists and hands.

After a while I couldn't scream. Only a hoarse, helpless, retching sound came out whenever I opened my mouth.

Did I hear their voices then? I couldn't be sure whether I heard them speak, or whether I dreamed that they spoke.

"He can't feel it any more now." That was Apollo's voice.

"Wake him up again," said the Crane. "Give him a shot."

"Oh, hell, I'm hungry," said Apollo.

"All right," said the Crane, "let's go get something to eat. We can always come back again."

Blackness, sweet blackness, and the sense of floating among the stars. Nothingness. It was exquisite now...even the touch of agony that still seeped through was exquisite.

How much of this, I don't know.

I heard a voice again, and at first I thought my precious blackness was leaving me. I struggled to keep it. I grasped out, clutching with my mind.

"Don't give up...we are coming..."

It was *her* voice. The low, seductive voice of my dreams. But I didn't want to hear it now; this was the last thing I wanted to hear. This voice had brought me here, and I never wanted to hear it again.

"No matter what they say...no matter what they offer you or tell you...don't give up."

I fought it off. I drove it away by sheer mind-power. Either that or it stopped of itself. I didn't know and didn't care; all I wanted was peace and blackness again if I could find it.

And then, after a while, I was awake, truly awake, and I knew this because I ached and burned all over. I could scarcely move. I lay on the table-like thing and stared at the gleaming metal ceiling, not really seeing it.

"How do you feel?" said somebody.

I TURNED my head. The somebody was sitting beside me. He was a man of about fifty, thickset and gray-haired with skin that looked like fine porcelain. His eyes were blue and they seemed able, intelligent. He was not exactly smiling, but his expression was pleasant. Poised—that was the word. Here was a man who would quietly control things wherever he would go.

I said, "Lousy. And you?"

Ghost of a smile. "Sorry you had to go through it. We pick the Deacons because they're sadistically inclined. That makes for efficiency in the long run. Some people suffer, of course, but it's for the common good."

I didn't say anything. If I had, it would have been insulting, unreasonable, blasphemous, obscene and treasonable. So I didn't say anything. I just kept staring at him.

He continued to smile. "I'm N-J-K-F one seven seven three four nine, Chief of the Office of Psychological Adjustment. I'm usually simply Chief. I want you to consider me your friend—within the limits of State good, that is."

I still didn't say anything.

"Yours is quite a case, and of course I understand it. I think I had a quick insight into it the moment I spotted the arrest report on you.

You're really lucky I happened to go through the arrest reports a little while ago, and got to you before the three Deacons who interviewed you returned. They were going to interview you some more."

"Yes. I'm very lucky." My voice was flat, lifeless.

He leaned back easily in the chair. For all that he was thickset, he was graceful. He was handsome. His head, and deep, pleasant voice, and the cut of his porcelain features all were handsome. Trust in me, said this handsomeness, I am a father to all men.

"Naturally, we want to excuse your actions, and all the infractions you have committed in your rather desperate struggle for escape from your situation. Of course we'll have to re-evaluate your Emotional Adjustment Category. It must be very low by now. And I think I'll be able to assign a new name to you, and have it justified."

Funny, here was the thing I'd sought and fought for, and now I had it, and this was the end of the long fight, and I didn't feel triumphant at all. I didn't even feel pleased. Funny.

The chief said, "You can undoubtedly find a post suitable to a lower E.A.C. You can work your way up again. At least you'll be on productive status and have all the privileges that go with it."

"Yes," I said. "Yes, I suppose so."

"So there's really nothing to worry about now, is there?"

"No, I suppose not."

"There's just one little thing I'd like to go into before I take the steps necessary to get you on your feet again." Even his magnificent poise couldn't conceal the feather touch of slyness then.

"One little thing?" I asked.

THE pain was with me again. My body wasn't flesh; it was all raw, clinging pain.

"We'll have to know who started you on your little quest. Who influenced you to try to have your name changed."

I said, "I don't understand what you're talking about."

He looked patient, smilingly patient. "It's rather obvious, you know. You wouldn't have acted as you did purely on your own impulses. I know that, because I cybed for your master file after I saw the report of arrest. Up until two days ago, your actions have always been satisfactorily conformal. A man doesn't change overnight like that without some sort of external influence."

"But there wasn't any," I protested. "I mean, nobody told me to do anything. Nobody real."

He chuckled. "Come now, you don't expect me to believe that, do you? After all, I deal with cases like this quite often. You're not the only one who has tried to upset the efficiency of the State. There's a pattern in these things, my friend. Almost invariably we find that a deliberate influence has gone to work on our infractor. There's a dangerous, organized underground movement that spends its time bringing these things about. One of its members unquestionably contacted you, suggested that you take the steps you have taken. Now, then, who was it?"

"Nobody." I looked blank because I felt blank.

The Chief sighed. "You've changed more than I thought. Probably you're emotionally angry with the State now, after that little interview with the Deacons. That's understandable. But you'll have to come back to your senses. Let's put it this way, old man. *If I don't get this information from you right now, the Deacons will.*"

"Listen," I said, "what I'm telling you is the truth. There was nobody who told me to do anything. There was—well, there was a kind of voice that used to come into my dreams. A woman's voice. It suggested, in my dreams, that I go ahead and try to get my name changed. That's all."

He wasn't smiling any more. "Do you really expect me to believe that?"

"It's the truth, I tell you. It's the truth!"

"Perhaps whoever influenced you did it subtly. Perhaps you never even realized it. Think back now. Who helped you? Who departed from standard and gave you any kind of aid?"

Realization came like a cold wash. There *had* been help. Lara. She had gone out of her way back there in N. & I. She had been warm and real and she had dropped the mask of efficiency. Could it have been with a purpose? No matter. Guilty or innocent, if I mentioned her name, she would be interviewed. I didn't want that to happen to Lara. I shook my head and said, "No one helped me. I did it all myself. You've got to believe that."

"I don't," said the Chief, and got up. He looked at me for just a moment before he turned away. He said, "The boys will be able to have their fun, after all. I suppose it's just as well. It keeps their morale up to be able to interview somebody once in a while."

"No! You can't! You can't send them in here again!" I shouted, without meaning to. I struggled to rise and found that I was strapped to the table. "No! No!"

He was standing at the doorway to the room. He held a key-box oscillator in his hand and I knew that a force screen held me in the cubicle here, and that without a key-box I could beat my head forever against that invisible barrier and never pass through that doorway. He said, "I'll give you one hour to decide. I'll be back. I'll ask you if you're ready to talk. If you aren't—well, you'll talk to the Deacons instead of me."

The key-box hummed and he walked through the doorway and turned and disappeared.

I stared after him and fought back my sudden nausea.

CHAPTER FIVE

How long, then, lying there before a key-box hummed again? I didn't know. My time sense had been dulled. Even the pain was dull now; it was something that had always existed.

I looked at the shining ceiling.

The glowlights began to dim and I supposed that since my arrest in the park another day had passed.

Most of all, I wondered. Something had happened to me, something that I could almost feel as a physical change, but I didn't know quite what it was. I knew its results. I knew that I was no longer standard, no longer conformal, no longer well behaved and moral and an efficient, useful citizen of the State. I hated the State. I hated all States. I hate all efficiency and common sense and hate.

It suddenly came to me that I didn't care whether I was in Southem or Northem, or which of them ruled the world.

I lay there.

And presently a key-box hummed and I didn't even look that way. The stink of my own burning flesh still clung to my nostrils, the dull pain was still with me, but I didn't care. It was too much. When horror becomes too great, it stops being horror. The mind is smart. It doesn't believe; it doesn't register. The curve of sensation flattens out, stops, almost.

When such horror looms, you go on doing whatever you are doing.

I was lying there, so I went on lying there.

"Don't speak," whispered a voice. "Don't ask questions."

Something fumbled at the straps.

I turned my head, and two people were in the room. They were thin, and their eyes were overlarge and they were naked and covered with bruises. The fugitives of the park last night!

"What are you doing here?"

Finger to the lips. That was the man. He was taking the straps from my legs. The woman was releasing my arms and shoulders.

"But—"

"Sh!" That was the woman.

In a moment they had me free. I started, confidently, to rise, and the pain streaked through me like a powder rocket. They helped me. I stood there, amazed that I could stand. They helped me go forward. I took several dizzy steps, and after that it wasn't as bad. We moved through the doorway; there was no force screen. The man held the key-box. He pressed it as we moved away, to bring the force screen into place once more.

I said, "Where are we—?"

I was shushed again. We went on through the corridors. Dead oyster white corridors. I walked as through a sea of marshmallow. Time sense was gone again and we were pushing on and on and there was no end in sight and we had already forgotten the beginning.

We took an automatic shaft to another level and walked more corridors.

ONCE we passed an opening and tunnelcars filled with people roared past. I had a flash glimpse of them. They sat there staring straight ahead, wearing the efficient expressions of good workers. State corpses.

Suddenly we emerged into the dark. It was the dark of night, but after the tunnels it was practically sunrise. The air was clean—no, it was not actually as clean as the conditioned air below. It was more than clean. It was *alive*.

We were on the edge of a great concrete paved area. About a hundred yards ahead, a massive, shining, fat needle rose into the air, and squatted there against the stars. It was a spaceship in its launching cradle. There were low buildings near it, a few floodlights, and people standing around. It took a moment to realize that the men walking up and down and along the groups of people, the men with rifles on their shoulders, were guards.

"Luck, now, that's all we need. A little luck," said the thin man beside me. It was the first time I had heard his voice. It was a low voice; he spoke with emotion. It was not approved standard.

The woman moved beside him and put her hand upon his arm.

I said, "May I talk now?"

He turned to me, smiling. The smile had something of that sadness I had first noticed when he sat a prisoner in the jetcopter. "You want an explanation, don't you? Of course you do. But I'm afraid I can't tell you very much, except that we were sent to get you."

"Sent? By whom? How did you have a key-box? And—"

He laughed. "Wait, one question at a time. I was a force screen technician before—before we were arrested. Cells are the same everywhere. I know how to short the screens out from the inside; it's troublesome, but it can be done. That's how we escaped the first time. Then they discovered we were gone, chased us, and *you* gave us our second chance. We came here to the rendezvous. There were six here, including our elected leader. When we told the leader what had happened, she arranged for us to return, find you, and help you escape. It wasn't any problem to lift a key-box from the rack where they're usually kept."

I FELT as though I had been put upon the end of a huge oscillating spring. I said, "The leader? She?"

"You'll meet her," he said. "After blastoff you'll meet her. Right now our problem is to slip in among those prisoners without being seen."

"Among the *prisoners*?"

"Haven't time to explain more. You'll have to trust us. Unless you want to stay here and have the Deacons hunt you till they find you."

He was right: wherever I was going, I had to go. I couldn't go back now. Ever. I said, "I trust you. Let's go."

Slipping in wasn't really difficult. There were only one or two guards for each group of prisoners, and they were looking for someone to escape, not join their flock. Some of the prisoners were dressed, some naked. Some looked bruised and beaten; some did not. It all depended on whether they had been questioned. They all looked dull-eyed, resigned. They paid remarkably little attention as we moved in among them, and stood there.

THE guards began to call out orders presently and the groups shuffled forward, and then single lines moved up the ramp and into the spaceship. The thin man and his woman were still with me. "They don't bother to count," he whispered, "so we won't be noticed."

I wanted to ask him other questions, but we were divided into groups and they weren't in mine.

Minutes later I found myself in the vast hull, sitting on one of the tiers that hold the seats vertical when the ship is tail-based for blastoff. It was very dim here and I couldn't readily make out the faces of the people on the same tier with me.

A loudspeaker came to life; a deep, impersonal voice. "Fasten your webbings carefully!"

I did that and heard the rustling sounds about me as the others did it, too.

"Stand by for blastoff!"

There was a dead pause, then a sudden low throbbing roar and the feeling of life in the floor plates and the bulkheads. I felt the slightest weight of pressure against the seat. The scat began to tilt slightly.

Suddenly a soft voice on my left spoke: *"We're on our way. They can't stop us now, can they?"*

It was the same low, provocative woman's voice that I had heard in my dreams!

I whirled my head. I could see only the shape of flowing hair, no features. "Who are you?"

She laughed. "No wonder you don't recognize me. The natural voice is different than approved standard, isn't it? Listen. Do you remember this?" The head cocked to one side and a crisp, formal voice came out. "Information you desire is in Bank 29."

"Lara!" I said. I pushed toward her, but the webbing held me back.

"Yes. It's I. And we're together now and we'll have a long, long time to find out about each other. It's ten weeks to Mars."

I RAN my hand over my forehead. "I don't get it. I don't get any of it. Your voice—I mean your real voice, not the standard one—I dreamed about it, and—"

"I know." I could see her nod. "It wasn't a dream, though. I was talking to you. Each time. That was the way we planned it from the beginning."

"Talking to me? But—but *how?* Through the sleep-learner?"

"No, we'd never have been able to arrange that. It was through your identity tag, which would almost always be in contact with your skin when you slept. It has a microscopic electrical circuit, both between its metal halves and painted on its surface. The same principle as the sleep-learner, tactile induction, and, of course, a highly selective one-channel receiver. All I needed to do was put my transmitter on that same frequency."

I shook my head. "I follow, I guess, but I'm still baffled. Why all this? When did—"

"Wait for me to finish," she said. "We've been organized and underground, just as the Deacons suspect, for some time. One of our members worked on the identity tags and, when renumbering came about, it was a perfect opportunity to plant the receivers. We picked our people carefully. We picked doctors and hydroponics experts and chemists and rocket pilots—and we picked you because of your knowledge of space drive theory. Someday we'll go on to the stars; someday you'll help us do that. Anyway, all these people we have picked—or most of them—are joining us on Mars. There's where mankind will begin again while Northem and Southem sit upon earth and glare at each other across the equator and wait for war."

"But Mars—there's an equator there, too.

She laughed. "Northern and Southern prisoners there mingle all the time. There aren't enough guards to notice it, or stop it if they did notice it. There have even been hundreds of intermarriages."

"Marriages? You mean like the pre-atomics?"

"Exactly. But we'll get to that later. We needed you for our colony, only it wasn't likely that you'd infract all by yourself. You were too standard, too adjusted. We had to give you something to shake you out of it, to make you realize that the security of the State was not security, but slavery. And so one of our members in the renumbering bureau arranged for you to have that four-letter word of yours for a name. One thing led to another, then, not always exactly as we'd planned it, but always in the same general direction. Our whole plan nearly failed when the Deacons nabbed you in the park. Fortunately, I'd come along to stowaway on this trip, and I sent those others back after you."

"But what if I'd actually managed to get my name changed?"

THE ship was swaying now, balanced on its rocket trail. The acceleration was increasing. The seat was swinging back. The roar was becoming louder.

"It was unlikely enough to take a chance on it. We felt at the very least you'd be kept on N/P status and then we could work on you some more until you infracted, and got sent to Marscol as a nonconform. Funny, that seems a terrible fate to most people. Actually, it's the only escape. From what I hear of Mars we'll like it there."

I was recovering a little now and I dared to say, "If you're there, too, I'll like it. I know that."

"Oh, you'll like other things. You'll like everything. And on Mars they'll call you by your present name if you wish, and no one will be at all shocked by it." There was a slight pause and then she said, "In fact, it's a very nice name. I wouldn't mind having it myself."

"Is that what the pre-atomics called a proposal?"

She laughed. "I'm not sure. But at least we have ten weeks to talk it over—"

And then the acceleration pressed hard and the gray curtain began to come, and I knew that when it was lifted we would be on our way through space. I thought in that moment of the name that had brought all this about—the unspeakable four letter word that no conformist would ever dare voice, or even think of; the word, the dangerous word inimical to all that the warring, efficient State meant and stood for.

The word, I realized, that eventually would destroy all that.

I dared to say it now. I spelled it out first, and then I pronounced it. Just loud enough for Lara to hear above the growing roar. "L-O-V-E," I said. "Love."

I heard Lara repeat it before the momentary blackout came.

THE END

Fresh Air Fiend

By KRIS NEVILLE

Sick and helpless, he was very lucky to have a faithful native woman to nurse him. Or was he?

HE rolled over to look at the plants. They were crinkled and dead and useless in the narrow flower box across the hut. He tried to draw his arm under his body to force himself erect. The reserve oxygen began to hiss in sleepily. He tried to signal Hertha to help him, but she was across the room with her back to him, her hands fumbling with a bowl of dark, syrupy medicine. His lips moved, but the words died in his throat.

He wanted to explain to her that scientists in huge laboratories with many helpers and millions of dollars had been unable to find a cure for liguna fever. He wanted to explain that no brown liquid, made like cake batter, would cure the disease that had decimated the crews of two expeditions to Sitari and somehow gotten back to cut down the population of Wiblanihaven.

But, watching her, he could understand what she thought she was doing. At one time she must have seen a pharmacist put chemicals into a mortar and grind them with a pestle. This, she must have remembered, was what people did to make medicine, and now she put what chemical-appearing substances she could locate—flour, powdered coffee, lemon extract, salt—into a bowl and mashed them together. She was very intent on her work and it probably made her feel almost helpful.

Finally she moved out of his field of vision; he found that he could not turn his head to follow her with his eyes. He lay conscious but inert, like waterlogged wood on a river bottom. He heard sounds of her movement. At last he slept.

HE awakened with a start. His head was clearer than it had been for hours. He listened to the oxygen hissing in again. He tried to read the dial on the far wall, but it blurred before his eyes.

"Hertha," he said.

She came quickly to his cot. "What does the oxygen register say?"

"Oxygen register?"

He gritted his teeth against the fever which began to shake his body mercilessly until he wanted to scream to make it stop. He became angry even as the fever shook him: angry not really at the doctors; not really at anyone thing. Angry because the mountains did not care if he saw them; angry that the air did not care if he breathed it. Angry because, between planets, between suns, the coldness of space merely waited, not giving a damn.

Several years ago—ten, twenty, perhaps more—some doctor had finally isolated a strain of the filterable virus of liguna fever that could be used as a vaccine: too weak to kill, but strong enough to produce immunity against its more virulent brother strains. That opened up the Sitari System for colonization and exploration and meant that the men who got there first would make fortunes.

So he went to the base at Ke, first selling his strip mine property and disposing of his tools and equipping his spaceship for the intersolar trip; and at Ke they shot him full of the disease. But his bloodstream built no antibodies. The weakened virus settled in his nervous system and there was no way of getting it out. The doctors were very sorry for him, and they assured him it was a one-in-ten-thousand phenomenon. Thereafter, he suffered recurrent paralytic attacks.

If it had not been for the advance warning—a pain at the base of his spine, a moment of violent trembling in his knees, he would have been forced to give up solitary strip mining altogether. As it was, whenever he felt the warning, he had to hurry to the nearest colony and be hospitalized for the duration of the attack. He had had four such warnings on this satellite, and three times he had gone to Pastiville on Helio and been cared for and come away with less money than he had gone with.

His bank credit, once large had slowly dribbled away, and now he made just about enough from his mining to care for himself during illness. He could not afford to hunt for less dangerous, less isolated work. It would not pay enough, for he knew how to do very little that civilization needed done. He was finally trapped; no longer could he afford a pilot for the long flight from Helio to a newer frontier, and he could not risk the trip alone.

He lay waiting for the new spasm of fever and stared at Hertha who, this time, would care for him here and he would not need to go to a hospital. Perhaps, after a little while, he would be able to save enough to push on, through the awful indifference of space, to some new world where, with luck, there would be a sudden fortune.

Then he could go back to civilization.

He realized bitterly that he was merely telling himself he would go back. He knew there was only one direction he could go, and that direction was not back.

Hertha waited, hurt-eyed, moving her pudgy hands helplessly. When the shaking subsided, he explained through chattering teeth about the oxygen register across the room, and she went away.

THE fever vanished completely leaving him listless. His hand, lying on the rough blanket, was abnormally white. He wiggled the fingers, but he could not feel the wool.

His mouth was dry and he wanted a drink of water.

Hertha moved out of his range of vision. He shifted his head on the damp pillow and watched her out of the corner of his eye.

He had never heard her real name, but she did not seem to object to his name for her.

> I am that which began;
> Out of me the years roll;
> Out of me God and man;
> am equal and whole;
> God changes, and man,
> And the form of them bodily;
> I am the soul.

He tried to sit up again, but he was very weak. He wanted to quote it to her and tell her what he had never told her: that the name of it was *Hertha* and that it had been written long ago by a man named Swinburne, and he wanted to explain why he had named her after a poem, because it was very funny.

The harsh light hurt his eyes and made him feel dizzy. He lay watching her as she bent toward the oxygen dial, wrinkling her face in animal concentration, trying to read it for him. Her puzzled expression was pathetic; it reminded him of the first time he had seen her.

The walls began to spin crazily, for the hut had been intended for only one person.

He remembered the first time he saw her, cowering in a filthy alleyway in the Miramus. At first he thought she had taken some food from a garbage pail and was trying to conceal it by holding it to her breast. But when the flare of a rocket leaving the field two blocks away lit the area for a moment, he saw that she was holding a tiny welikin, terribly mangled, looking as if it had just been run over by a heavy transport truck. He took it away from her and threw it into the darkness, shuddering.

"It was dead," he said.

She continued to stare at him, starting to cry silently, big, round, salt tears that she brushed at with reddened hands.

"My—my—" she stammered.

He had an eerie feeling that she was trying to say, "My baby," and he felt a little chill of pity creep up his spine.

"What do you do?" he asked kindly.

"Sweep floors. I work a little for the Commander's wife. Around her home."

"How did you get here?"

Still crying, she said, "On a rocket."

"Of course. What I meant was…" But he did not need to ask how she had gotten past the emigration officers. Some influential man—such things could happen, especially when the destination was a relatively new frontier, such as Helio, where there was little danger of investigation—had seen to it that certain answers were falsified; and a little money and a corrupt official had conspired to produce a passport which read, "Mentally and physically fit for colonization."

The influential man had, in effect, bought and paid for a personal slave to bring with him to the stars. She would not know of her legal rights. She would be easily frightened and confused.

And then something had happened, and for some reason she had been abandoned to shift for herself. Perhaps she had run away.

He looked away from her face. This was none of his affair.

"Never mind," he said. He reached into his pocket and gave her a few coins and then turned and walked rapidly away, suddenly anxious to see the bright, remembered face of the young colonist, Doris, Den's friend; a face that would chase away the memory of this pathetic creature.

After a moment, he heard the pad of her feet hopefully, fearfully following him.

SHE was standing beside his cot again, and he concentrated to make the walls stop spinning.

"It had a blue line."

"Yes, I know. Where?"

She showed him with her fingers. "This much."

"Halfway up?" he prompted.

Dumbly, she nodded.

He looked at the plants. "Hertha, listen. I've got to talk before the paralysis comes back. You'll have to listen very carefully and try to understand. I'll be all right in about ten days. You know that?"

She nodded again.

He took a deep breath that seemed to catch in his throat. "But you'll have to go outside before then."

Hertha whimpered and fluttered her hands nervously.

"I know you're afraid," he said. "I wouldn't ask you, but it has to be done. I can't go. You can see that, can't you? It has to be done."

"Afraid!"

"Nonsense," he said harshly. "There's nothing to be afraid of. Put on the outside suit and nothing can hurt you." Moaning in fear, she shook her head.

"Listen, Hertha. You've *got* to do it. For *me!*" He did not like to make the appeal personal. He would have preferred to convince her that fear of the outside was groundless. It was not possible. He had attempted, again and again, to explain that the tiny satellite with its poison air was completely harmless as long as she wore a

96

surface suit. There was no alien life, no possible danger, outside this tiny square of insulated hut and breathable air. But it was useless. And the personal appeal was the only course remaining. It was as much for her sake as his; she also needed oxygen, but she could never understand that fact.

"For you?" she asked.

He nodded, feeling the fever rise. His face twisted in pain, and he stared pleadingly into her cow-like eyes: dumb eyes, animal eyes, brown and trusting and...loyal. The paralysis struck. His voice would not come up out of his chest and the dizziness swamped his mind, and, in fever, he was once again in Pastiville, the nearest planet with an oxygen atmosphere.

HERTHA followed him up the alley, out into the cheap glitter of Windopole Avenue, a rutted, smelly street, which was the center of the port-workers' section. She followed him across Windopole, up Venus, across Nineshime. He turned into the Lexo Building, which had become shabby since he had seen it last, when it had been freshly painted. She did not follow him inside, and he breathed a sigh of relief and tried to put her out of his mind as he walked up the stairs to the room 17B.

After a moment's hesitation, his heart knocking with pleasant anticipation, he pressed the buzzer.

"Come in."

He found the knob, twisted open the door, entered.

"Why Jimmy!" the girl said in what seemed to be surprise and heavy delight. She crossed to him quickly and offered her lips to be kissed. "It's good to see you."

He took half a step backward trying to keep the shock out of his face.

"Oh, it's *so* good to see you Jimmy! Sit down. Tell me all about it, about everything. Did you make loads and loads of money? When did you get back? How's the lig fever?"

He sat down, scarcely listening, studying the apartment, feeling vaguely ill. She was chattering, he realized, to overcome her embarrassment.

"The books you ordered came. I've got them right here. They're all there but some poetry or other. There was a letter about that, but the people just said they didn't have it in stock. I opened it to see if it required an answer. Just a sec, I'll get them for you." She left the room with quick, nervous strides.

The apartment had been redone since he had seen it. There were now expensive drapes at the windows, imported from somewhere; a genuine Earth tapestry hung above the door. Plump silken, pillows scattered on the floor and, a late model phono-general in the corner, with a gleaming cabinet and record spool accessory box.

She came back with the books, neatly done up in a bundle.

"I guess you still read as much as ever? Don said you always were a great reader."

Uncomfortably, he stood up.

She put the books on a low serving table, moistened her lips to make them glistening red. "Sit *down*, Jimmy."

He still stood.

"*Jimmy!*" she said in mock anger. "Sit down! Goodness, it's good to have a fellow Earthman talk to. I was so busy when I came by the other time, we rarely had a *minute* to talk. I'd got here, you remember... Well, I'm settled now, so we'll just have to have a nice, long talk."

He shifted on his feet.

"I don't suppose you've heard from Don?" Her voice was strained, almost desperate. "Isn't it the oddest thing, him knowing you and me, and both of us right here?"

"He told me to write how you were getting along?"

"...Oh."

He smiled without humor and felt like an old man. He wanted to explain how he had looked forward to seeing a person from his own planet again. Now he wanted to remind her of the girl he remembered: When she had just arrived, still unpacking, eager to start as a junior secretary for the League.

"Thank you for letting me send the books here," he said. The sickness was heavy in the pit of his stomach, and suddenly he was hard and bitter. He quoted softly:

> "The world forsaken,
> And out of mind

Honor and labor,
We shall not find
The star's unkind."

"Old poetry? I guess you really do read a—" Then understanding made her eyes wince. "That wasn't intended to be very complimentary, was it, Jimmy?"

Her name was no longer Doris; it was any of a thousand, and her perfume, heavy in his nostrils, was not her perfume or any individual's. She was there before him; she was real. But along with her were a thousand names and a thousand scents. There was the painful nostalgia of recognizing a strange room.

Awkwardly he said, "I really must go. I'd like to have a long talk, but—"

Her lips parting in sudden artificiality, she crossed to him, reached for his hand with her own.

In his mind was the heavy futility of repeating the same thing senselessly until it lost all meaning.

"I apologize about the poem," he said, because he knew that it was not his place to speak of it.

"That's all right," she said with hollow cheerfulness. Her mouth jerked and her eyes darkened. "Please don't go yet."

The palms of his hands were moist. He looked around the apartment again, and he did not want to ask, to bring it out in cruel words. It was not the sort of thing one asked.

"I really must go," he repeated levelly.

She put her hands on his shoulders. "Please…"

And then he saw that she intended to bribe him in the only way she knew how, and he said, "Don't worry, I won't tell Don."

He saw relief on her face, and then he was out of the apartment, shaken. He felt as if he had been kicked in the stomach, and he was sickened and his hand trembled. He wanted to talk to someone and try to explain it.

Hertha was waiting when he came out to the street.

THE fever passed; control of his body returned.

"For you?" Hertha asked.

He half propped himself up on the cot. He waved his hand weakly. "Those dead plants. You must throw them out and bring in more."

He listened tensely, imagining that he could hear the precious oxygen hiss in from the emergency tank to freshen and revitalize the dead air. Halfway down on the dial. Not enough for ten days, even for one person, unless the air was replenished by bringing in plants.

"Hertha, we've got to purify this air. Now Listen. Listen carefully, Hertha. You've seen me dig up those plants on the outside?"

"Yes, I watch when you go out. I always watch, Jimmy."

"Good. You've got to do the same thing. You've got to go out and dig up some plants. You've got to bring them in here and plant them the way I did. You know which ones they are?"

"Yes," she said.

He closed his eyes, trying to think of a way to make her see how vital a thing a tiny plant could be. The complex chemistry of it bubbled to the surface of his mind. He wanted to tell her why the plants died in the artificial human atmosphere and had to be replaced every week or so. He wanted to tell her, but he was growing weaker.

"They purify the air by releasing oxygen. You understand?"

She nodded her head dumbly.

"You must bring in a great many plants, Hertha. Remember that—a *great* many. Don't forget that. When you go outside, through the locks, we lose air. Air is very precious, so you must bring in a great many plants."

"Yes, Jimmy."

"And you must plant them as I did."

"Yes, Jimmy."

He began to talk faster, in a race with the growing fever.

"I've gathered most of the oxygenating plants around the hut. So you may have to go into the forest to get enough."

"The—the forest?"

"You *must*, Hertha! You *must!*"

Her mouth twisted as if she were ready to cry. "For you. Yes, for you I will go into the forest."

The fever came back. His mind wandered away.

HE was walking in the open air. He walked from Nineshime to Venus, down Venus to Windopole, up Windopole to "The Grand Eagle and Barrel." He went in. Hertha came with him and sat down by his side at the bar.

The bartender looked at him oddly. "She with you, Mac?"

He turned to look at her; her dumb, brown eyes met his. He wanted to snarl: "Get the hell away. Leave me alone." But he choked back the words. It was not Hertha he was angry with. She had done him no injury. She had merely followed him, perhaps because she knew of nothing else to do; perhaps because of temporary gratitude for the coins; perhaps in hope that he would buy her a drink. When the anger passed, he felt sorry for her again.

He said, "Want a drink?"

She shook her head without changing expression.

He looked at her and shrugged and thought that after a while she would get tired and go away. He ordered, and the bartender brought a bottle and one glass.

Hertha continued to stare at him; he tried to ignore her.

He drank. He thought it would get easier to ignore her as the level of the bottle fell. It didn't. He drank some more. It grew late.

"I gotta explain," he said, the liquor swirling in his mind.

She waited, cow-eyed.

"Ernest Dowson. Man's name. He wrote a poem—*Beata Solitudo*. I wanna explain this. Man lived long, long, long, long time ago. You listenin'? Okay. That's good. That's fine. He said—it's ver' importan' you should unnerstan' this—he said how you put honor and labor out of your mind when you...you're out here. What he meant, it's...it's...you see... Now I gotta make you see all this. So you listen real close while I tell it to you. There was a man named..."

He wanted to explain how the frontier does things to people. He wanted to explain how society is a tight little box that keeps everything locked up and hidden, but how society breaks down and becomes fluid in the stars, and how people explode and forget what they learned in civilization, and how everything is unstable.

"This man, his name's—" he said.

He wanted to explain how the harsh elements and brute nature and space, the God-awful emptiness and indifference and the sense of aloneness and selfishness and...

There were a thousand things he wanted to tell her. They were all the things he had thought about as he followed the frontier. If he could get it all down right, he could make her see why he had to follow the frontier as long as there was anything left inside of him.

Maybe the rest of the people out here were that way, too. Maybe he had seen it in Doris' eyes tonight. Maybe that was why society broke down in the stars and civilization came only when men and women like him were gone.

He did not want to know how the rest felt. He did not know whether it would be more terrifying to learn that he was alone, or that he was not atone.

But just for tonight, he could tell the alien creature beside him. It would be safe to tell her—if the idea had not rusted inside of him so long that there were no longer any words to fit it.

But first he had to make her see his home planet and the great cities and the landscaped valleys and the majestic mountains and the people. He had to make her see the vast sweep of the explorers who first carried the race to a million planets, who devised faster-than-light ships and metals to make the ships out of metals to hold their forms in the crucible beyond normal space. He had to make her see the colonists who tied all the world together with spans of steel commerce and then moved on in ever-widening circles. He wanted to give her the whole picture.

Then he wanted to explain the surge, the restlessness of the men at the frontier. Different men, he thought; from the womb of civilization, but unlike their brothers. The men who pushed out and out. Searching, always searching. He was afraid to find out if their reasons were the same as his. For himself, he had seen a thousand planets and a thousand new lifeforms. But it was not enough. There were the vast, blank, empty, indifferent reaches of space beyond him, and that was what drove him on.

This he wanted to say to Hertha: No matter how far you go, the thing that gets you is that there's nothing that cares; no matter how far, the thing is that nothing cares; the thing is that nothing cares. It gets you. And you have to go on because some day, somewhere, there may be—something.

But he lost the trend of his thoughts completely, and he had another drink.

"Decent people come out here..."

What was he going to say about decent people?

"Stupid," he cried, slapping her in the face.

She rubbed her cheek. "Stupid?"

He wanted to cry, for he had not known that he was brutal. "Can't you see?" he screamed, and it was necessary to explain it to her; and then it was not necessary. "You're like the awful, indifferent, mindless blackness of space, unreasoning!"

"Unreasoning," she repeated carefully.

"You're *Hertha!*"

"I'm Hertha," she said.

THE period of calmness that returned after the fever was crystal and lucid, preceding, he knew, a severe, prolonged seizure.

"I'm afraid," she told him, shivering, "but I will go."

He watched her get into the light surface suit, clamp down the helmet with trembling hands. He was shaking with nervousness as she hesitated at the lock. Then she pulled it open. It clicked behind her. He heard the brief hiss of the oxygen replacing the air that had whooshed out.

And he felt sorry for her, alone, terrified, on the scaly, hard surface of the tiny satellite. He closed his eyes, pictured her walking past his strip mine, past the gleaming heap of minerals ready for the transport.

He felt tears in his eyes and yet he could not entirely explain his feelings toward her—half fear, sometimes half affection. But more important than that: Why was she with him? What were her feelings? Had some sense of gratitude made her come? Affection?

He could not understand her. At times she seemed beyond all understanding. Her responses were mindless, almost mechanical, and that frightened him.

He remembered her dumb, apologetic caresses and her pathetically clumsy tenderness—or reflex; he could never be sure—and her eager yet reluctant hands and the always slightly hurt, slightly accusing look in her eyes, as if at every instant she was ready for a stinging blow, and her great sighs, muted as if fearing to be heard and...

He was drunk, screaming meaninglessly, and the bartender threw him out. The pavement cut his face. When he awoke, it was morning and he was in a strange room and she was in bed beside him.

She said. "I am Hertha. I brought you home. I will go with you."

The paralysis set in. He could not move. The tears froze on his cheeks, and he lay inert, thinking of her almost mindlessly fighting for his life in the alien outside.

Then she was back in the hut. So soon?

She looked at him, smiled through the transparent helmet at him. He could hear the precious oxygen hiss in to compensate for the air that had been lost when she entered.

He could see her eyes. They were proud. Relieved, too, as if she had been afraid he would be gone when she returned. He felt she had hurried back to be sure that he was still there.

She knelt by the flowerbed and, without removing her suit, she held up the plant proudly. He could see the hard-packed dirt in the roots. Fascinated, he watched her scrape a planting hole. He watched her set the plant delicately and pat the soil with care.

Then she stood up.

He tried to move, to cry out. He could not.

He watched her until she went out of the range of his fixed eyes. She was going to the airlock again.

After a moment he heard the familiar hiss of oxygen.

She was going to get a great number of plants.

But one at a time.

THE END

The Next Logical Step

By BEN BOVA

Ordinarily the military least wants to have the others know the final details of their war plans. But, logically, there would be times—

"I don't really see where this problem has anything to do with me," the CIA man said. "And, frankly, there are a lot of more important things I could be doing."

Ford, the physicist, glanced at General LeRoy. The general had that quizzical expression on his face, the look that meant he was about to do something decisive.

"Would you like to see the problem first-hand?" the general asked, innocently.

The CIA man took a quick look at his wristwatch. "O.K., if it doesn't take too long. It's late enough already."

"It won't take very long, will it, Ford?" the general said, getting out of his chair.

"Not very long," Ford agreed. "Only a lifetime."

The CIA man grunted as they went to the doorway and left the general's office. Going down the dark, deserted hallway, their footsteps echoed hollowly.

"I can't overemphasize the seriousness of the problem," General LeRoy said to the CIA man. "Eight ranking members of the General Staff have either resigned their commissions or gone straight to the violent ward after just one session with the computer."

The CIA man scowled. "Is this area secure?"

General LeRoy's face turned red. "This entire building is as secure as any edifice in the Free World, mister. And it's empty. We're the only living people inside here at this hour. I'm not taking any chances."

"Just want to be sure."

"Perhaps if I explain the computer a little more," Ford said, changing the subject, "you'll know what to expect."

"Good idea," said the man from CIA.

"We told you that this is the most modern, most complex and delicate computer in the world...nothing like it has ever been attempted before...anywhere."

"I know that. *They* don't have anything like it," the CIA man agreed.

"And you also know, I suppose, that it was built to simulate actual war situations. We fight wars in this computer...wars with missiles and bombs and gas. Real wars, complete down to the tiniest detail. The computer tells us what will actually happen to every missile, every city, every man...who dies, how many planes are lost, how many trucks will fail to start on a cold morning, whether a battle is won or lost..."

General LeRoy interrupted. "The computer runs these analyses for both sides, so we can see what's happening to Them, too."

The CIA man gestured impatiently. "War games simulations aren't new. You've been doing them for years."

"Yes, but this machine is different," Ford pointed out. "It not only gives a much more detailed war game, it's the next logical step in the development of machine-simulated war games," he hesitated dramatically.

"Well, what is it?"

"We've added a variation of the electro-encephalograph..."

The CIA man stopped walking. "The electro-what?"

"Electro-encephalograph. You know, a recording device that reads the electrical patterns of your brain. Like the electro-cardiograph."

"Oh."

"But you see, we've given the EEG a reverse twist. Instead of using a machine that makes a recording of the brain's electrical wave output, we've developed a device that will take the computer's readout tapes, and turn them into electrical patterns that are put *into* your brain."

"I don't get it."

General LeRoy took over. "You sit at the machine's control console. A helmet is placed over your head. You set the machine in operation. You *see* the results."

"Yes," Ford went on. "Instead of reading rows of figures from the computer's printer you actually see the war being fought.

Complete visual and auditory hallucinations. You can watch the progress of the battles, and as you change strategy and tactics you can see the results before your eyes."

"The idea, originally, was to make it easier for the General Staff to visualize strategic situations," General LeRoy said.

"But every one who's used the machine has either resigned his commission or gone insane," Ford added.

The CIA man cocked an eye at LeRoy. "You've used the computer."

"Correct."

"And you have neither resigned nor cracked up."

General LeRoy nodded. "I called you in."

Before the CIA man could comment, Ford said, "The computer's right inside this doorway. Let's get this over with while the building is still empty."

They stepped in. The physicist and the general showed the CIA man through the room-filling rows of massive consoles.

"It's all transistorized and subminiaturized, of course," Ford explained. "That's the only way we could build so much detail into the machine and still have it small enough to fit inside a single building."

"A single building?"

"Oh yes; this is only the control section. Most of this building is taken up by the circuits, the memory banks, and the rest of it."

"Hmm..."

They showed him finally to a small desk, studded with control buttons and dials. The single spotlight above the desk lit it brilliantly, in harsh contrast to the semidarkness of the rest of the room.

"Since you've never run the computer before," Ford said, "General LeRoy will do the controlling. You just sit and watch what happens."

The general sat in one of the well-padded chairs and donned a grotesque headgear that was connected to the desk by a half-dozen wires. The CIA man took his chair slowly.

When they put one of the bulky helmets on him, he looked up at them, squinting a little in the bright light. "This...this isn't going to...well, do me any damage, is it?"

"My goodness, no," Ford said. "You mean mentally? No, of course not. You're not on the General Staff, so it shouldn't...it won't...affect you the way it did the others. Their reaction had nothing to do with the computer *per se*..."

"Several civilians have used the computer with no ill effects," General LeRoy said. "Ford has used it many times."

The CIA man nodded, and they closed the transparent visor over his face. He sat there and watched General LeRoy press a series of buttons, then turn a dial.

"Can you hear me?" The general's voice came muffled through the helmet.

"Yes," he said.

"All right. Here we go. You're familiar with Situation One-Two-One? That's what we're going to be seeing."

Situation One-Two-One was a standard war game. The CIA man was well acquainted with it. He watched the general flip a switch, then sit back and fold his arms over his chest. A row of lights on the desk console began blinking on and off, one, two, three...down to the end of the row, then back to the beginning again, on and off, on and off...

And then, somehow, he could see it!

He was poised incredibly somewhere in space, and he could see it all in a funny, blurry-double-sighted, dream-like way. He seemed to be seeing several pictures and hearing many voices, all at once. It was all mixed up, and yet it made a weird kind of sense.

For a panicked instant he wanted to rip the helmet off his head. *It's only an illusion*, he told himself, forcing calm on his unwilling nerves. *Only an illusion.*

But it seemed strangely real.

He was watching the Gulf of Mexico. He could see Florida off to his right, and the arching coast of the southeastern United States. He could even make out the Rio Grande River.

Situation One-Two-One started, he remembered, with the discovery of missile-bearing Enemy submarines in the Gulf. Even as he watched the whole area—as though perched on a satellite— he could see, underwater and close-up, the menacing shadowy figure of a submarine gliding through the crystal blue sea.

He saw, too, a patrol plane as it spotted the submarine and sent an urgent radio warning.

The underwater picture dissolved in a bewildering burst of bubbles. A missile had been launched. Within seconds, another burst—this time a nuclear depth charge—utterly destroyed the submarine.

It was confusing. He was everyplace at once. The details were overpowering, but the total picture was agonizingly clear.

Six submarines fired missiles from the Gulf of Mexico. Four were immediately sunk, but too late. New Orleans, St. Louis and three Air Force bases were obliterated by hydrogen-fusion warheads.

The CIA man was familiar with the opening stages of the war. The first missile fired at the United States was the signal for whole fleets of missiles and bombers to launch themselves at the Enemy. It was confusing to see the world all at once; at times he could not tell if the fireball and mushroom cloud was over Chicago or Shanghai, New York or Novosibirsk, Baltimore or Budapest.

It did not make much difference, really. They all got it in the first few hours of the war; as did London and Moscow, Washington and Peking, Detroit and Delhi, and many, many more.

The defensive systems on all sides seemed to operate well, except that there were never enough anti-missiles. Defensive systems were expensive compared to attack rockets. It was cheaper to build a deterrent than to defend against it.

The missiles flashed up from submarines and railway cars, from underground silos and stratospheric jets; secret ones fired off automatically when a certain airbase command post ceased beaming out a restraining radio signal. The defensive systems were simply overloaded. And when the bombs ran out, the missiles carried dust and germs and gas. On and on. For six days and six firelit nights. Launch, boost, coast, re-enter, death.

And now it was over, the CIA man thought. The missiles were all gone. The airplanes were exhausted. The nations that had built the weapons no longer existed. By all the rules he knew of, the war should have been ended.

Yet the fighting did not end. The machine knew better. There were still many ways to kill an enemy. Time-tested ways. There were armies fighting in four continents, armies that had marched overland, or splashed ashore from the sea, or dropped out of the skies.

Incredibly, the war went on. When the tanks ran out of gas, and the flame throwers became useless, and even the prosaic artillery pieces had no more rounds to fire, there were still simple guns and even simpler bayonets and swords.

The proud armies, the descendents of the Alexanders and Caesars and Temujins and Wellingtons and Grants and Rommels, relived their evolution in reverse.

The war went on. Slowly, inevitably, the armies split apart into smaller and smaller units, until the tortured countryside that so recently had felt the impact of nuclear war once again knew the tread of bands of armed marauders. The tiny savage groups, stranded in alien lands, far from the homes and families that they knew to be destroyed, carried on a mockery of war, lived off the land, fought their own countrymen if the occasion suited, and revived the ancient terror of hand-wielded, personal, one-head-at-a-time killing.

The CIA man watched the world disintegrate. Death was an individual business now, and none the better for no longer being mass-produced. In agonized fascination he saw the myriad ways in which a man might die. Murder was only one of them. Radiation, disease, toxic gases that lingered and drifted on the once-innocent winds, and—finally—the most efficient destroyer of them all: starvation.

Three billion people (give or take a meaningless hundred million) lived on the planet Earth when the war began. Now, with the tenuous thread of civilization burned away, most of those who were not killed by the fighting itself succumbed inexorably to starvation.

Not everyone died, of course. Life went on. Some were lucky.

A long darkness settled on the world. Life went on for a few, a pitiful few, a bitter, hateful, suspicious, savage few. Cities became pestholes. Books became fuel. Knowledge died. Civilization was completely gone from the planet Earth.

The helmet was lifted slowly off his head. The CIA man found that he was too weak to raise his arms and help. He was shivering and damp with perspiration.

"Now you see," Ford said quietly, "why the military men cracked up when they used the computer."

General LeRoy, even, was pale. "How can a man with any conscience at all direct a military operation when he knows that *that* will be the consequence?"

The CIA man struck up a cigarette and pulled hard on it. He exhaled sharply. "Are all the war games...like that? Every plan?"

"Some are worse," Ford said. "We picked an average one for you. Even some of the 'brushfire' games get out of hand and end up like that."

"So...what do you intend to do? Why did you call me in? What can *I* do?"

"You're with CIA," the general said. "Don't you handle espionage?"

"Yes, but what's that got to do with it?"

The general looked at him. "It seems to me that the next logical step is to make damned certain that *They* get the plans to this computer...and fast!"

THE END

The Man Who Hated Mars

By RANDALL GARRETT

To escape from Mars, all Clayton had to do was the impossible. Break out of a crack-proof exile camp—get onto a ship that couldn't be boarded—smash through an impenetrable wall of steel. Perhaps he could do all these things, but he discovered that Mars did evil things to men; that he wasn't even Clayton any more...

"I want you to put me in prison!" the big, hairy man said in a trembling voice.

He was addressing his request to a thin woman sitting behind a desk that seemed much too big for her. The plaque on the desk said:

LT. PHOEBE HARRIS
TERRAN REHABILITATION SERVICE

Lieutenant Harris glanced at the man before her for only a moment before she returned her eyes to the dossier on the desk; but long enough to verify the impression his voice had given. Ron Clayton was a big, ugly, cowardly, dangerous man.

He said: "Well? Dammit, say something!"

The lieutenant raised her eyes again. "Just be patient until I've read this." Her voice and eyes were expressionless, but her hand moved beneath the desk.

Clayton froze. *She's yellow!* he thought. She's turned on the trackers! He could see the pale greenish glow of their little eyes watching him all around the room. If he made any fast move, they would cut him down with a stun beam before he could get two feet.

She had thought he was going to jump her. *Little rat!* he thought, *somebody ought to slap her down!*

113

He watched her check through the heavy dossier in front of her. Finally, she looked up at him again.

"Clayton, your last conviction was for strong-arm robbery. You were given a choice between prison on Earth and freedom here on Mars. You picked Mars."

He nodded slowly. He'd been broke and hungry at the time. A sneaky little rat named Johnson had bilked Clayton out of his fair share of the Corey payroll job, and Clayton had been forced to get the money somehow. He hadn't mussed the guy up much; besides, it was the sucker's own fault. If he hadn't tried to yell—

Lieutenant Harris went on: "I'm afraid you can't back down now."

"But it isn't fair! The most I'd have got on that frame-up would've been ten years. I've been here fifteen already!"

"I'm sorry, Clayton. It can't be done. You're here. Period. Forget about trying to get back. Earth doesn't want you." Her voice sounded choppy, as though she was trying to keep it calm.

Clayton broke into a whining rage. "You can't do that! It isn't fair! I never did anything to you! I'll go talk to the Governor! He'll listen to reason! You'll see! I'll—"

"*Shut up!*" the woman snapped harshly. "I'm getting sick of it! I personally think you should have been locked up—permanently. I think this idea of forced colonization is going to breed trouble for Earth someday, but it is about the only way you can get anybody to colonize this frozen hunk of mud.

"Just keep it in mind that I don't like it any better than you do—*and I didn't strong-arm anybody to deserve the assignment!* Now get out of here."

She moved a hand threateningly toward the manual controls of the stun beam.

Clayton retreated fast. The trackers ignored anyone walking away from the desk; they were set only to spot threatening movements toward it.

Outside the Rehabilitation Service Building, Clayton could feel the tears running down the inside of his facemask. He'd asked again and again—God only knew how many times—in the past fifteen years. Always the same answer. No.

When he'd heard that this new administrator was a woman, he'd hoped she might be easier to convince. She wasn't. If anything, she was harder than the others.

The heat-sucking frigidity of the thin Martian air whispered around him in a feeble breeze. He shivered a little and began walking toward the recreation center.

There was a high, thin piping in the sky above him, which quickly became a scream in the thin air.

He turned for a moment to watch the ship land, squinting his eyes to see the number on the hull.

Fifty-two. Space Transport Ship Fifty-two.

Probably bringing another load of poor suckers to freeze to death on Mars.

That was the thing he hated about Mars—the cold. The everlasting damned cold! And the oxidation pills; take one every three hours or smother in the poor, thin air.

The government could have put up domes; it could have put in building-to-building tunnels, at least. It could have done a hell of a lot of things to make Mars a decent place for human beings.

But no—the government had other ideas. A bunch of bigshot scientific characters had come up with the idea nearly twenty-three years before. Clayton could remember the words on the sheet he had been given when he was sentenced.

"Mankind is inherently an adaptable animal. If we are to colonize the planets of the Solar System, we must meet the conditions on those planets as best we can.

"Financially, it is impracticable to change an entire planet from its original condition to one which will support human life as it exists on Terra.

"But man, since he is adaptable, can change himself—modify his structure slightly—so that he can live on these planets with only a minimum of change in the environment."

So they made you live outside and like it. So you froze and you choked and you suffered.

Clayton hated Mars. He hated the thin air and the cold. More than anything, he hated the cold.

Ron Clayton wanted to go home.

The Recreation Building was just ahead; at least it would be warm inside. He pushed in through the outer and inner doors, and he heard the burst of music from the jukebox. His stomach tightened up into a hard cramp.

They were playing Heinlein's *Green Hills of Earth*.

There was almost no other sound in the room, although it was full of people. There were plenty of colonists who claimed to like Mars, but even they were silent when that song was played.

Clayton wanted to go over and smash the machine—make it stop reminding him. He clenched his teeth and his fists and his eyes and cursed mentally. *God, how I hate Mars!*

When the hauntingly nostalgic last chorus faded away, he walked over to the machine and fed it full of enough coins to keep it going on something else until he left.

At the bar, he ordered a beer and used it to wash down another oxidation tablet. It wasn't good beer; it didn't even deserve the name. The atmospheric pressure was so low as to boil all the carbon dioxide out of it, so the brewers never put it back in after fermentation.

He was sorry for what he had done—really and truly sorry. If they'd only give him one more chance, he'd make good. Just one more chance. He'd work things out.

He'd promised himself that both times they'd put him up before, but things had been different then. He hadn't really been given another chance, what with parole boards and all.

Clayton closed his eyes and finished the beer. He ordered another.

He'd worked in the mines for fifteen years. It wasn't that he minded work really, but the foreman had it in for him. Always giving him a bad time; always picking out the lousy jobs for him.

Like the time he'd crawled into a side boring in Tunnel 12 for a nap during lunch and the foreman had caught him. When he promised never to do it again if the foreman wouldn't put it on report, the guy said, "Yeah. Sure. Hate to hurt a guy's record."

Then he'd put Clayton on report anyway. Strictly a rat.

Not that Clayton ran any chance of being fired; they never fired anybody. But they'd fined him a day's pay. A whole day's pay.

He tapped his glass on the bar, and the barman came over with another beer. Clayton looked at it, then up at the barman. "Put a head on it."

The bartender looked at him sourly. "I've got some soapsuds here, Clayton, and one of these days I'm gonna put some in your beer if you keep pulling that gag."

That was the trouble with some guys. No sense of humor.

Somebody came in the door and then somebody else came in behind him, so that both inner and outer doors were open for an instant. A blast of icy breeze struck Clayton's back, and he shivered. He started to say something, then changed his mind; the doors were already closed again, and besides, one of the guys was bigger than he was.

The iciness didn't seem to go away immediately. It was like the mine. Little old Mars was cold clear down to her core—or at least down as far as they'd drilled. The walls were frozen and seemed to radiate a chill that pulled the heat right out of your blood.

Somebody was playing *Green Hills* again, damn them. Evidently all of his own selections had run out earlier than he'd thought they would.

Hell! There was nothing to do here. He might as well go home.

"Gimme another beer, Mac."

He'd go home as soon as he finished this one.

He stood there with his eyes closed, listening to the music and hating Mars.

A voice next to him said: "I'll have a whiskey."

The voice sounded as if the man had a bad cold, and Clayton turned slowly to look at him. After all the sterilization they went through before they left Earth, nobody on Mars ever had a cold, so there was only one thing that would make a man's voice sound like that.

Clayton was right. The fellow had an oxygen tube clamped firmly over his nose. He was wearing the uniform of the Space Transport Service.

"Just get in on the ship?" Clayton asked conversationally.

The man nodded and grinned. "Yeah. Four hours before we take off again." He poured down the whiskey. "Sure cold out."

Clayton agreed. "It's always cold." He watched enviously as the spaceman ordered another whiskey.

Clayton couldn't afford whiskey. He probably could have by this time, if the mines had made him a foreman, like they should have.

Maybe he could talk the spaceman out of a couple of drinks.

"My name's Clayton. Ron Clayton."

The spaceman took the offered hand. "Mine's Parkinson, but everybody calls me Parks."

"Sure, Parks. Uh—can I buy you a beer?"

Parks shook his head. "No, thanks. I started on whiskey. Here, let me buy you one."

"Well—thanks. Don't mind if I do."

They drank them in silence, and Parks ordered two more.

"Been here long?" Parks asked.

"Fifteen years. Fifteen long, long years."

"Did you—uh—I mean—" Parks looked suddenly confused.

Clayton glanced quickly to make sure the bartender was out of earshot. Then he grinned. "You mean am I a convict? Nah. I came here because I wanted to. But—" He lowered his voice. "—we don't talk about it around here. You know." He gestured with one hand—a gesture that took in everyone else in the room.

Parks glanced around quickly, moving only his eyes. "Yeah. I see," he said softly.

"This your first trip?" asked Clayton.

"First one to Mars. Been on the Luna run a long time."

"Low pressure bother you much?"

"Not much. We only keep it at six pounds in the ships. Half helium and half oxygen. Only thing that bothers me is the oxy here. Or rather, the oxy that *isn't* here." He took a deep breath through his nose tube to emphasize his point.

Clayton clamped his teeth together, making the muscles at the side of his jaw stand out.

Parks didn't notice. "You guys have to take those pills, don't you?"

"Yeah."

"I had to take them once. Got stranded on Luna. The cat I was in broke down eighty some miles from Aristarchus Base and I had to walk back—with my oxy low. Well, I figured—"

Clayton listened to Parks' story with a great show of attention, but he had heard it before. This "lost on the moon" stuff and its variations had been going the rounds for forty years. Every once in a while, it actually did happen to someone; just often enough to keep the story going.

This guy did have a couple of new twists, but not enough to make the story worthwhile.

"Boy," Clayton said when Parks had finished, "you were lucky to come out of that alive!"

Parks nodded, well pleased with himself, and bought another round of drinks.

"Something like that happened to me a couple of years ago," Clayton began. "I'm supervisor on the third shift in the mines at Xanthe, but at the time, I was only a foreman. One day, a couple of guys went to a branch tunnel to—"

It was a very good story. Clayton had made it up himself, so he knew that Parks had never heard it before. It was gory in just the right places, with a nice effect at the end.

"—so I had to hold up the rocks with my back while the rescue crew pulled the others out of the tunnel by crawling between my legs. Finally, they got some steel beams down there to take the load off, and I could let go. I was in the hospital for a week," he finished.

Parks was nodding vaguely. Clayton looked up at the clock above the bar and realized that they had been talking for better than an hour. Parks was buying another round.

Parks was a hell of a nice fellow.

There was, Clayton found, only one trouble with Parks. He got to talking so loud that the bartender refused to serve either one of them any more.

The bartender said Clayton was getting loud, too, but it was just because he had to talk loud to make Parks hear him.

Clayton helped Parks put his mask and parka on and they walked out into the cold night.

Parks began to sing *Green Hills*. About halfway through, he stopped and turned to Clayton.

"I'm from Indiana."

Clayton had already spotted him as an American by his accent.

"Indiana? That's nice. Real nice."

"Yeah. You talk about green hills, we got green hills in Indiana. What time is it?"

Clayton told him.

"Jeez-krise! Ol' spaship takes off in an hour. Ought to have one more drink first."

Clayton realized he didn't like Parks. But maybe he'd buy a bottle.

Sharkie Johnson worked in Fuels Section, and he made a nice little sideline of stealing alcohol, cutting it, and selling it. He thought it was real funny to call it Martian Gin.

Clayton said: "Let's go over to Sharkie's. Sharkie will sell us a bottle."

"Okay," said Parks. "We'll get a bottle. That's what we need: a bottle."

It was quite a walk to the Shark's place. It was so cold that even Parks was beginning to sober up a little. He was laughing like hell when Clayton started to sing.

"We're going over to the Shark's to buy a jug of gin for Parks! Hi ho, hi ho, hi ho!"

One thing about a few drinks; you didn't get so cold. You didn't feel it too much, anyway.

The Shark still had his light on when they arrived. Clayton whispered to Parks: "I'll go in. He knows me. He wouldn't sell it if you were around. You got eight credits?"

"Sure I got eight credits. Just a minute, and I'll give you eight credits." He fished around for a minute inside his parka, and pulled out his notecase. His gloved fingers were a little clumsy, but he managed to get out a five and three ones and hand them to Clayton.

"You wait out here," Clayton said.

He went in through the outer door and knocked on the inner one. He should have asked for ten credits. Sharkie only charged five, and that would leave him three for himself. But he could have got ten—maybe more.

When he came out with the bottle, Parks was sitting on a rock, shivering.

"Jeez-krise!" he said. "It's cold out here. Let's get to someplace where it's warm."

"Sure. I got the bottle. Want a drink?"

Parks took the bottle, opened it, and took a good belt out of it.

"Hooh!" he breathed. "Pretty smooth."

As Clayton drank, Parks said: "Hey! I better get back to the field. I know. We can go to the men's room and finish the bottle before the ship takes off. Isn't that a good idea? It's warm there."

They started back down the street toward the spacefield.

"Yep, I'm from Indiana. Southern part, down around Bloomington," Parks said. "Gimme the jug. Not Bloomington, Illinois—Bloomington, Indiana. We really got green hills down there." He drank, and handed the bottle back to Clayton. "Persnally, I don't see why anybody'd stay on Mars. Here y'are, practic'ly on the equator in the middle of the summer, and it's colder than hell. Brrr!

"Now if you was smart, you'd go home, where it's warm. Mars wasn't built for people to live on, anyhow. I don't see how you stand it."

That was when Clayton decided he really hated Parks.

And when Parks said: "Why be dumb, friend? Whyn't you go home?" Clayton kicked him in the stomach, hard.

"And that, that—" Clayton said as Parks doubled over.

He said it again as he kicked him in the head. And in the ribs. Parks was gasping as he writhed on the ground, but he soon lay still.

Then Clayton saw why. Parks' nose tube had come off when Clayton's foot struck his head.

Parks was breathing heavily, but he wasn't getting any oxygen.

That was when the Big Idea hit Ron Clayton. With a nosepiece on like that, you couldn't tell who a man was. He took another drink from the jug and then began to take Parks' clothes off.

The uniform fit Clayton fine, and so did the nose mask. He dumped his own clothing on top of Parks' nearly nude body, adjusted the little oxygen tank so that the gas would flow properly through the mask, took the first deep breath of good air he'd had in fifteen years, and walked toward the spacefield.

He went into the men's room at the Port Building, took a drink, and felt in the pockets of the uniform for Parks' identification. He found it and opened the booklet. It read:

PARKINSON, HERBERT J.
Steward 2nd Class, STS

Above it was a photo, and a set of fingerprints.

Clayton grinned. They'd never know it wasn't Parks getting on the ship.

Parks was a steward, too. A cook's helper. That was good. If he'd been a jetman or something like that, the crew might wonder why he wasn't on duty at takeoff. But a steward was different.

Clayton sat for several minutes, looking through the booklet and drinking from the bottle. He emptied it just before the warning sirens keened through the thin air.

Clayton got up and went outside toward the ship.

"Wake up! Hey, you! Wake up!"

Somebody was slapping his cheeks. Clayton opened his eyes and looked at the blurred face over his own.

From a distance, another voice said: "Who is it?"

The blurred face said: "I don't know. He was asleep behind these cases. I think he's drunk."

Clayton wasn't drunk—he was sick. His head felt like hell. Where the devil was he?

"Get up, bud. Come on, get up!"

Clayton pulled himself up by holding to the man's arm. The effort made him dizzy and nauseated.

The other man said: "Take him down to sick bay, Casey. Get some thiamin into him."

Clayton didn't struggle as they led him down to the sick bay. He was trying to clear his head. Where was he? He must have been pretty drunk last night.

He remembered meeting Parks. And getting thrown out by the bartender. Then what?

Oh, yeah. He'd gone to the Shark's for a bottle. From there on, it was mostly gone. He remembered a fight or something, but that was all that registered.

The medic in the sick bay fired two shots from a hypo-gun into both arms, but Clayton ignored the slight sting.

"Where am I?"

"Real original. Here, take these." He handed Clayton a couple of capsules, and gave him a glass of water to wash them down with.

When the water hit his stomach, there was an immediate reaction.

"Oh, Christ!" the medic said. "Get a mop, somebody. Here, bud; heave into this." He put a basin on the table in front of Clayton.

It took them the better part of an hour to get Clayton awake enough to realize what was going on and where he was. Even then, he was plenty groggy.

It was the First Officer of the STS-52 who finally got the story straight. As soon as Clayton was in condition, the medic and the quartermaster officer who had found him took him up to the First Officer's compartment.

"I was checking through the stores this morning when I found this man. He was asleep, dead drunk, behind the crates."

"He was drunk, all right," supplied the medic. "I found this in his pocket." He flipped a booklet to the First Officer.

The First was a young man, not older than twenty-eight with tough-looking gray eyes. He looked over the booklet.

"Where did you get Parkinson's ID booklet? And his uniform?"

Clayton looked down at his clothes in wonder. "I don't know."

"You *don't know*? That's a hell of an answer."

"Well, I was drunk," Clayton said defensively. "A man doesn't know what he's doing when he's drunk." He frowned in concentration. He knew he'd have to think up some story.

"I kind of remember we made a bet. I bet him I could get on the ship. Sure—I remember, now. That's what happened; I bet him I could get on the ship and we traded clothes."

"Where is he now?"

"At my place, sleeping it off, I guess."

"Without his oxy-mask?"

"Oh, I gave him my oxidation pills for the mask."

The First shook his head. "That sounds like the kind of trick Parkinson would pull, all right. I'll have to write it up and turn you both in to the authorities when we hit Earth." He eyed Clayton. "What's your name?"

"Cartwright. Sam Cartwright," Clayton said without batting an eye.

"Volunteer or convicted colonist?"

"Volunteer."

The First looked at him for a long moment, disbelief in his eyes.

It didn't matter. Volunteer or convict, there was no place Clayton could go. From the officer's viewpoint, he was as safely imprisoned in the spaceship as he would be on Mars or a prison on Earth.

The First wrote in the logbook, and then said: "Well, we're one man short in the kitchen. You wanted to take Parkinson's place; brother, you've got it—without pay." He paused for a moment.

"You know, of course," he said judiciously, "that you'll be shipped back to Mars immediately. And you'll have to work out your passage both ways—it will be deducted from your pay."

Clayton nodded. "I know."

"I don't know what else will happen. If there's a conviction, you may lose your volunteer status on Mars. And there may be fines taken out of your pay, too.

"Well, that's all, Cartwright. You can report to Kissman in the kitchen."

The First pressed a button on his desk and spoke into the intercom. "Who was on duty at the airlock when the crew came aboard last night? Send him up. I want to talk to him."

Then the quartermaster officer led Clayton out the door and took him to the kitchen.

The ship's driver tubes were pushing it along at a steady five hundred centimeters per second squared acceleration, pushing her steadily closer to Earth with a little more than half a gravity of drive.

There wasn't much for Clayton to do, really. He helped to select the foods that went into the automatics, and he cleaned them out after each meal was cooked. Once every day, he had to partially dismantle them for a really thorough going-over.

And all the time, he was thinking.

Parkinson must be dead; he knew that. That meant the Chamber. And even if he wasn't, they'd send Clayton back to Mars. Luckily, there was no way for either planet to communicate with the ship; it was hard enough to keep a beam trained on a planet without trying to hit such a comparatively small thing as a ship.

But they would know about it on Earth by now. They would pick him up the instant the ship landed. And the best he could hope for was a return to Mars.

No, by God! He wouldn't go back to that frozen mud-ball! He'd stay on Earth, where it was warm and comfortable and a man could live where he was meant to live. Where there was plenty of air to breathe and plenty of water to drink. Where the beer tasted like beer and not like slop. Earth. Good green hills, the like of which exists nowhere else.

Slowly, over the days, he evolved a plan. He watched and waited and checked each little detail to make sure nothing would go wrong. It *couldn't* go wrong. He didn't want to die, and he didn't want to go back to Mars.

Nobody on the ship liked him; they couldn't appreciate his position. He hadn't done anything to them, but they just didn't like him. He didn't know why; he'd *tried* to get along with them. Well, if they didn't like him, the hell with them.

If things worked out the way he figured, they'd be damned sorry.

He was very clever about the whole plan. When turnover came, he pretended to get violently spacesick. That gave him an opportunity to steal a bottle of chloral hydrate from the medic's locker.

And, while he worked in the kitchen, he spent a great deal of time sharpening a big carving knife.

Once, during his off time, he managed to disable one of the ship's two lifeboats. He was saving the other for himself.

The ship was eight hours out from Earth and still decelerating when Clayton pulled his getaway.

It was surprisingly easy. He was supposed to be asleep when he sneaked down to the drive compartment with the knife. He pushed open the door, looked in, and grinned like an ape.

The Engineer and the two jetmen were out cold from the chloral hydrate in the coffee from the kitchen.

Moving rapidly, he went to the spares locker and began methodically to smash every replacement part for the drivers. Then he took three of the signal bombs from the emergency kit, set them for five minutes, and placed them around the driver circuits.

He looked at the three sleeping men. What if they woke up before the bombs went off? He didn't want to kill them though. He wanted them to know what had happened and who had done it.

He grinned. There was a way. He simply had to drag them outside and jam the door lock. He took the key from the Engineer, inserted it, turned it, and snapped off the head, leaving the body of the key still in the lock. Nobody would unjam it in the next four minutes.

Then he began to run up the stairwell toward the good lifeboat.

He was panting and out of breath when he arrived, but no one had stopped him. No one had even seen him.

He clambered into the lifeboat, made everything ready, and waited.

The signal bombs were not heavy charges; their main purpose was to make a flare bright enough to be seen for thousands of miles in space. Fluorine and magnesium made plenty of light—and heat.

Quite suddenly, there was no gravity. He had felt nothing, but he knew that the bombs had exploded. He punched the LAUNCH switch on the control board of the lifeboat, and the little ship leaped out from the side of the greater one.

Then he turned on the drive, set it at half a gee, and watched the STS-52 drop behind him. It was no longer decelerating, so it would miss Earth and drift on into space. On the other hand, the lifeship would come down very neatly within a few hundred miles of the spaceport in Utah, the destination of the STS-52.

Landing the lifeship would be the only difficult part of the maneuver, but they were designed to be handled by beginners. Full instructions were printed on the simplified control board.

Clayton studied them for a while, then set the alarm to waken him in seven hours and dozed off to sleep.

He dreamed of Indiana. It was full of nice, green hills and leafy woods, and Parkinson was inviting him over to his mother's house for chicken and whiskey. And all for free.

Beneath the dream was the calm assurance that they would never catch him and send him back. When the STS-52 failed to show up, they would think he had been lost with it. They would never look for him.

When the alarm rang, Earth was a mottled globe looming hugely beneath the ship. Clayton watched the dials on the board, and began to follow the instructions on the landing sheet.

He wasn't too good at it. The accelerometer climbed higher and higher, and he felt as though he could hardly move his hands to the proper switches.

He was less than fifteen feet off the ground when his hand slipped. The ship, out of control, shifted, spun, and toppled over on its side, smashing a great hole in the cabin.

Clayton shook his head and tried to stand up in the wreckage. He got to his hands and knees, dizzy but unhurt, and took a deep breath of the fresh air that was blowing in through the hole in the cabin.

It felt just like home.

Bureau of Criminal Investigation
Regional Headquarters
Cheyenne, Wyoming
20 January 2102
To: Space Transport Service
Subject: Lifeship 2, STS-52
Attention Mr. P. D. Latimer

Dear Paul,

I have on hand the copies of your reports on the rescue of the men on the disabled STS-52. It is fortunate that the Lunar radar stations could compute their orbit.

The detailed official report will follow, but briefly, this is what happened:

The lifeship landed—or, rather, crashed—several miles west of Cheyenne, as you know, but it was impossible to find the man who was piloting it until yesterday because of the weather.

He has been identified as Ronald Watkins Clayton, exiled to Mars fifteen years ago.

Evidently, he didn't realize that fifteen years of Martian gravity had so weakened his muscles that he could hardly walk under the pull of a full Earth gee.

As it was, he could only crawl about a hundred yards from the wrecked lifeship before he collapsed.

Well, I hope this clears up everything.

I hope you're not getting the snowstorms up there like we've been getting them.

John B. Remley
Captain, CBI

THE END

The Murder Machine

By HUGH B. CAVE

Four lives lay helpless before the murder machine, the uncanny device by which hypnotic thought-waves are filtered through men's minds to mold them into murdering tools!

It was dusk, on the evening of December 7, 1906, when I first encountered Sir John Harmon. At the moment of his entrance I was standing over the table in my study, a lighted match in my cupped hands and a pipe between my teeth. The pipe was never lit.

I heard the lower door slam shut with a violent clatter. The stairs resounded to a series of unsteady footbeats, and the door of my study was flung back. In the opening, staring at me with quiet dignity, stood a young, careless fellow, about five feet ten in height and decidedly dark of complexion. The swagger of his entrance branded him as an adventurer. The ghastly pallor of his face, which was almost colorless, branded him as a man who has found something more than mere adventure.

"Doctor Dale?" he demanded.

"I am Doctor Dale."

He closed the door of the room deliberately, advancing toward me with slow steps.

"My name is John Harmon—Sir John Harmon. It is unusual, I suppose," he said quietly, with a slight shrug, "coming at this late hour. I won't keep you long."

He faced me silently. A single glance at those strained features convinced me of the reason for his coming. Only one thing can bring such a furtive, restless stare to a man's eyes. Only one thing—fear.

"I've come to you, Dale, because—" Sir John's fingers closed heavily over the edge of the table, "because I am on the verge of going mad."

"From fear?"

"From fear, yes. I suppose it is easy to discover. A single look at me…"

"A single look at you," I said simply, "would convince any man that you are deadly afraid of something. Do you mind telling me just what it is?"

He shook his head slowly. The swagger of the poise was gone; he stood upright now with a positive effort, as if the realization of his position had suddenly surged over him.

"I do not know," he said quietly. "It is a childish fear—fear of the dark, you may call it. The cause does not matter; but if something does not take this unholy terror away, the effect will be madness."

I watched him in silence for a moment, studying the shrunken outline of his face and the unsteady gleam of his narrowed eyes. I had seen this man before. All London had seen him. His face was constantly appearing in the sporting pages, a swaggering member of the upper set—a man who had been engaged to nearly every beautiful woman in the country—who sought adventure in sport and in night life, merely for the sake of living at top speed. And here he stood before me, whitened by fear, the very thing he had so deliberately laughed at!

"Dale," he said slowly, "for the past week I have been thinking things that I do not want to think and doing things completely against my will. Some outside power—God knows what it is—is controlling my very existence."

He stared at me, and leaned closer across the table.

"Last night, some time before midnight," he told me, "I was sitting alone in my den. Alone, mind you—not a soul was in the house with me. I was reading a novel; and suddenly, as if a living presence had stood in the room and commanded me, I was forced to put the book down. I fought against it, fought to remain in that room and go on reading. And I failed."

"Failed?" My reply was a single word of wonder.

"I left my home because I could not help myself. Have you ever been under hypnotism, Dale? Yes? Well, the thing that gripped me was something similar—except that no living person came near me in order to work his hypnotic spell. I went alone, the whole way. Through back streets, alleys, filthy dooryards—never once striking a main thoroughfare—until I had crossed the entire city and reached the west side of the square. And there, before a big gray townhouse, I was allowed to stop my mad wandering. The power, whatever it was, broke. I—well, I went home."

Sir John got to his feet with an effort, and stood over me.

"Dale," he whispered hoarsely, "what was it?"

"You were conscious of every detail?" I asked. "Conscious of the time, of the locality you went to? You are sure it was not some fantastic dream?"

"Dream? Is it a dream to have some damnable force move me about like a mechanical robot?"

"But... You can think of no explanation?" I was a bit skeptical of his story.

He turned on me savagely.

"I have no explanation, Doctor," he said curtly. "I came to you for the explanation. And while you are thinking over my case during the next few hours, perhaps you can explain this: when I stood before that gray mansion on After Street, alone in the dark, there was murder in my heart. I should have killed the man who lived in that house had I not been suddenly released from the force that was driving me forward!"

Sir John turned from me in bitterness. Without offering any word of departure, he pulled open the door and stepped across the sill. The door closed, and I was alone.

That was my introduction to Sir John Harmon. I offer it in detail because it was the first of a startling series of events that led to the most terrible case of my career. In my records I have labeled the entire case "The Affair of the Death Machine."

Twelve hours after Sir John's departure—which will bring the time, to the morning of December 8—the headlines of the Daily Mail stared up at me from the table. They were black and heavy those headlines, and horribly significant. They were:

FRANKLIN WHITE Jr. FOUND
MURDERED
Midnight Marauder Strangles
Young Society Man in West-End
Mansion

I turned the paper hurriedly, and read:

Between the hours of one and two o'clock this morning, an unknown murderer entered the home of Franklin White, Jr., well known West-End sportsman, and escaped, leaving behind his strangled victim.

Young White, who is a favorite in London upper circles, was discovered in his bed this morning, where he had evidently lain dead for many hours. Police are seeking a motive for the crime, which may have its origin in the fact that White only recently announced his engagement to Margot Vernee, young and exceedingly pretty French débutante.

Police say that the murderer was evidently an amateur, and that he made no attempt to cover his crime. Inspector Thomas Drake of Scotland Yard has the case.

There was more, much more. Young White had evidently been a decided favorite, and the murder had been so unexpected, so deliberate, that the Mail reporter had made the most of his opportunity for a story. But aside from what I have reprinted, there was only a single short paragraph that claimed my attention. It was this:

The White home is not a difficult one to enter. It is a huge gray townhouse, situated just off the square, in After Street. The murderer entered by a low French window, leaving it open.

I have copied the words exactly as they were printed. The item does not call for any comment.

But I had hardly dropped the paper before she stood before me. I say "she"—it was Margot Vernee, of course—because for some peculiar reason I had expected her. She stood quietly before me, her cameo face, set in the black of mourning, staring straight into mine.

"You know why I have come?" she said quickly.

I glanced at the paper on the table before me, and nodded. Her eyes followed my glance.

"That is only part of it, Doctor," she said. "I was in love with Franklin—very much—but I have come to you for something more. Because you are a famous psychologist, and can help me."

She sat down quietly, leaning forward so that her arms rested on the table. Her face was white, almost as white as the face of that young adventurer who had come to me on the previous evening. And when she spoke, her voice was hardly more than a whisper.

"Doctor, for many days now I have been under some strange power. Something frightful, that compels me to think and act against my will."

She glanced at me suddenly, as if to note the effect of her words. Then:

"I was engaged to Franklin for more than a month, Doctor: yet for a week now I have been commanded—*commanded*—by some awful force, to return to—to a man who knew me more than two years ago. I can't explain it. I did not love this man; I hated him bitterly. Now comes this mad desire, this hungering, to go to him. And last night—"

Margot Vernee hesitated suddenly. She stared at me searchingly. Then, with renewed courage, she continued.

"Last night, Doctor, I was alone. I had retired for the night, and it was late, nearly three o'clock. And then I was strangely commanded, by this awful power that has suddenly taken possession of my soul to go out. I tried to restrain myself, and in the end I found myself walking through the square. I went straight to Franklin White's home. When I reached there, it was half past three—I could hear Big Ben. I went in—through the wide French window at the side of the house. I went straight to Franklin's room—because I could not prevent myself from going."

A sob came from Margot's lips. She had half risen from her chair, and was holding herself together with a brave effort. I went to her side and stood over her. And she, with a half-crazed laugh, stared up at me.

"He was dead when I saw him!" she cried. "Dead! Murdered! That infernal force, what ever it was, had made me go straight to my lover's side, to see him lying there, with those cruel finger marks on his throat—dead, I tell you, I—oh, it is horrible!"

She turned suddenly.

"When I saw him," she said bitterly, "the sight of him—and the sight of those marks—broke the spell that held me. I crept from the house as if I had killed him. They—they will probably find out that I was there, and they will accuse me of the murder. It does not matter. But this power—this awful thing that has been controlling me—is there no way to fight it?"

I nodded heavily. The memory, of that unfortunate fellow who had come to me with the same complaint was still holding me. I was prepared to wash my hands of the whole horrible affair. It was clearly not a medical case, clearly out of my realm.

"There is a way to fight it," I said quietly. "I am a doctor, not a master of hypnotism, or a man who can discover the reasons behind that hypnotism. But London has its Scotland Yard, and Scotland Yard has a man who is one of my greatest comrades..."

She nodded her surrender. As I stepped to the telephone, I heard her murmur, in a weary, troubled voice:

"Hypnotism? It is not that. God knows what it is. But it has always happened when I have been alone. One cannot hypnotize through distance..."

And so, with Margot Vernee's consent, I sought the aid of Inspector Thomas Drake, of Scotland Yard. In half an hour Drake stood beside me, in the quiet of my study. When he had heard Margot's story, he asked a single significant question. It was this:

"You say you have a desire to go back to a man who was once intimate with you. Who is he?"

Margot looked at him dully.

"It is Michael Strange," she said slowly. "Michael Strange, of Paris. A student of science."

Drake nodded. Without further questioning he dismissed my patient; and when she had gone, he turned to me.

"She did not murder her sweetheart, Dale" he said. "That is evident. Have you any idea who did?"

And so I told him of that other young man. Sir John Harmon, who had come to me the night before. When I had finished Drake stared at me—stared through me—and suddenly turned on his heel.

"I shall be back, Dale," he said curtly. "Wait for me."

Wait for him? Well, that was Drake's peculiar way of going about things. Impetuous, sudden—until he faced some crisis. Then, in the face of danger, he became a cold, indifferent officer of Scotland Yard.

And so I waited. During the twenty-four hours that elapsed before Drake returned to my study, I did my best to diagnose the case before me. First, Sir John Harmon—his visit to the home of Franklin White. Then—the deliberate murder. And, finally, young Margot Vernee, and her confession. It was like the revolving whirl of a pinwheel, this series of events: continuous and mystifying, but without beginning or end. Surely, somewhere in the procession of horrors, there would be a loose end to cling to. Some loose end that would eventually unravel the pinwheel!

It was plainly not a medical affair, or at least only remotely so. The thing was in proper hands, then, with Drake following it through. And I had only to wait for his return.

He came at last, and closed the door of the room behind him. He stood over me with something of a swagger.

"Dale, I have been looking into the records of this Michael Strange," he said quietly. "They are interesting, those records. They go back some ten years, when this fellow Strange was beginning his study of science. And now Michael Strange is one of the greatest authorities in Paris on the subject of mental telegraphy. He has gone into the study of human thought with the same thoroughness that other scientists go into the subject of radiotelegraphy. He has written several books on the subject."

Drake pulled a tiny black volume from the pocket of his coat and dropped it on the table before me. With one hand he opened it to a place which he had previously marked in pencil.

"Read it," he said significantly.

I looked at him in wonder, and then did as he ordered. What I read was this:

"Mental telegraphy is a science, not a myth. It is a very real fact, a very real power which can be developed only by careful research. To most people it is merely a curiosity. They sit, for instance, in a crowded room at some uninteresting lecture, and stare continually at the back of some unsuspecting companion until that companion, by the power of suggestion, turns suddenly around. Or they think heavily of a certain person nearby, perhaps commanding him mentally to hum a certain popular tune, until the victim, by the power of their will, suddenly fulfills the order. To such persons, the science of mental telegraphy is merely an amusement.

"And so it will be, until science has brought it to such a perfection that these waves of thought can be broadcast—that they can be transmitted through the ether precisely as radio waves are transmitted. In other words, mental telegraphy is at present merely a mild form of hypnotism. Until it has been developed so that those hypnotic powers can be directed through space, and directed accurately to those individuals to whom they are intended, this science will have no significance. It remains for scientists of today to bring about that development."

I closed the book. When I looked up, Drake was watching me intently, as if expecting me to say something.

"Drake," I said slowly, more to myself than to him, "the pinwheel is beginning to unravel. We have found the beginning thread. Perhaps, if we follow that thread…"

Drake smiled.

"If you'll pick up your hat and coat, Dale," he interrupted, "I think we have an appointment. This Michael Strange, whose book you have just enjoyed so immensely, is now residing on a certain quiet little side street about three miles from the square, in London."

I followed Drake in silence, until we had left Cheney Lane in the gloom behind us. At the entrance to the square my companion called a cab; and from there on we rode slowly, through a heavy darkness which was blanketed by a wet, penetrating fog. The cabby, evidently one who knew my companion by sight (and what London cabby does not know his Scotland Yard men!) chose a route that twisted through gloomy, uninhabited side streets, seldom winding into the main route of traffic.

As for Drake, he sank back in the uncomfortable seat and made no attempt at conversation. For the entire first part of our journey he said nothing. Not until we had reached a black, unlighted section of the city did he turn to me.

"Dale," he said at length, "have you ever hunted tiger?"

I looked at him and laughed.

"Why?" I replied. "Do you expect this hunt of ours will be something of a blind chase?"

"It will be a blind chase, no doubt of it," he said. "And when we have followed the trail to its end, I imagine we shall find something very like a tiger to deal with. I have looked rather deeply into Michael Strange's life, and unearthed a bit of the man's character. He has twice been accused of murder—murder by hypnotism—and has twice cleared himself by throwing scientific explanations at the police. That is the nature of his entire history for the past ten years."

I nodded, without replying. As Drake turned away from me again, our cab poked its laboring nose into a narrowing, gloomy street. I had a glimpse of a single unsteady street lamp on the corner, and a dim sign, "Mate Lane." And then we were dragging along the curb. The cab stopped with a groan.

I had stepped down and was standing by the cab door when suddenly, from the darkness in front of me, a strange figure advanced to my side. He glanced at me intently; then, seeing that I was evidently not the man he sought, he turned to Drake. I heard a whispered greeting and an undertone of conversation. Then, quietly, Drake stepped toward me.

"Dale," he said. "I thought it best that I should not show myself here tonight. No, there is no time for explanation; you will understand later. Perhaps"—significantly—"sooner than you anticipate. Inspector Hartnett will go through the rest of this pantomime with you."

I shook hands with Drake's man, still rather bewildered at the sudden substitution. Then, before I was aware of it, Drake had vanished and the cab was gone. We were alone, Hartnett and I, in Mate Lane.

The home of Michael Strange—number seven—was hardly inviting. No light was in evidence. The big house stood like a huge, unadorned vault set back from the street, some distance from its adjoining buildings. The heavy steps echoed to our footbeats as we mounted them in the darkness; and the sound of the bell, as Hartnett pressed it came sharply to us from the silence of the interior.

We stood there, waiting. In the short interval before the door opened, Hartnett glanced at his watch (it was nearly ten o'clock), and said to me:

"I imagine, Doctor, we shall meet a blank wall. Let me do the talking, please."

That was all. In another moment the big door was pulled slowly open from the inside, and in the entrance, glaring out at us, stood the man we had come to see. It is not hard to remember that first impression of Michael Strange. He was a huge man, gaunt and haggard, moulded with the hunched shoulders and heavy arms of a gorilla. His face seemed to be unconsciously twisted into a snarl. His greeting, which came only after he had stared at us intently, for nearly a minute, was curt and rasping.

"Well, gentlemen? What is it?"

"I should like a word with Dr. Michael Strange," said my companion quietly.

"I am Michael Strange."

"And I," replied Hartnett, with a suggestion of a smile, "am Raoul Hartnett, from Scotland Yard."

I did not see any sign of emotion on Strange's face. He stepped back in silence to allow us to enter. Then closing the big door after us, he led the way along a carpeted hall to a small, ill-lighted room just beyond. Here he motioned us to be seated, he himself standing upright beside the table, facing us.

"From Scotland Yard," he said, and the tone was heavy with dull sarcasm. "I am at your service, Mr. Hartnett."

And now, for the first time, I wondered just why Drake had insisted on my coming here to this gloomy house in Mate Lane. Why he had so deliberately arranged a substitute so that Michael Strange should not come face to face with him directly. Evidently Hartnett had been carefully instructed as to his course of action—but why this seemingly unnecessary caution on Drake's part? And now, after we had gained admission, what excuse would Hartnett offer for the intrusion? Surely he would not follow the bull-headed rôle of a common policeman!

There was no anger, no attempt at dramatics, in Hartnett's voice. He looked quietly up at our host.

"Dr. Strange," he said at length, "I have come to you for your assistance. Last night, some time after midnight, Franklin White was strangled to death. He was murdered, according to substantial evidence, by the girl he was going to marry—Margot Vernee. I come to you because you know this girl rather well, and can perhaps help Scotland Yard in finding her motive for killing White."

Michael Strange said nothing. He stood there, scowling down at my companion in silence. And I, too, I must admit, turned upon Hartnett with a stare of bewilderment. His accusation of Margot had brought a sense of horror to me. I had expected almost anything from him, even to a mad accusation of Strange himself. But I had hardly foreseen this cold-blooded declaration.

"You understand, Doctor," Hartnett went on, in that same ironical drawl, "that we do not believe Margot Vernee did this thing herself. She had a companion, undoubtedly, one who accompanied her to the house on After Street, and assisted her in the crime. Who that companion was, we are not sure; but there is decidedly a case of suspicion against a certain young London sportsman. This fellow is known to have prowled about the White mansion both on the night of the murder and the night before."

Hartnett glanced up casually. Strange's face was a total mask. When he nodded, the nod was the most even and mechanical thing I have ever seen. Certainly this man could control his emotions!

"Naturally, Doctor," Hartnett said, "we have gone rather deeply into the past life of the lady in question. Your name appears, of course, in a rather unimportant interval when Margot Vernee resided in Paris. And so we come to you in the hope that you can perhaps give us some slight bit of information—something that seems insignificant, perhaps, to you, but which may put us on the right track."

It was a careful speech. Even as Hartnett spoke it, I could have sworn that the words were Drake's, and had been memorized. But Michael Strange merely stepped back to the table and faced us without a word. He was probably, during that brief interlude, attempting to realize his position, and to discover just how much Raoul Hartnett actually knew.

And then, after his interim of silence, he came forward sullenly and stood over my comrade.

"I will tell you this much, Mr. Hartnett of Scotland Yard," he said bitterly: "My relations with Margot Vernee are not an open book to be passed through the clumsy fingers of ignorant police officers. As to this murder, I know nothing. At the time of it, I was seated in this room in company with a distinguished group of scientific friends. I will tell you, on authority, that Margot did not murder her lover. Why? Because she loved him!"

The last words were heavy with bitterness. Before they had died into silence, Michael Strange had opened the door of his study.

"If you please, gentlemen," he said quietly.

Hartnett got to his feet. For an instant he stood facing the gorilla-like form of our host; then he stepped over the sill, without a word. We passed down the unlighted corridor in silence, while Strange stood in the door of his study, watching us. I could not help but feel, as we left that gloomy house, that Strange had suddenly focused his entire attention upon me, and had ignored my companion. I could feel those eyes upon me, and feel the force of the will behind them. A decided feeling of uneasiness crept over me, and I shuddered.

A moment later the big outer door had closed shut after us, and we were alone in Mate Lane. Alone, that is, until a third figure joined us in the shadows, and Drake's hand closed over my arm.

"Capital, Dale," he said triumphantly. "For half an hour you entertained him, you and Hartnett. And for half an hour I've had the unlimited freedom of his inner rooms, with the aid of an unlocked window on the lower floor. Those inner rooms, gentlemen, are significant—very!"

As we walked the length of Mate Lane, the gaunt, sinister home of Michael Strange became an indistinct outline in the pitch behind us. Drake said nothing more on the return trip, until we had nearly reached my rooms. Then he turned to me with a smile.

"We are one up on our friend, Dale," he said. "He does not know, just now, which is the bigger fool—you or Hartnett here. However, I imagine Hartnett will be the victim of some very unusual events before many hours have passed."

That was all. At least, all of significance. I left the two Scotland Yard men at the opening of Cheney Lane, and continued alone to my rooms. I opened the door and let myself in quietly. And there some few hours later, began the last and most horrible phase of the case of the murder machine.

It began—or to be more accurate, I began to react to it—at three o'clock in the morning. I was alone, and the rooms were dark. For hours I had sat quietly by the table, considering the significant events of the past few days. Sleep was impossible with so many unanswered questions staring into me, and so I sat there wondering.

Did Drake actually believe that Margot Vernee's simple story had been a ruse—that she had in truth killed her lover on that midnight intrusion of his home? Did he believe that Michael Strange knew of that intrusion—that he had possibly planned it himself, and aided her, in order that Margot might be free to return to him? Did Strange know of that other intrusion, and of the uncanny power which had driven Sir John Harmon, and supposedly driven Margot to that house on After Street?

Those were the questions that still remained without answers: and it was over those questions that I pondered, while my surroundings became darker and more silent as the hour became more advanced. I heard the clock strike three, and heard the answering drone of Big Ben from the square.

And then it began. At first it was little more than a sense of nervousness. Before I had been content to sit in my chair and doze. Now, in spite of myself, I found myself pacing the floor, back and forth like a caged animal. I could have sworn, at the time, that some sinister presence had found entrance to my room. Yet the room was empty. And I could have sworn, too, that some silent power of will was commanding me, with undeniable force, to go out—out into the darkness of Cheney Lane.

I fought it bitterly. I laughed at it, yet even through my laugh came the memory of Sir John Harmon and Margot, and what they had told me. And then, unable to resist that unspoken demand, I seized my hat and coat and went out.

Cheney Lane was deserted, utterly still. At the end of it, the street lamp glowed dully, throwing a patch of ghastly light over the side of the adjoining building. I hurried through the shadows, and as I walked, a single idea had possession of me. I must hurry, I thought, with all possible speed, to that grim house in Mate Lane—number seven.

Where that deliberate desire came from I did not know. I did not stop to reason. Something had commanded me to go at once to Michael Strange's home. And though I stopped more than once, deliberately turning in my tracks, inevitably I was forced to retrace my steps and continue.

I remember passing through the square, and prowling through the unlightened side streets that lay beyond. Three miles separated Cheney Lane from Mate Lane, and I had been over the route only once before, in a cab. Yet I followed that route without a single false turn, followed it instinctively. At every intersecting street I was dragged in a certain direction and not once was I allowed to hesitate. It was as though some unseen demon perched on my shoulders, as the demon of the sea rode Sinbad, and pointed out the way.

Only one disturbing thing occurred on that night journey through London. I had turned into a narrow street hardly more than a quarter mile from my destination; and before me, in the shadows, I made out the form of a shuffling old man. And here, as I watched him, I was conscious of a new, mad desire. I crept upon him stealthily, without a sound. My hands were outstretched, clutching for his throat. At that moment I should have killed him!

I cannot explain it. During that brief interval I was a murderer at heart. I wanted to kill. And now that I remember it, the desire had been pregnant in me ever since the lights of Cheney Lane had died behind me. All the time that I prowled through those black streets, murder lurked in my heart. I should have killed the first man who crossed my path.

But I did not kill him. Thank God, as my fingers twisted toward the back of his throat, that mad desire suddenly left me. I stood still, while the old fellow, still unsuspecting, shuffled, away into the darkness. Then, dropping my hands with a sob of helplessness, I went forward again.

And so I reached Mate Lane, and the huge gray house that awaited me. This time, as I mounted the stone steps, the old house seemed even more repulsive and horrible. I dreaded to see that door open, but I could not retreat.

I dropped the knocker heavily. A moment passed, and then, precisely as before, the huge door swung inward. Michael Strange stood before me.

He did not speak. Perhaps, if he had spoken, that fiendish spell would have been broken, and I should have returned, even then, to my own peaceful little rooms in Cheney Lane. No—he merely held the door for me to enter, and as I passed him he stood there, watching me with a significant smile.

Straight to that familiar room at the end of the hall I went, with Strange behind me. When we had entered, he closed the door cautiously. For a moment he faced me without speaking.

"You came very close to committing a murder on your way here, did you not, Dale?"

I stared at him. How, in God's name, could this man read my thoughts so completely?

"You would have completed the murder," he said softly, "had I wished it. I did not wish it."

I did not answer. There was no reply to such a mad declaration. As for my companion, he watched me for an instant and then laughed. He was not mad. I am doctor enough to know that.

But the laugh was not long in duration. He stepped forward suddenly and took my arm in a steel grip, dragging me toward the half-hidden door at the farther end of the room.

"I shall not keep you long, Dale," he said harshly. "I could have killed you—could have made you kill yourself, and in fact, I intended to do so—but after all, you are merely a poor stumbling fool who has meddled in things too deep for you."

He pulled open the door and pushed me forward. The room was dark, and not until he had closed the door again and switched on a dim light, could I see its contents.

Even then I saw nothing. At least, nothing of importance to an unscientific mind. There was a low table against the wall, with a profusion of tiny wires emanating from it. I was aware that a cup shaped microphone—or something very similar—hung over the table, about on a level with my eyes, had I been sitting in the chair. Beyond that I saw nothing, until Strange had moved forward and drawn aside a curtain that hung beside the table.

"I made you come here tonight, Dale," he murmured, "because I was a bit afraid of you. Your comrade, Hartnett, was an ignorant police officer. He has not the intellect to connect the series of events of the past day or two, and so I did not trouble myself with him. But you are an educated man. You have made no demonstrations of your ability in the field of science, but—"

He stopped speaking abruptly. From the room behind us came the sound of a warning bell. Strange turned quickly and went to the door.

"You will wait here, Doctor," he said. "I have another caller tonight. Another one who came the same way as you."

He vanished. For a short interlude I was alone, with that peculiar radio-like apparatus before me. It was, for all the world, like a miniature control room in some small broadcasting station. Except for the odd shape of the microphone, if it was such I could detect no radical difference in equipment.

However, I had little time for conjecture. A patter of footsteps interrupted me from the next room, and a frightened, feminine voice broke the stillness of the outer study. Even before the owner of that voice stepped in to my presence, I knew her.

And when she came, with white, fearful face and trembling body, I could not withhold a shudder of apprehension. It was the young woman who had come to my office—Margot Vernee. Evidently, at last, she had yielded to the horrible impulse that had drawn her back to Michael Strange, an impulse that, I now understood, had originated from the man himself.

He pressed her forward. There was nothing tender in his touch: it was cruel and triumphant.

"So you have succeeded—at last," I said bitterly.

He turned to me with a sneer.

"I have brought her here, yes," he replied. "And now that she has come, she shall hear what I have to tell you. It will perhaps give her a respect for me, and this time she will not have the power to turn me away."

He pointed to the table, to the apparatus that lay there.

"I'm telling you this, Dale," he said, "because it gives me pleasure to do so. You are enough of a scientist to appreciate and understand it. And if, when I have finished, I have told you too much, there is a very easy way to keep your tongue silent. You have heard of hypnotism, Dale? You have heard also of radio? Have you ever thought of combining the two?"

He faced me directly. I made no effort to reply.

"Radio," he said quietly, "is broadcast by means of sound waves. That much you know. But hypnotism too, can be transmitted through distance, if an instrument delicate enough to transmit thought waves can be invented. For twenty years I have worked on that instrument, and for twenty years I have studied hypnotism. You understand, of course, that this instrument is worthless unless it is operated by a mastermind. Thought waves are useless; they will not control the actions of even a cat. But hypnotic waves or concentrated thought waves—will control the world."

There was no denying him. He faced me with the savage triumph of a wild beast. He was glorying in his power, and in my amazement.

"I wanted Franklin White to die!" he cried. "It was I who murdered him. Why? Because he was about to take the girl I desired. Is that not reason enough for murder? And so I killed him. It was not Margot Vernee who strangled her lover: it was a complete stranger, a London sportsman, who had no reason for committing the murder, except that I wished him to!

"Franklin died on the night of December seventh, murdered by Sir John Harmon, the sportsman. Why? Because, of all London, Sir John would be the last man to be suspected. I have a keen appreciation for the irony of fate. White would have died the night before, Dale, except that I lacked the courage to kill him. His murderer was standing, under my power, outside his very house—and then I suddenly thought it best that I should have an alibi. Your Scotland Yard is clever, and it was best that I have protection. And so, on the following night, I sent Sir John to the house once again. This time, while I sat here and controlled the actions of my puppet, a group of men sat here with me. They believed that I was experimenting with a new type of radio receiver!"

Michael Strange laughed, laughed harshly, in utter triumph, as a cat laughs at the antics of his mouse victims.

"When that murder was done," he said, "I sent Margot to the scene, so that she might see her lover strangled, dead. I repeat, Dale, that I enjoy the irony of fate, especially when I can control it. And as for you—I brought you here tonight merely so that you would realize the intensity of the powers that control you. When you leave here, you will be unharmed—but after the exhibition I shall give you, I am sure that you will make no further attempt to interfere with things out of your realm of understanding."

I heard a sob from Margot. She had retreated to the door, and clung there. For myself, I did not move. Strange's recital had revealed to me the horrible lust that gripped him, and now I watched him in fascination. He would not harm the girl; that much I was sure of. In his distorted fashion he loved her. In his crazed, murderous way he would attempt to win her love, even though she had once scorned him.

I saw him step toward the table. Saw him drop heavily into the chair, and stare directly into that microphonic thing that hung before his eyes. As he stared, he spoke to me.

"Science, in its intricate forms, is probably above the mind of a common medical man, Dale," he said. "It would be useless to explain to you how my thoughts—and my will—can be transmitted through space. Perhaps you have sat in a theater and stared at a certain person until that person turned to face you. You have? Then you will perhaps understand how I can control the minds of any human creature within the radius of my power. You see, Dale, this intricate little machine gives me the power to transform London into a city of stark murder. I could bring about such a horrible wave of crime that Scotland Yard would be scorned from one end of the world to the other. I could make every man murder his neighbor, until the streets of the city were running with blood."

Strange turned quietly to look at me. He spoke deliberately.

"And now for the little exhibition of which I spoke, Dale," he murmured. "Your detective friend, Hartnett, has been under my power for the past three hours. You see, it was safer to control his movements, and be sure of him. And now, to be doubly sure of him, perhaps you would like to see him kill himself?"

I stepped forward with a sudden cry. Strange said nothing: his eyes merely burned into mine. Once again I felt that strange, all-powerful control forcing me back. I retreated, step by step, until the wall stopped me. Yet even as I retreated, a childish hope filled me. How could Strange, working his terrible murder machine, concentrate his power on any individual, when the whole of London lay before him?

He answered my question. He must have read it as it came over me.

"Have you ever been in a crowd, Dale, and watched a certain individual intently, until that particular individual turned to look at you? The rest of the crowd pays no attention, of course, but that one man. And now we shall make that one man murder himself!"

Strange turned slowly. I saw his fingers creep along the rim of the table, touching certain wires that came together there. I heard a dull, droning hum fill the room, and, over it, Strange's penetrating voice.

"When I am finished, Dale, I shall probably kill you. I brought you here merely to frighten you, but I believe I have told you too much."

With that new horror upon me, I saw my captor's lips move slowly...

And then, from the shadows at the other end of the small room, came a low, unemotional voice.

"Before you begin, Strange—"

Michael Strange whipped about in his chair like a tiger. His hand dropped to his pocket, so swiftly that my eyes did not follow it. And as it dropped, a single staccato shot split the darkness of the room. The scientist slumped forward in his chair.

The dull, whirring sound of that hellish machine had stopped abruptly, cut short by the sudden weight of Strange's lunging body as he fell upon it. I saw the livid, fiery snake of white light twist suddenly upward through that coil of wires and in another moment the entire apparatus shattered by a blinding crash of flame.

After that I turned away. Whether the bullet killed Strange or not, I do not know but the sight of his charred face, hanging over that table of destruction, told its own story.

It was Inspector Drake who came across the room toward me, and took my arm. The smoking revolver still lay in his hand, and as he led me into the adjoining room, I saw that Margot had already found refuge there.

"You see now, Dale," Drake said quietly, "why I let Hartnett go with you before? If Strange had suspected me, I should have been merely another victim. As for Hartnett, he has been under constant guard down at headquarters. He's safe. They've kept him there, at my instructions, in spite of all his terrific efforts to leave them."

I was listening to my companion in admiration. Even then I did not quite understand.

"I was wrong in just one thing, Dale. I left you alone, without protection. I believed Strange would ignore you, because, after all, you are not a Scotland Yard man. Thank God I had the sense to follow Margot—to trail her here—and get here soon enough."

And so ended the horrible series of events that began with Sir John Harmon's chance visit to my study. As for Harmon, he was later cleared of all guilt, upon the charred evidence in Michael Strange's house in Mate Lane. The girl, I believe, has left London, where she can be as far as possible from memories that are all too terrible.

As for me, I am back once again in my quiet rooms in Cheney Lane, where the routine of common medical practice has wiped out many of those vivid horrors. In time, I believe, I shall forget, unless Inspector Drake, of Scotland Yard, insists upon bringing the affair up again!

THE END

When The People Fell

By CORDWAINER SMITH

The biggest news story in all history had happened centuries ago—but he was an eyewitness!

"CAN you imagine a rain of people through an acid fog? Can you imagine thousands and thousands of human bodies, without weapons, overwhelming the unconquerable monsters? Can you—"

"Look, sir," interrupted the reporter.

"Don't interrupt me! You ask me silly questions. I tell you I saw the Goonhogo itself. I saw it take Venus. Now ask me about that!"

The reporter had called to get an old man's reminiscences about bygone ages. He did not expect Dobyns Bennett to flare up at him.

Dobyns Bennett thrust home the psychological advantage he had gotten by taking the initiative. "Can you imagine showhices in their parachutes, a lot of them dead, floating out of a green sky? Can you imagine mothers crying as they fell? Can you imagine people pouring down on the poor helpless monsters?"

Mildly, the reporter asked what showhices were.

"That's old Chinesian for children," said Dobyns Bennett. "I saw the last of the nations burst and die, and you want to ask me about fashionable clothes and things. Real history never gets into the books. It's too shocking. I suppose you were going to ask me what I thought of the new striped pantaloons for women!"

"No," said the reporter, but he blushed. The question was in his notebook and he hated blushing.

"Do you know what the Goonhogo did?"

"What?" asked the reporter, struggling to remember just what a Goonhogo might be.

"It took Venus," said the old man, somewhat more calmly.

Very mildly, the reporter murmured, "It *did?*"

"You bet it did," said Dobyns Bennett belligerently.

"Were you there?" asked the reporter.

"You bet I was there when the Goonhogo took Venus," said the old man. "I was there and it's the damnedest thing I've ever seen. You know who I am. I've seen more worlds than you can count, boy, and yet when the nondies and the needies and the showhices came pouring out of the sky, that was the worst thing that any man could ever see. Down on the ground, there were the loudies the way they'd always been—"

The reporter interrupted, very gently. Bennett might as well have been speaking a foreign language. All of this had happened three hundred years before. The reporter's job was to get a feature from him and to put it into a language which people of the present time could understand.

RESPECTFULLY he said, "Can't you start at the beginning of the story?"

"You bet. That's when I married Terza. Terza was the prettiest girl you ever saw. She was one of the Vomacts, a great family of scanners, and her father was a very important man. You see, I was thirty-two, and when a man is thirty-two, he thinks he is pretty old, but I wasn't really old, I just thought so, and he wanted Terza to marry me because she was such a complicated girl that she needed a man's help. The Court back home had found her unstable and the Instrumentality had ordered her left in her father's care until she married a man who then could take on proper custodial authority. I suppose those are old customs to you, boy—"

The reporter interrupted again. "I am sorry, old man," said he. "I know you are over four hundred years old and you're the only person who remembers the time the Goonhogo took Venus. Now the Goonhogo was a government, wasn't it?"

"Anyone knows that," snapped the old man. "The Goonhogo was a sort of separate Chinesian government. Seventeen billion of them all crowded in one small part of Earth. Most of them spoke English the way you and I do, but they spoke their own language, too, with all those funny words that have come on down to us. They hadn't mixed in with anybody else yet. Then, you see, the Waywanjong himself gave the order and that is when the people started raining. They just fell right out of the sky. You never saw anything like it—"

The reporter had to interrupt him again and again to get the story bit by bit. The old man kept using terms that he couldn't seem to realize were lost in history and that had to be explained to be intelligible to anyone of this era. But his memory was excellent and his descriptive powers as sharp and alert as ever...

YOUNG Dobyns Bennett had not been at Experimental Area A very long, before he realized that the most beautiful female he had ever seen was Terza Vomact. At the age of fourteen, she was fully mature. Some of the Vomacts did mature that way. It may have had something to do with their being descended from unregistered, illegal people centuries back in the past. They were even said to have mysterious connections with the lost world back in the age of nations when people could still put numbers on the years.

He fell in love with her and felt like a fool for doing it. She was so beautiful, it was hard to realize that she was the daughter of Scanner Vomact himself. The scanner was a powerful man.

Sometimes romance moves too fast and it did with Dobyns Bennett because Scanner Vomact himself called in the young man and said, "I'd like to have you marry my daughter Terza, but I'm not sure she'll approve of you. If you can get her, boy, you have my blessing."

Dobyns was suspicious. He wanted to know why a senior scanner was willing to take a junior technician.

All that the scanner did was to smile. He said, "I'm a lot older than you, and with this new santaclara drug coming in that may give people hundreds of years, you may think that I died in my prime if I die at a hundred and twenty. You may live to four or five hundred. But I know my time's coming up. My wife has been dead for a long time and we have no other children and I know that Terza needs a father in a very special kind of way. The psychologist found her to be unstable. Why don't you take her outside the area? You can get a pass through the dome anytime. You can go out and play with the loudies."

Dobyns Bennett was almost as insulted as if someone had given him a pail and told him to go play in the sandpile. And yet he realized that the elements of play in courtship were fitted together and that the old man meant well.

The day that it all happened, he and Terza were outside the dome. They had been pushing loudies around.

Loudies were not dangerous unless you killed them. You could knock them down, push them out of the way, or tie them up; after a while, they slipped away and went about their business. It took a very special kind of ecologist to figure out what their business was. They floated two meters high, ninety centimeters in diameter, gently just above the land of Venus, eating microscopically. For a long time, people thought there was radiation on which they subsisted. They simply multiplied in tremendous numbers. In a silly sort of way, it was fun to push them around, but that was about all there was to do.

They never responded with intelligence.

Once, long before, a loudie taken into the laboratory for experimental purposes had typed a perfectly clear message on the typewriter. The message had read, "Why don't you Earth people go back to Earth and leave us alone? We are getting along all—"

And that was all the message that anybody had ever got out of them in three hundred years. The best laboratory conclusions was that they had very high intelligence if they ever chose to use it, but that their volitional mechanism was so profoundly different from the psychology of human beings that it was impossible to force a loudie to respond to stress as people did on Earth.

THE name *loudie* was some kind of word in the old Chinesian language. It meant the "ancient ones." Since it was the Chinesians who had set up the first outposts on Venus, under the orders of their supreme boss the Waywanjong, their term lingered on.

Dobyns and Terza pushed loudies, climbed over the hills and looked down into the valleys where it was impossible to tell a river from a swamp. They got thoroughly wet, their air converters stuck, and perspiration itched and tickled along their cheeks. Since they could not eat or drink while outside—at least not with any reasonable degree of safety—the excursion could not be called a picnic. There was something mildly refreshing about playing child with a very pretty girl-child—but Dobyns wearied of the whole thing.

Terza sensed his rejection of her. Quick as a sensitive animal, she became angry and petulant. "You didn't have to come out with me!"

"I wanted to," he said, "but now I'm tired and want to go home."

"You treat me like a child. All right, play with me. Or you treat me like a woman. All right, be a gentleman. But don't seesaw all the time yourself. I just got to be a little bit happy and you have to get middle-aged and condescending. I won't take it."

"Your father—" he said, realizing the moment he said it that it was a mistake.

"My father this, my father that. If you're thinking about marrying me, do it yourself." She glared at him, stuck her tongue out, ran over a dune, and disappeared.

Dobyns Bennett was baffled.

He did not know what to do. She was safe enough. The loudies never hurt anyone. He decided to teach her a lesson and to go on back himself, letting her find her way home when she pleased. The Area Search Team could find her easily if she really got lost.

He walked back to the gate.

When he saw the gates locked and the emergency lights on, he realized that he had made the worst mistake of his life.

HIS heart sinking within him, he ran the last few meters of the way, and beat the ceramic gate with his bare hands until it opened only just enough to let him in.

"What's wrong?" he asked the doortender.

The doortender muttered something that Dobyns could not understand.

"Speak up, man!" shouted Dobyns. "What's wrong?"

"The Goonhogo is coming back and they're taking over."

"That's impossible," said Dobyns. "They couldn't—" He checked himself. *Could* they?

"The Goonhogo's taken over," the gatekeeper insisted. "They've been given the whole thing. The Earth Authority has voted it to them. The Waywanjong has decided to send people right away. They're sending them."

"What do the Chinesians want with Venus? You can't kill a loudie without contaminating a thousand acres of land. You can't push them away without them drifting back. You can't scoop them up. Nobody can live here until we solve the problem of these things. We're a long way from having solved it," said Dobyns in angry bewilderment.

The gatekeeper shook his head. "Don't ask me. That's all I hear on the radio. Everybody else is excited too."

Within an hour, the rain of people began.

Dobyns went up to the radar room, saw the skies above. The radar man himself was drumming his fingers against the desk. He said, "Nothing like this has been seen for a thousand years or more. You know what there is up there? Those are warships, the warships left over from the last of the old, dirty wars. I knew the Chinesians were inside them. Everybody knew about it. It was sort of like a museum. Now they don't have any weapons in them. But do you know—there are millions of people hanging up there over Venus and I don't know what they are going to do!"

He stopped and pointed at one of the screens. "Look, you can see them running in patches. They're behind each other, so they cluster up solid. We've never had a screen look like that."

Dobyns looked at the screen. It was, as the operator said, full of blips.

As they watched, one of the men exclaimed, "What's that milky stuff down there in the lower left? See, it's—it's pouring," he said, "it's pouring somehow out of those dots. How can you pour things into a radar? It doesn't really show, does it?"

The radar man looked at his screen. He said, "Search me. I don't know what it is, either. You'll have to find out. Let's just see what happens."

Scanner Vomact came into the room. He said, once he had taken a quick, experienced glance at the screens, "This may be the strangest thing we'll ever see, but I have a feeling they're dropping people. Lots of them. Dropping them by the thousands, or by the hundreds of thousands, or even by the millions. But people are coming down there. Come along with me, you two. We'll go out and see it. There may be somebody that we can help."

BY this time, Dobyns' conscience was hurting him badly. He wanted to tell Vomact that he had left Terza out there, but he had hesitated—not only because he was ashamed of leaving her, but because he did not want to tattle on the child to her father. Now he spoke.

"Your daughter's still outside."

Vomact turned on him solemnly. The immense eyes looked very tranquil and very threatening, but the silky voice was controlled.

"You may find her." The scanner added, in a tone which sent the thrill of menace up Dobyns' back, "And everything will be well if you bring her back."

Dobyns nodded as though receiving an order.

"I shall," said Vomact, "go out myself, to see what I can do, but I leave the finding of my daughter to you."

They went down, put on the extra-long-period converters, carried their miniaturized survey equipment so that they could find their way back through the fog, and went out. Just as they were at the gate, the gatekeeper said, "Wait a moment, sir and Excellency. I have a message for you here on the phone. Please call Control."

Scanner Vomact was not to be called lightly and he knew it. He picked up the connection unit and spoke harshly.

The radar man came on the phone screen in the gatekeeper's wall. "They're overhead now, sir."

"Who's overhead?"

"The Chinesians are. They're coming down. I don't know how many there are. There must be two thousand warships over our heads right here and there are more thousands over the rest of Venus. They're down now. If you want to see them hit ground, you'd better get outside quick."

Vomact and Dobyns went out.

Down came the Chinesians. People's bodies were raining right out of the milk-cloudy sky. Thousands upon thousands of them with plastic parachutes that looked like bubbles. Down they came.

Dobyns and Vomact saw a headless man drift down. The parachute cords had decapitated him.

A woman fell near them. The drop had torn her breathing tube loose from her crudely bandaged throat and she was choking in her own blood. She staggered toward them, tried to babble but only drooled blood with mute choking sounds, and then fell face forward into the mud.

Two babies dropped. The adult accompanying them had been blown off course. Vomact ran, picked them up and handed them to a Chinesian man who had just landed. The man looked at the babies in his arms, sent Vomact a look of contemptuous inquiry, put the weeping children down in the cold slush of Venus, gave them a last impersonal glance and ran off on some mysterious errand of his own.

Vomact kept Bennett from picking up the children. "Come on, let's keep looking. We can't take care of all of them."

THE world had known that the Chinesians had a lot of unpredictable public habits, but they never suspected that the nondies and the needies and the showhices could pour down out of a poisoned sky. Only the Goonhogo itself would make such a reckless use of human life. *Nondies* were men and *needies* were women and *showhices* were the little children. And the *Goonhogo* was a name left over from the old days of nations. It meant something like republic or state or government. Whatever it was, it was the organization that ran the Chinesians in the Chinesian manner, under the Earth Authority.

And the ruler of the Goonhogo was the Waywanjong.

The Waywanjong didn't come to Venus. He just sent his people. He sent them floating down into Venus, to tackle the Venusian ecology with the only weapons which could make a settlement of that planet possible—people themselves. Human arms could tackle the loudies, the loudies who had been called "old ones" by the first Chinesian scouts to cover Venus.

The loudies had to be gathered together so gently that they would not die and, in dying, each contaminate a thousand acres. They had to be kept together by human bodies and arms in a gigantic living corral.

Scanner Vomact rushed forward. A wounded Chinesian man hit the ground and his parachute collapsed behind him. He was clad in a pair of shorts, had a knife at his belt, canteen at his waist. He had an air converter attached next to his ear, with a tube running into his throat. He shouted something unintelligible at them and limped rapidly away.

People kept on hitting the ground all around Vomact and Dobyns.

The self-disposing parachutes were bursting like bubbles in the misty air, a moment or two after they touched the ground. Someone had done a tricky, efficient job with the chemical consequences of static electricity.

And as the two watched, the air was heavy with people. One time, Vomact was knocked down by a person. He found that it was two Chinesian children tied together.

Dobyns asked, "What are you doing? Where are you going? Do you have any leaders?"

He got cries and shouts in an unintelligible language. Here and there someone shouted in English "This way!" or "Leave us alone!" or "Keep going..." but that was all.

The experiment worked.

Eighty-two million people were dropped in that one day.

AFTER four hours, which seemed barely short of endless, Dobyns found Terza in a corner of the cold hell. Though Venus was warm, the suffering of the almost-naked Chinesians had chilled his blood.

Terza ran toward him. She could not speak.

She put her head on his chest and sobbed. Finally she managed to say, "I've—I've—I've tried to help, but they're too many, too many, too many!" And the sentence ended as shrill as a scream.

Dobyns led her back to the experimental area.

They did not have to talk. Her whole body told him that she wanted his love and the comfort of his presence, and that she had chosen that course of life, which would keep them together.

As they left the drop area, which seemed to cover all of Venus so far as they could tell, a pattern was beginning to form. The Chinesians were beginning to round up the loudies.

Terza kissed him mutely after the gatekeeper had let them through. She did not need to speak. Then she fled to her room.

The next day, the people from Experimental Area A tried to see if they could go out and lend a hand to the settlers. It wasn't possible to lend a hand; there were too many settlers. People by the millions were scattered all over the hills and valleys of Venus, sludging through the mud and water with their human toes, crushing the alien mud, crushing the strange plants. They didn't know what to eat. They didn't know where to go. They had no leaders.

All they had were orders to gather the loudies together in large herds and hold them there with human arms.

The loudies didn't resist.

After a time-lapse of several Earth days, the Goonhogo sent small scout cars. They brought a very different kind of Chinesian—these late arrivals were uniformed, educated, cruel, smug men. They knew what they were doing. And they were willing to pay any sacrifice of their own people to get it done.

They brought instructions. They put the people together in gangs. It did not matter where the nondies and needies had come from on Earth; it didn't matter whether they found their own showhices or somebody else's. They were shown the jobs to do and they got to work. Human bodies accomplished what machines could not have done—they kept the loudies firmly but gently encircled until every last one of the creatures was starved into nothingness.

Rice fields began to appear miraculously.

Scanner Vomact couldn't believe it. The Goonhogo biochemists had managed to adapt rice to the soil of Venus. And yet the seedlings came out of boxes in the scout cars and weeping people walked over the bodies of their own dead to keep the crop moving toward the planting.

Venusian bacteria could not kill human beings, nor could they dispose of human bodies after death. A problem arose and was solved. Immense sleds carried dead men, women and children—those who had fallen wrong, or drowned as they fell, or had been trampled by others—to an undisclosed destination. Dobyns suspected the material was to be used to add Earthtype organic waste to the soil of Venus, but he did not tell Terza.

The work went on.

The nondies and needies kept working in shifts. When they could not see in the darkness, they proceeded without seeing—keeping in line by touch or by shout. Foremen, newly trained, screeched commands. Workers lined up, touching fingertips. The job of building the fields kept on.

"THAT'S a big story," said the old man, "eighty-two million people dropped in a single day. And later I heard that the Waywanjong said it wouldn't have mattered if seventy million of them had died. Twelve million survivors would have been enough to make a spacehead for the Goonhogo. The Chinesians got Venus, all of it.

"But I'll never forget the nondies and the needies and the showhices falling out of the sky, men and women and children with their poor scared Chinesian faces. That funny Venusian air made them look green instead of tan. There they were, falling all around.

"You know something, young man?" said Dobyns Bennett approaching his fifth century of age.

"What?" said the reporter.

"There won't be things like that happening on any world again. Because now, after all, there isn't any separate Goonhogo left. There's only one Instrumentality and they don't care what a man's race may have been in the ancient years. Those were the rough old days, the ones I lived in. Those were the days *men* still tried to do things."

Dobyns almost seemed to doze off, but he roused himself sharply and said, "I tell you, the sky was full of people. They fell like water. They fell like rain. I've seen the awful ants in Africa, and there's not a thing among the stars to beat them for prowling horror. Mind you, they're worse than anything the stars contain. I've seen the crazy worlds near Alpha Centauri, but I never saw anything like the time the people fell on Venus. More than eighty-two million in one day and my own little Terza lost among them.

"But the rice did sprout. And the loudies died as the walls of people held them in with human arms. Walls of people, I tell you, with volunteers jumping in to take the places of the falling ones.

"They were people still, even when they shouted in the darkness. They tried to help each other even while they fought a fight that had to be fought without violence. They were people still. And they did so win. It was crazy and impossible, but they won. Mere human beings did what machines and science would have taken another thousand years to do...

"The funniest thing of all was the first house that I saw a nondie put up, there in the rain of Venus. I was out there with Vomact and with a pale sad Terza. It wasn't much of a house, shaped out of twisted Venusian wood. There it was. *He* built it, the smiling half-naked Chinesian nondie. We went to the door and said to him in English, 'What are you building here, a shelter or a hospital?'

"The Chinesian grinned at us. 'No,' he said, 'gambling.'

"Vomact wouldn't believe it: 'Gambling?'

"'Sure,' said the nondie. 'Gambling is the first thing a man needs in a strange place. It can take the worry out of his soul."

"Is that all?" said the reporter.

DOBYNS Bennett muttered that the personal part did not count. He added, "Some of my great-great-great-great-great-grand-sons may come along. You count those greats. Their faces will show you easily enough that I married into the Vomact line. Terza saw what happened. She saw how people build worlds. This was the hard way to build them. She never forgot the night with the dead Chinesian babies lying in the half-illuminated mud, or the parachute ropes dissolving slowly. She heard the needies weeping and the helpless nondies comforting them and leading them off to nowhere. She remembered the cruel, neat officers coming out of the scout cars. She got home and saw the rice come up, and saw how the Goonhogo made Venus a Chinesian place."

"What happened to you personally?" asked the reporter.

"Nothing much. There wasn't any more work for us, so we closed down Experimental Area A. I married Terza.

"Any time later, when I said to her, 'You're not such a bad girl!' she was able to admit the truth and tell me she was not. That night in the rain of people would test anybody's soul and it tested hers. She had met a big test and passed it. She used to say to me, 'I saw it once. I saw the people fall, and I never want to see another person suffer again. Keep me with you, Dobyns, keep me with you forever.'

"And," said Dobyns Bennet, "it wasn't forever, but it was a happy and sweet three hundred years. She died after our fourth diamond anniversary. Wasn't that a wonderful thing, young man?"

The reporter said it was. And yet, when he took the story back to his editor, he was told to put it into the archives. It wasn't the right kind of story for entertainment and the public would not appreciate it any more.

THE END

Earthman's Choice

By ROGER DEE

Cameron and his wife were left stranded on Venus when the old madness of the human race struck across all the millions of miles of space at them. The Droon Mind offered them shelter—of a kind!

For seconds after the roar of the blast rolled up the mountain-side to them Cameron and his wife stood frozen beside their caterpillar ore sled and stared palely at each other, neither daring to voice their inevitable first thought.

"That was the *Astra's* fuel pile letting go," Cameron said finally. "We found what we came to Venus for, Helen, but we'll never take it away."

She answered him indirectly, displaying for the thousandth time the characteristic commonsense that made her a perfect balance-wheel to his driving impatience.

"Miilak!" she called.

The Droon worker came out of the ore pit toward them, his silvery eye-discs glowing like bland, cryptic windows against the violet oval of his face. The flood of white light from the mist-ceiling overhead sank into his flesh without highlight or reflection, causing Cameron to think irrelevantly of a purple California grape, translucent but with an odd quality of absorbing and drowning light.

Unerringly Miilak read the question in their minds and droned his answer in the English, which he and the millions of his kind swarming the planet had learned in a single day.

"The star-ship is destroyed," he said. "The men are all dead but Jansen."

Cameron stared, feeling again the instinctive prickle of unease that had been his first reaction to a creature so human in form yet so alien of nature. He knew the infallibility of the Droon's communal telepathic sense, but for the moment it seemed to him that more than simple awareness lay behind the enigmatic eye-discs. Anticipation, triumph?

Impatiently he discarded the thought, knowing that in spite of his improbable abilities the Droon worker was utterly amenable to an Earthman's will—a four-foot puppet with a faculty of telepathic rapport, and nothing more.

"What happened?" Cameron demanded. "How did Jansen escape?"

The mellow drone was placid, disinterested. "A message came from your own world and made the crew like madmen. Afterward, Jansen destroyed the ship and the men in it."

"*A message*," Helen breathed. Hope sprang up in her eyes. "Vic, maybe it isn't all—"

He knew her thought: World Council might have finished a second ship ahead of schedule to assist the *Astra* in her last-ditch attempt to augment Earth's dwindling stockpile of radioactives. Perhaps another expedition was on its way already, and they were not marooned after all. Jansen, taut with the eternal strain that rode the crew, might have gone mad from simple relief of tension and...

"There is no second star-ship," Miilak said, answering Cameron's unspoken query. "There is war on Earth. Jansen destroyed the ship because his country ordered it."

Helen came into Cameron's arms and began to cry quietly, her face hidden against his chest. He held her with detached tenderness, thinking bitterly that the agony of waiting was over at last. The *Astra's* precious cargo would never reach Earth to swing the balance from unrest to peace; the *Astra* was gone, and with her had gone Earth's chance.

Their foolhardy argosy into space was done, and for nothing. Earth by now would be broken into a hundred warring factions, locked in a vicious struggle that might tear down all that the ages had built.

"We could have prevented this war, except for Jansen and his kind," Cameron said thickly. Futility sickened him—and was displaced, characteristically, by an instant and overpowering need for revenge. "The filthy spy!"

Miilak read his thought and climbed obediently to the ore-sled's seat to start the motor. Helen raised a startled, tear-streaked face when Cameron vaulted up beside the native.

"Vic! What are you going to do?"

"I'm going to find Jansen," he said grimly, "and kill him."

Knowing him, she did not argue. Instead she mounted the sled and sat beside him in silent misery, her soft mouth quivering.

The sled took them swiftly downward through masses of mica-flecked boulders, past yawning burrows of the Droon workers' tunnels, past groves of yellow-leaved trees that rose taller and thicker as the green plain below came up to meet them. Across the valley floor wound a clear, shallow river, its placid surface gleaming like silver. In the distance another mountain range rose, lofty peaks hidden in the mist ceiling.

At the valley's upper end loomed the deserted city, rising tier upon massive tier, conical towers reaching for the mists.

Helen's hand found Cameron's, and from its trembling he sensed that she shared the feeling of pygmy inconsequence that fell upon him with each fresh sight of the empty city. And with reason, he thought, for it was more than a city. It was a monument, a towering testimonial to the greatness of the race that had built and then abandoned it.

Pervading light drenched it and made it a place without shadow, a featureless pile of polished planes that gleamed like glass, unbroken by any aperture. For the thousandth time Cameron pondered that illogical blankness, wondering why a creation so perfect should turn upon its world a face so blind.

"But they *had* to see," he muttered. "A race must visualize before it can build beauty like that..."

He felt the puzzled weight of Helen's regard and broke off, recalling the purpose that drove him. There was no time now to consider a dead city's riddle. He had to find Jansen.

In a bend of the river below they saw the crater where the *Astra* had lain, a great raw pit gouged out of the green meadow, dust still swirling lazily at its bottom. There was no trace of the ship. Even the second, and larger, ore-sled was now gone.

They stared in dreary silence at the crater until a flash of movement farther up the valley caught Cameron's eye. A man-made dot crawled across the plain, sunlight winking on angular, metallic surfaces—the second sled, making straight for the dead city.

"The fool!" Cameron said. "Does he think he can hide from me here, with a million Droons broadcasting every move he makes?"

The bright dot grew rapidly larger when they gave chase.

Cameron's sled was faster, so much faster that by the time Jansen reached the city they could distinguish the pale blur of the saboteur's backward-turned face. Once Jansen shook a clenched fist, and Cameron grunted with satisfaction.

"He's unarmed, or he'd have opened on us by now," he said. "All our weapons were locked away to prevent trouble, remember?"

Helen touched his arm, pleading with him. "Don't follow into the city, Vic, please. If anything should happen—"

He squeezed her fingers absently, knowing that she was not afraid for herself but for him. A moment later they were at the city gates.

The city stretched before them in vast ordered divisions like the segments of a gigantic disc, silent avenues converging like spokes toward a central hub; a place heavy with the silence of millenia, deserted beyond the meaning of time. The only sound was the jangling of the sleds, echoing through canyoned, empty streets.

The *Astra's* crew had never penetrated here, bending every energy toward gathering a full hold of ore before Earth should recede beyond reach. Cameron had no eye for detail now, his whole attention centered upon the vehicle ahead.

The city-segments narrowed, the empty streets drew more sharply toward their common center. Jansen's sled was no more than a hundred feet ahead when it clanked into the final confluence and halted.

It was a place of utter desertion, a vast circular arena lying naked and empty except for a towering block of native stone that gleamed like pale, polished marble. The stone was the city's hub, and in each of its four vertical surfaces black tunnel-mouths gaped, angling downward.

Into the planet itself? Cameron felt his scalp prickle at the thought. Was that where the city builders had gone—inside?

Jansen did not hesitate. He chose the danger he did not know, and plunged directly into the first black opening.

Miilak halted the sled beside Jansen's and waited passively. Helen clung to Cameron, hampering him. "Please, Vic—we don't know what maybe down there!"

He shook her off. "Jansen went in. I'm going after him."

He strode into the orifice, Helen and Miilak at his heels.

The tunnel sloped gently downward, and it was not dark. A faint glow lighted the way, growing sharply brighter at the farther end where Jansen had vanished, swallowed up by whatever lay beyond.

At the glow, Cameron paused. "What's ahead there, Miilak?"

Something like ecstasy warmed the native's mellow drone. "The Hive is there, and the Droon Soul guiding Its people through the eternal Cycle."

Cameron swore, startled by the inference. "So *that's* why you're all in rapport! I should have known—you're like a termite colony or an ant-hive, a composite intelligence!"

Helen pressed against him, her eyes on the Droon worker's placid face. "Miilak, what will happen if we follow Jansen?"

For the first time the answer was oblique. "That lies between the Earth people and the Droon. I may not say."

"Rot," Cameron said shortly.

He moved into the light, down a short incline that dropped away to a circular chamber whose polished walls gaped with the mouths of a dozen other corridors leading deeper into the planet's heart. Light flooded from a low-arched ceiling, falling without shadow upon a circle of kneeling Droon people.

They ignored his entrance, their silver eye-discs fixed raptly upon a globe of milky radiance that rested upon a pedestal in the center of the room. The globe pulsed and changed, mottled with strange shadows and seethed with alien motion.

Cameron ignored it, centering his attention upon the tense figure of Jansen crouching against the farther wall.

"The burrows are open," Cameron said. "Why don't you run, Jansen? Have you lost your nerve?"

The saboteur raised a thin, frantic face. His eyes rolled, pale with terror.

"I won't go!" he said shrilly. "You can't drive me out, Cameron—I know what is down there now!"

"I see you've found out about the hive-brain," Cameron said. His lip curled. "Facing a thing like that *is* harder than murdering a crew of unsuspecting men, isn't it ?"

Jansen's eyes begged, mute as a dog's. "I'm sorry about the *Astra*, Cameron… Can't you forgive me now when we're alone here with this thing, when we'll never get off the planet alive?"

Cameron moved in, circling the ring of kneeling Droon people. The globe on its pedestal spun a flickering web of light and shadow, sucking at his attention like an insistent, hypnotic vortex.

"No," he said. "You're going to pay for the *Astra*, Jansen."

A shadow welled out of the globe, assumed a shape defying definition. It caught Cameron and froze him in midstride, his consciousness recoiling in stark panic from the overwhelming intelligence that threatened to swallow his.

Fading vision told him that Jansen had surrendered control already; the placidity that lay across the saboteur's face was as alien as the round-eyed serenity of the Droon people.

Darkness swept Cameron into a void stippled with icy pinpoints of light. He heard Helen's stifled scream and fought to reach her, and could not. The grip on his mind closed tighter…

He drifted like a disembodied soul, powerless to shut out the scene unfolding below him.

A jungle world that steamed with primeval mists, a-crawl with alien life monstrous beyond his conception. Under his eyes the jungles thinned, the mists lifted, the monsters gave way before smaller and less feral fauna. A new race, violet-skinned and silver-eyed, rose to swarm across the planet.

The Droon people.

Parallel to their evolution grew a formless shadow, shot through with myriad tiny sparkling's like moonlight on snow crystals. It waxed and swelled and became the pulsing thing Cameron had seen emerge from the globe of light in the Droon-circle.

In the depths of his consciousness a soundless voice implanted a conviction; this was the hive-mind, the racial soul. The light-points were Droon people, cells of its being.

The concept revolted him, and he rejected angrily the postulation of a race without liberty.

His own people fought to the death against restraint—the suicidal war raging on Earth at the moment was, paradoxically, an end result of that principle. No man who had ever known freedom could ever *belong* body and soul to a tyrannical race-master, drowning his personal ego in termitic regimentation...

But this was perfection, his conviction told him. All other ways must lead to insanity and to death.

Violently he denied it. The individual is more important than the whole, personal liberty a greater thing than the culture that bears it. He, Victor Cameron, was a discrete entity, and he would rather die than be a part of such a corporate monster.

Yet you must join us or perish, the voice said. *Your own race is dying, the end of your world is at hand. Take your place in the circle before it is too late. Your companions understand—look and see.*

Sight and speech returned, and he saw Helen and Jansen kneeling side by side in the Droon-circle. Their unnatural stillness startled him; the alien calm that lay like a veil across Helen's face sent him taut with horror.

"Helen!" His voice was a hoarse half-shout. "You didn't—"

She stood erect at the sound of his voice, her slim hands raised against his fury.

"Jansen and I joined the Cycle because we understand what the Droon offers," she said. The voice was Helen's, but rounded to an impersonal evenness totally foreign to the girl he had known. "We have entered the Hive, Vic, but it's not the bondage you think. It's release, the ultimate peace. Join us quickly, before it is too late."

He fought with all his strength to break the stasis that held him, and his futility only fanned the rage higher in him.

"Join you?" he shouted. "Come into that slave-chain willingly? I'll see you damned first—even you, Helen!"

"Hurry, Vic," Helen said, as if he had not spoken. "Earth is dying. Unless you join us you will die with her."

He hesitated, finding behind her words a stark mental picture of Earth shriveling and cracking, spewing out atomic fires in a blazing, cosmic holocaust.

Helen came toward him, her wide eyes glowing like the sight-discs of the Droon people. "You have glimpsed the truth, Vic. Join us now, while there is still time."

He made his voice savage, pushing back the fearful concept growing at the back of his mind.

"I can't knuckle under to this hive-brute—if I'm going to die I'll die free, as an Earthman should!"

"Please, Vic," she begged. "The Droon is right. It knows— everything."

"Then it knows how we climbed up out of the slime," he said. "It knows that men came up the hard way, alone, and built a culture that might have reached the stars. Our ancestors went out with their heads up and their bare hands for weapons, and fought their way through a world that would have swallowed the Droons overnight!"

She shook her head, and the familiar toss of her dark hair wrung him sharply with the ache of remembered intimacy.

"We were a proud people," she said, "but a dull and savage one. The Droons built and abandoned the city above us, because they had outgrown it, ages before our recorded history began."

You were great once, the soundless voice said, *but what you have known is only a clumsy, apish mockery of the older culture that was yours before some cosmic accident to Earth destroyed it. What you have now is a patchwork of degeneracy, bound from the first to fail.*

"Degeneracy?" Cameron raged. "Do you know what you're saying, Helen? Does the Droon Soul that speaks through your mouth know?"

"Men were always like the Droon people, Vic, though they never knew it. There are no free individuals anywhere, except in dissolution. We are units too in an all-encompassing Man-soul."

Stunningly the concept flared in his mind, beating down the feeble protests his stubborn hope raised against it. His eyes went from Helen to Jansen, who knelt in rapt serenity with the rest of the circle and communed with the vast, throbbing intelligence that was the complete Droon.

"But if Earth has a Man-soul," Cameron whispered, "then how can we be at each other's throats now? How could we ever have blundered into the atomic trap that is destroying us?"

The truth came of itself, numbing him with its crushing simplicity, and he saw with final clarity the gibbering unreason behind man's tortured idealism and blind ferocity. Earth's Man-soul, maimed by that ancient, cosmic catastrophe, was helpless to control its own ragings...*mad*.

"You're right," Cameron said. "I should have seen it long ago."

Then he knelt, between Helen and Jansen, in the circle.

THE END

Incomplete Superman

By POUL ANDERSON

"We want our place in the sun, but it isn't only Man who is holding us back; there's another power as strong as we are."

CHAPTER ONE

THE MAN said, "I'm sorry, Mr. Kennedy; I know it's unethical, and I wouldn't ever play such a trick on you myself. But it's orders."

"Whose orders?"

"I got them from the sales chief. Don't ask me where *he* got them." The man leaned forward, so that his face seemed almost to project from the visiscreen. "If you want my private guess, Mr. Kennedy, the government bought those parts. Want them for some top secret project."

"You don't *know* who got them?"

"No. Nor did my boss, when I asked him. It's just orders from higher up. And who swings that much influence, except the government?"

I could name a few— "What chance is there of our getting them later?"

"Not much, I'm afraid. I gather all of our production of those particular items will be going to this unidentified client."

"You couldn't find out who it is? Maybe we could make a deal with them."

The man looked frightened. "It'd cost me my job if I got nosy."

"Perhaps we could find you a better job with our outfit."

"No!"

"Well—never mind, then. If necessary, we can always make the parts ourselves."

"I'm really very sorry about all this. Murchison Laboratories has been one of our best clients. We hate to disappoint you this way. Hope you won't hold it against us in future purchases—"

"Of course not." *Like hell we won't! We can't make further use of that company—not when it too has come under their control.*

Presently the man ended the conversation and the screen went dark. For a moment the being who called himself Will Kennedy sat alone in his office, thinking.

So Murchison Labs wouldn't get its electronic parts. This had been the last source of supply for such delicate and unusual apparatus—all the others had been taken over, one by one, and on some or other pretext had quit selling anything to Murchison which couldn't be obtained from any ordinary source. Now this one, too—the secret research would be held up indefinitely while Kennedy got his plant organized to manufacture all its own needs.

Except that that wasn't the worst of it. If *they* simply happened to be engaged in some parallel work, had merely beaten out the supermen in the course of normal competition for scarce material, it didn't matter. They might even have thought that the various projects they nullified were being carried on by humans, and had throttled them as undesirable. The supermen themselves had had occasion to do that to humans.

In either case, the thing to do was to affect a rapprochement, convince them of their incredible error, and join forces.

But more and more the conflict didn't look accidental. There was too much interference, all along the line, for all of it to be due to chance collisions with *their* unknown purposes. If they were so thoroughly aware of what the supermen were doing, how could they be ignorant of the nature of the workers? And if they knew that, they would only remain hidden if they were hostile!

And in that case—

It was high time for another meeting of the Council.

KENNEDY got up, a tall lean dark-haired man with a deep inward bitterness far behind his eyes, and put on his coat. He had to go home to call the others; the special circuit was there, and it was about quitting time anyway.

Old Tom Murchison hailed him as he left the office. "What luck, Will?"

"None," shrugged Kennedy. "Somebody's got in ahead of us and contracted for their entire output. I couldn't find out whom. May be the government, working on something secret." He might as well let the old man think that. "Looks like we'll just have to start making our own stuff."

"That's a mighty big investment, especially in something so long range as this subelectronic generator—when you're not even sure it'll work!"

"Research is what keeps us ahead, chief," said Kennedy. "You founded these labs to do nothing but research. There's no point in sticking to petty industrial problems. We don't want to be just glorified consultants; this is a chance to get in on the ground floor of something as fundamental and important as atomic energy."

The old scientist nodded. "You're right, of course—as usual. Okay, I'll see if I can't dig up a spare million dollars or two for you to play with."

"We'll get it back tenfold in five or ten years."

"Maybe. At least—it'll be fun!" The faded blue eyes twinkled.

"Sure. Well, goodnight, chief." Kennedy paused. "I might not be around tomorrow. I'd like to see a chap in Seattle sometime soon; he had some interesting ideas that I think we can use."

"No need to tell me, Will. You know you've got a free hand here. Goodnight."

The superman walked out onto the graveled driveway. The early winter dusk had fallen, and snow was drifting softly out of a lowering sky. He was alone in a world of white and gray and gathering darkness.

The faint pulse of life tingled in his nerves. He could sense the impulses of men in the building behind him, a little ragged now with weariness at the end of the day. A deeper subliminal current came from the town ahead, smoothed and muted by distance, the life forces of several thousand humans going about their business. A different pattern came briefly near, a dog loping through the snow. He felt the sudden tension as it sensed him. Few dogs liked a superman, they could smell a subtle difference.

He caught the fragment of a thought, some human's unsystematic rambling—*not time tomorrow and dentist bill and straight up and*—it faded back into the formless swirling of nervous energy.

Telepathy—but maddeningly incomplete, unreliable, brief flashes of clear reception and then darkness again. It was a sense the supermen should have had, but it was rudimentary in those few who possessed it at all. Even as psychosomatic control was imperfect, as the endocrine system still wasn't much better than man's, as—

The incomplete superman. Evolution, he supposed, would in time have produced perfection of all that of which the present generation had only the beginnings. Only there wasn't going to be any evolution; there wouldn't be any future generations.

The supermen were sterile.

HE FOUND his car and sent it whispering along the street toward his house. Thought filled his brain, the enormous logic of a brain with an I.Q. of 250—not that I.Q. meant much when it got that high—thought only partially translatable into human terms. It was swift, that thought—hard, cold, and rapid as lightning flickering in a summer night; it held to its purpose without wandering; and it integrated more factors than a human brain could ever handle at once.

He knew of the interference with his own work and with some of the projects carried on by others of his species; he had bits of information hinting at trouble in almost every field. But it wasn't coordinated and there wasn't enough of it. More important, no decision had been made as to what should be done about it.

Definitely, the Council would have to meet.

Snow whirled blindingly in the beam of his headlights. The rising wind seemed to hoot at him. It had been wandering the earth before man rose up on two feet and took the wind in his face; it would still be wandering when man was in his grave.

Man—and superman.

Why do we bother? There's no real hope for us. We're doomed, we'll go down into oblivion and be forgotten—unless—

Unless! We may be able to overcome the sterility, somehow. And meanwhile, supermen are being born to human mothers, there's always a new generation of sorts. He had a brief vision of a world controlled by his species, with a few select humans left as slaves and breeding stock. It wasn't a pleasant thought.

The house loomed before him. He slid the car into the garage and got out.

As he entered, the music met him, and he scowled in annoyance. Anna was composing again. There wasn't time.

But it held him, regardless. This was music for a superman, music such as no human had ever imagined; there were the tones above and below audibility, shivering along his sensitive nerves, raising his hackles with the return of old forgotten instincts, blowing a wind upon him as if he looked into the cold depths of space itself.

It was stark, that music. It was an underground river flowing through lightless caverns with blind fish swimming past ice floes, it was a wind howling over empty moors; it was the mad dance of witches on the Brocken; the cold glass-smooth brain of a creature older than the universe and a wild beast stirring to life and flexing its claws down in the darkness of his subconscious. It laughed and sneered and roared at him, it flickered with little cold flames, it danced and mocked and lured. It was Anna's.

She heard him enter and her long fingers paused over the multiplex. The music snarled into silence, but it took a minute before the effects died within him, before the room seemed real again.

"Like it?" she asked. *"Symphonie Diabolique."*

"It's good," said Kennedy. "It's appropriate for us, isn't it?" He smiled wryly. "From the human viewpoint, I mean. We are the old Enemy, you know, the unhuman being that walks in darkness and strives for possession of man's world. We even deal in human souls, in a way." He shrugged. "Enough of that. There's more urgent business at hand."

They did not speak to each other in those words. Supermen never did, except in the presence of humans—it wasn't necessary. A phrase, a gesture, even a silence in the right place, could convey enough information for one of those minds instantly to grasp the whole. And that whole was not entirely expressible in human terms, it involved formulations found in no language of *homo sapiens* because no human brain could really comprehend them. An integrated totality, a trans-sensory visualization, a probability manifold—clumsy words, barely hinting at the immensity of events behind them.

How would you explain tensor analysis to a chimpanzee?

But roughly, supermen's thoughts and words could be rendered in human terms. Their intelligence, in the ordinary sense, was not fantastically far above that of *homo sapiens*—a few humans had even gotten that high, been as bright as a mediocre superman. It was the extra components of their minds which made the essential difference, abilities possessed, if at all, only in the most rudimentary and distorted form by humans; and this difference, rather than the greater powers of sheer memory and reason, was what made comparison between the intellects of man and superman meaningless.

ANNA GOT up and came over to him. She was tall and gaunt like himself, like most others of their species, and a human would not consider her beautiful—nor, for that matter, did Kennedy. But there was a fascination in her white skin and slant blue eyes and the aureole of frosty-gold hair about her high-cheeked face. You couldn't hide that tremendous personality; it blazed from both of them with almost a physical force. No matter how inconspicuous a superman tried to be, he remained the sort whom humans automatically obeyed.

Like old Murchison, for instance.

The scientist knew nothing about Kennedy except that he was a brilliant young physicist and administrator. Technically, he was no more than the owner's chief assistant, vice president of the firm and director of research. Murchison himself wasn't aware of it, but Kennedy ran the place. Which suited the superman—most of his breed preferred to be the power behind the throne, to have a human figurehead.

Partly it was sheer ability, which got a superman into a key position. Partly it was the overwhelming, unstoppable personality. Partly it was semi-telepathic control—not complete, for *homo superior* didn't have the senses or the projective ability except as a weak embryo of something that would never develop fully, but sufficient. A damping of certain impulses, an insertion of certain others—that was enough.

"There's trouble," said Anna. "Someone else has blocked off your supplies again."

Kennedy nodded. "The same parties, no doubt, who've been balking me for the past three years. It begins to look very much as if someone doesn't want us to do work in subelectronics. And that's a matter for the Council."

He went over to the house visiphone. Ostensibly it was an ordinary instrument, but he had built subelectronic circuits into it. No human would ever detect his calls to the Councillors.

No human.

Anna turned back to her multiplex, but didn't play it while he called. Her eyes grew dreamy; she was composing in her head now, a silent immensity of tones sliding through her brain and singing deep in her nerves.

Artists were as much in demand as scientists and administrators among the supermen. They were starved for expression suitable to themselves. Human works were all trivial, and not entirely comprehensible to a race with radically different emotional patterns. The *Symphonie Disbolique* would be—appreciated. She smiled, a slow secret curving of chiseled lips.

Kennedy's set sputtered and whined with interference. He didn't know enough about the huge new field of subelectronics to eliminate it, or even be very sure of its cause. Perhaps the motion of the planets themselves, varying gravitational fields through the Solar System, had something to do with it. The processes involved were perhaps the most fundamental of the physical universe.

He got a dozen of the twenty-odd present members of the Council. The rest could be contacted soon enough. They shifted into the artificial language they had developed, but Kennedy didn't trust it any more. If the unknowns were listening in—well, even such a code could be broken.

"I think we should meet physically, at Rendezvous Number Ten," he said. "That way we'll be safe from spies."

"They might possibly trace you and find out where we are," objected Li Wang from Canton.

"Quite so. But it won't do them much good; they won't be able to listen in on us."

"Very well." The agreement went around the world, a few muttered syllables on the whispering beam. "Midnight tomorrow, then; ten's local time."

KENNEDY turned off his set and looked back to Anna. "So much for that," he said. "I'll start tomorrow and follow an evasive path, just in case someone is trying to shadow us."

"We will," she corrected.

"But—don't be a fool! Someone has to stay here. Leaving the house unguarded would be an invitation for them to come in and see what—"

"Let them. If they know enough to search this place, they won't learn anything else by spying here. All you have lying about are some notes on subelectronics, and you said yourself you think they know as much about that as you do—or maybe more."

Kennedy scowled. "Even so—"

"I'm going. I haven't seen anyone of the species except you for months now. You can bury yourself in the lab—I have to be polite to the *humans* that call and chatter—I've had about enough of it!" Anna's eyes flashed cold and arrogant.

Kennedy shrugged. It wasn't much use arguing with her, and he didn't want her to leave him just yet.

Since there was no chance of propagating, most males and females of *homo superior* remained without ties. He thought wistfully that human love must be a wonderful thing, but it wasn't for his race. Respect, friendship, affection of a sort, yes—but they couldn't lose themselves in the wonder of another, no one else could become all the world to them. Whether it was a basic trait of the highly intellectualized breed, love simply man's version of an animal passion that superman had left behind him or whether it was related to their sterility, he didn't know.

The male and female *homo superior* usually had a succession of human mistresses or lovers—they were easy to deceive and dominate; they were convenient housekeepers or breadwinners and fronts in human society, leaving the superbeing free for other things. But he liked to have Anna around. He could talk to her.

"Very well," he said.

And it might be just as well, he reflected. She had an uncanny faculty for intuitive grasping at realities, she might be able to make valuable suggestions. And they'd need all the help they could get.

Snow whirled against the windows. He felt a sudden immense loneliness. The supermen were so few, so few, in a world of two-legged beasts. And somewhere out in that night lay their unknown enemy.

CHAPTER TWO

KENNEDY'S plane looked like an ordinary human vehicle, but he had installed modifications. As soon as he was well out of sight from the town he sealed the cabin, went up into the stratosphere, and headed for the meeting place at a thousand miles an hour.

Earth slipped away far below him, green wonderful Earth, the only world in the Solar System where any of her children could really be at home. Unless they developed the faster-than-light spaceship for which some of them hoped, the supermen would have to stay here and slowly wring a place on the planet from man. Even if they did find means of going out among the stars, he wondered if they would care to abandon their birthplace.

Even supposing they did that, they would still have to keep control on Earth, make provision for the new supermen who would be born to human parents, see that the human race didn't have a chance to interfere.

A world of our own— Briefly, he wondered what it was like to be a man, to think oneself belonging on Earth, to walk freely beneath the sky and look up to the far planets and think, *This is ours.*

But man had hope, as a race, and superman did not. A world of *homo superior* would never know the laughter of children; there would only be age and death and oblivion. Unless—

But still we must control. The greater cannot remain subservient to the lesser, the very thought is intolerable. We need man, but we cannot bow to him. We don't want to enslave, but we must control, or all our purposes, which they can not comprehend, will fall into dust.

Anna sat quietly, looking out into the stratospheric dusk with unseeing eyes. He wondered what chords and harmonies were streaming through her head.

Rendezvous Ten was simply an apartment building in Rio de Janeiro, owned by a Brazilian superman and inhabited by others of the race. Kennedy set his plane down on whispering jets into the fragrance of a roof garden. In the darkness around him, he saw the parked vehicles of the other Councillors, with more arriving. Below him, the lights of the city winked and blazed an answer to the swarming stars.

They went inside, to the room where the meeting was to be. The Councillors sat informally, conversing or lost in their own thoughts. To the outward eye, they were simply human beings, men and women of various races with little to distinguish them save the brilliant eyes and high sharp features. But inwardly—

Any superman who wished could sit in on such a meeting, and not few of the tenants had chosen to do so. But generally they were glad enough to delegate their mutual problems to the Council and be free to carry, on their private affairs.

Kennedy nodded greetings, found a seat and a drink, and waited for the rest to arrive. It didn't take long. As the one who had called the meeting, he presided.

IT WAS A strange conference. They sat so quietly, all of them, and spoke only short phrases in their special language. A gesture, a nuance of expression, a few words here and there with a subtle shift in tone—but it was enough. Precise and tremendous, the meanings stood forth.

Kennedy described his frustrations through the latest one. He finished with what could be rendered into English as: "This merely clinches my conviction that someone is opposing the project. I would like to hear any other information any of you may have which bears on the subject."

"Question," said an African. "I've been in the Congo a long time, gotten out of touch with things, and also I'm not a scientist. Why is this subelectronic work of such practical importance to anyone? The humans already have some small knowledge of the phenomena, so it's not a monopoly of ours by any means. You'd expect them to work on it too."

"They do," said Kennedy. "But as yet they find it only an interesting theoretical problem. I've carried the mathematics farther than any human has—or ever can, with their present techniques—and I can assure you that the field is basic. It seems to underlie all physical processes and integrate them in some fashion. For instance, my work gives the best explanation to date of gyromagnetism. I think it will provide a basis for many developments, including the complete and controlled disintegration of matter and the building of a spaceship, which can circumvent the light-speed barrier.

"Now obviously we can't allow humans to have that information, yet; and certain of my associates are taking care of that. We'll see to it that we become the recognized authorities on subelectronics. The devices which I shall allow my ostensible employer to have, for instance, will apparently exhaust the possibilities of one branch of the field, though actually *we* will be getting certain much more powerful mechanisms which I can have made without anyone's realizing their true purpose. Thus most humans will listen to us when we tell them that further work in the field will be fruitless; and we have the usual means for discouraging any who persist in being curious. Very much the same means that are being used against me right now!

"The point is this: No humans can be the opponents because none of them know about this work—at least, enough for them to have any conceivable reason, including simple competition for supplies, to hinder it. Even if that were the case, we would soon be able to track down the offenders and evade them. Humans simply can't hide their activities from us. But here all investigation has come to a dead end. It is always someone else who is responsible, who is putting on pressure here and there. I can't get a certain tube element because it's all being bought by another company, which wants it for someone else whose directors have decided on a line of research requiring that part because a bottleneck in production of something else makes them look for a substitute; and the bottleneck is due to a similar complex of interlocking causes…and so on as far as we can trace it.

"Sheer chance cannot account for it. I have been frustrated too many times, too thoroughly, and always with the same power and efficiency. Too many others of our race whom I know about have been having similar troubles. *Someone is out to stop us!*"

THEY TOOK that quietly, but the room seethed and crackled with nervous tension. Li Wang said slowly: "I have been having similar difficulties. As you know, we've been infiltrating the Chinese government for the past ten years. And bit by bit, as our men got higher and higher, there have been troubles. Their orders are countermanded; underlings prove obstreperous; the execution of policies fail because of unforeseen and improbable factors. And certain other policies, which we vigorously oppose, are pushed through in spite of all out efforts. For instance, we wanted no action taken to develop the Yunnanese uranium strike. Humans have too much uranium to play with right now; moreover, it should be saved for *our* use later. Nevertheless, that uranium is being mined. I have not been able to find out where all of it is going. Somebody wants that uranium *now*."

They began to tell what they knew then, report after report of difficulty, failure, an opposition hidden by the sheer complexity of its organization. It would have seemed fantastic to a human. A few supermen could control a nation by holding the key posts—or better yet, by being the indispensable advisors of the men who held those jobs. A human mind could not grasp the totality of the gigantic fluid web, which was society; to him, its sheer complexity dissolved into chaos. A superman could; he would know precisely what button to push somewhere to effect, through an inexorable chain of events, a desired happening somewhere else.

So they could appreciate the fact that someone was following their own methods—and doing it more efficiently.

Even in the minds of men—Pierre Charmant said to them: "As most of you know, I am trying to produce a general trend in music which will influence human minds toward certain desired ends. You may not all be aware of the extent to which the mathematical theory of *homo sapiens* psychology has been worked out, but I assure you that our understanding is very precise. A different type of mentality enjoys, say, classical music from one that favors the latest cacophony; but conversely, the pervasive influence of one type of music will tend to mold a mind into the corresponding pattern." He smiled at Anna. "Not for humans are your fiendish and beautiful compositions, my dear. We want them to have music that will make them soothed, amenable, easy-going. It won't do that all by itself, of course, but among many other influences it will help. In the course of a century or two—"

"And you've been having trouble," flashed Anna.

"Exactly. Other schools are rising. Valdurian's style is especially bad for our purposes. I've investigated his background. He is clear enough himself, but he seems to have been under strange influences in his past. We appeal to snobbery through the critics, we give concerts, buy radio time—but someone else is doing the same. *Someone* is very interested in promoting Valdurian."

"I've found writings here and there," said Professor Gunnarsson. "Obscure works for the most part, but bearing marks of not having been written by humans. And the philosophers and scientists and political theorists whom we sponsor are meeting unexpectedly vigorous opposition from certain quarters whose background I cannot exactly trace."

"I think that's enough," said Kennedy. "It's plain that there is some organization parallel to ours; apparently better set up and more thoroughly entrenched. They, too, want to manipulate and control man for their own purposes—which apparently conflict at important points with ours. They seem to have some awareness of us; just how much I do not know. They may suspect our true nature, or they may crack down on general principles. If, for instance they don't want anyone not under their direct control to do subelectronic research, they'd try to stop me whether they knew I was a superman or not.

"The trouble is, we know nothing about them. They remain shadows: we encounter only their puppets."

THE PAUSE that followed was long by superman standards, while they turned the information over in their minds, but it lasted only a second or two by chronological time. Then Hallmyer said thoughtfully: "The most obvious answer is that they are of our race but have built up a parallel organization without knowing about us. After all, we only began to realize our true nature and to band together about fifty years ago. We could easily have missed many of the race—we must have done so. If some of these went through a similar development, the two groups could be quite unaware of each other's existence—especially when each is trying to be as secretive as possible."

"By now they must begin to suspect the same about us that we think about them," said Charmant. "Why aren't they trying to contact us? There is no earthly reason for conflict within the race."

"Isn't there?" asked Gunnarsson, "I can imagine any number of possible reasons for a clash, including the hypothesis that these unknowns represent some sort of variant of the mutation and therefore do not belong to the race at all. Suppose they have some radically different purpose. We want simply to gain control of mankind's world. They may want something entirely different; they may want the control for themselves alone."

"If they're friendly, we needn't worry," said Kennedy. "Sooner or later, contact will be made from one side or the other and agreement reached. But in view of the facts, and of our own precarious position on Earth, we'll have to assume they're somehow hostile. Then it becomes a problem of finding them, spying them out—and destroying their power."

"I don't think they are of the race at all," said Anna suddenly.

They looked at her in some surprise. Her strange eyes went beyond them, out to the darkness beyond the window, and her few voiced words were very quiet. "I've seen some of those writings Gunnarsson talks about," she whispered. "I've heard some of the music, seen paintings and poems and sculpture. And there's the whole way in which they've gone about all this.

"It doesn't *feel* right."

There was a longer silence now. They could sense the tension in her nerves, catch a fragment of thought more on the subconscious than the conscious level. It was weirdly convincing, the more so since all of them had bits and pieces of undeveloped abilities—and intuition or precognition or whatever it was might well be one of them.

A stocky, space-burned male spoke from a corner. "Sophoulis," he introduced himself. "I came along when Kyrenberg told me there was to be a meeting. I've got a hunch of my own about these beings."

THEY TURNED to him, and the enormous truth was in their minds even before he spoke. He nodded grimly.

Kennedy lifted his eyebrows. The gesture could have been rendered as, "What evidence have you?"

"I've been exploring on Mars lately. Geological survey. I got off by myself in the Syrtis Minor, a long ways from anyone else or any usual visitors. And I saw a spaceship.

"It came low over the sand—a huge thing, at least a thousand feet long. It was of some shining coppery metal I couldn't identify, and its design was different from anything I'd ever seen or imagined before. For one thing, it had no vision ports that I could see. For another thing, it had no jets. It just seemed to glide along with no motive power at all—and fast!

"I hunched low in the sand and tried to hide, but as soon as it was over the horizon I got out my instruments. There were some pretty sensitive detectors there. I could have spotted any ship in the Solar System by the radiations from its atomic and electronic equipment, shielded or not. But this thing didn't make the needles flicker even once. On the other hand, it was emitting quite a lot of subelectronic stuff.

"When I got back to Sandy Landing, I tried to organize an expedition into the Syrtis country. I meant to find their base. I would have gone alone if I could have gotten a Mars-tractor and the rest of the things I needed. But it was the same old story you've been telling. So sorry, all the tractors are spoken for. No, I'm afraid we can't get any from Aresport or Schiaparelli either. When I tried to buy one from a private party at an outrageous price, something tied up the communications to Earth, I couldn't get funds from my bank. And so on. I had to give up finally. And that's all I know—but I think it's enough."

They looked at each other, the supermen, and finally Kennedy laughed, a harsh bark in the explosive silence. "It's not conclusive," he said. "But it's certainly indicative. If there are beings from the stars who want to control Earth for their own purposes it would explain a lot of things.

"And in that case, we have to find them. And overcome them. Because they surely aren't going to let us go through with our own plans."

"It might be done," said Anna softly. "I think perhaps they could be found." Decision firmed her mouth. "You'll take a vacation from the lab, Will. Then our first job will be to disappear so that they can't possibly know where we are. Then we have to start looking for them—without ever revealing ourselves. And then we have to communicate the information, preferably without their knowing it."

Her eyes swept the room. "And the rest of you will have to organize an attack. I don't know yet what kind it will be. I rather think physical force would be useless against these creatures, whatever they are—men or supermen or nonhumans from the stars. But we have to be ready for anything. We'll need all the supermen of Earth ready to strike in any fashion that may be necessary."

They nodded, bleakly.

When Kennedy and Anna emerged onto the roof, only an hour or so had passed. He was vaguely surprised to find it still near the middle of the night.

He looked up to the grandly glittering stars and a shiver ran down his spine. The darkness seemed suddenly cold.

CHAPTER THREE

KENNEDY had set up a small supersonic vibrator to soundproof the room. Now they were as alone in it as they could be on Earth.

Alone, alone—it was dark outside; the early night had fallen and a heavy spring rain washed out of the lowering sky and rivered along the empty street. The dim yellow lamps gleamed on the wet pavement. A dull glow of city lights flimmered behind the looming buildings, and he could feel the rumble of traffic and sense the pulsing nervous flow of millions of lives. But in this district the ways were deserted the hotel was quiet, they were alone.

Anna was playing her violin. The music rose and fell, wailing an eerie desolation through him, swirling in the air like dead leaves hurrying before a gale. He sat at the window, staring into the rain. It ran down the glass, a slow dark stream, he seemed to be looking out at a drowned world.

The music filled the cheap, dreary room with a song that was wild and desolate, calling to the nighted sky and mumbling over a barren ground. There was darkness in the music, night and wind and a quenchless bitter longing: it hunted up and down the scale with hunger in its heart. Anna was lost in it; her eyes were unseeing and her silvery-gold head was bent over the violin as if it whispered something to her.

Kennedy sat half-listening, half-thinking his own thoughts. The long months of work were done, and now the climax was on him. Unless—unless this, too, were a blind alley; unless he should go into the building and find only emptiness. He wondered. More and more, his opponents seemed shadows, ghostly hands moving a piece on a chessboard and then retreating into darkness. He wondered if he would ever really find them.

But the trail seemed clear. It had taken a long time of slow patient investigation, feeling their way along the tangled net of the enemy organization, and the need for secrecy had hampered them still further and tautened their nerves to the breaking point. But— it could be done.

One could find out that a certain company was controlled by unknowns in another city, who in turn were puppets of someone else—not that they knew it, but economic and social strings were pulled, they reacted accordingly, and so the will of the hidden masters was done. These threads were themselves manipulated from some other place, and of course there was a reaction such that the organizations they controlled had influence on them—the sheer immensity of the web put it beyond even Kennedy's full understanding; but it worked, it worked, and with a minimum of direct supervision.

And some or other important human, politician or scientist or writer, could be shown to be under the influence of someone else whose antecedents were vague. And the superman's telepathy, maddeningly incomplete and unreliable as it was, revealed evidence of direct mental tampering in those advisors, their encephalic currents weren't quite normal—

There were other traces: a brilliantly written political treatise, a scientific paper, a symphony or painting, which somehow didn't feel right, didn't fit in with the times. One could try to locate the author or artist—and that trail ended in a controlled human or a blank anonymity, but one could still hazard a guess—

There were gaps in the trail, dead ends where no human detective could have gone further. But always Anna's intuition suggested some other approach, leaping beyond facts to a conclusion she could not justify rationally but which turned out to be right more often than not. *"The author of this paper is an amateur musician...classical mostly...I don't know why it feels as if he must be..."* And there had been Kennedy's logic, piecing together seemingly unrelated data, slowly evolving a complete picture—

And ultimately one thread led to New York and the Terran Import Company. An unostentatious firm not openly wealthy or powerful, but doing more business than it should, spreading tentacles into every corner of the Solar System. The management was all human, very respectable, entirely above suspicion. But Kennedy had seen the president and felt the curious impulses superimposed on the normal nervous rhythms, which meant that some sort of compulsion, had been put on him.

THE ALIENS had to have some kind of front. In the last analysis, they had to have a definite headquarters. More likely they had many, and the Terran Import Company was one.

And if this was the end of the long hunt then he had to enter their stronghold and find out what they really were and try to get back alive.

"Tonight," he said. "Tonight I'll go in; the building is empty after midnight except for a watchman. I've made certain of that."

He felt the small subelectronic communicator in his pocket. Anna had another tuned to his, and one of their trunks held a larger unit, which could reach the Council all over Earth. Given one minute to flash his information to her, he could let all the race know who the enemy was. After that—

Well, he hoped to escape with his life and sanity, but it didn't matter too much. Life under that shadow would not be worth a great deal to a being with his power compulsion.

The supermen had to control Earth, otherwise life became an empty farce and it was better to lie in the ground.

Anna put her violin aside and came over to him. "Still not a trace," she murmured. "We've run them down, I'm sure of it, but still not a hint what they are. Who are they, to hide that well?"

Kennedy shrugged. "Who knows? They could be from any of the stars."

"Maybe. But still—it doesn't feel that way. They don't really act the way aliens should. There's something—terrestrial—about them, Will. I don't know what it is, but I know it's there."

He smiled crookedly. "But you don't like the theory that they're of our race or a similar mutation," he pointed out.

"No. That doesn't seem right either, somehow." She shuddered and laid a hand on his. The lazy mockery had worn from her in the last months, her cool self-possession had dropped away and she was frightened. "I can't imagine what they are. I just can't imagine anything that fits."

"I still favor the notion that they're from the stars," he said, "another mutation like ours just violates probability."

"We ourselves do that," she replied.

"True. It's still the most baffling scientific mystery I know of." He looked out into the rainy night and his laugh was harsh. "Why are we trying to track down these aliens? What do we care what they're like? We still don't really know what we are."

"Doesn't Lomonosov think our mutation involves some new biological principle?"

"Yes. But he's never been able to work out just what the principle is," Kennedy swung around to face her. "Look, let's go over everything we know about ourselves. Once again, for the millionth time. It may give us a clue. It may hint at what the aliens are."

HE TICKED the points off on his fingers. "Externally, we look human, except that some of us lack wisdom teeth and little toes and all males have a tendency to early baldness. Internally, we're definitely not human; we're superior to man in many ways. We lack the vermiform appendix, of course; the arch of the foot is stronger; the vertebrae of the lumbar region have fused; the pelvis is different; the sinus drains downward; certain muscles differ, the circulatory system is more efficient; the eyes are keener and stand the strain of close work better—in general, we're mechanically superior to man. We do, though, have less sense of smell—again, about what you'd expect in the next stage of human evolution. There is also a tendency to brachycephaly and a tall, slender build though that does have exceptions.

"Metabolism is different, more efficient as a rule. We have partial voluntary control of involuntary functions when we want it; for instance, we can set up a nerve bloc to cut off pain impulses from the brain, and a few of us seem able even to control regeneration—it's handy to be able to will the absorption of a tumor! We can handle all this because we have the intelligence and self-control to make proper use of it, which other animals, including most men, couldn't. A primitive human who could will to cease feeling pain would simply ignore those danger signals, and soon die.

"The nervous system is the vital point of difference. Our brains aren't larger than human, but they're better organized. We don't go insane, though we're not all free from neuroses, without therapy. The average I.Q. insofar as it means anything in relation to us, is well over 200, and we are capable of totally different types of thought from human logic. And then we have fragments of still other abilities, telepathy and precognition and perfect intuition and more—but all in the most rudimentary form, as if we were still evolving them.

"And, of course, we're sterile." Bitterness twisted his mouth. "We're sterile!"

"And why is that?" she asked softly, though she had heard the answer often enough before.

"It's a matter of chromosome defects. A union of gametes, in our case, just doesn't produce a viable cell. I don't think there's anything that can be done about it. Our best bet would be some form of synthetic reproduction, exogenetic development of artificially created cells." He made a wry face. "I don't like that much better."

The rain poured down, slow and dark and still.

"Now as to our origin," went on Kennedy after a moment, "we're all born of human parents—human mothers, at least. We appear in all races with about the same—low—frequency, and usually don't suspect our nature until one of the Council's investigators finds us, routes us through therapy, then takes us into the organization. Feeling ourselves, then—casting off the armor and fictitious loyalties of most humans, we're glad to join our own species.

"It was only about fifty years ago that a few of us reached the true conclusion as to their nature and began to look for others. Since then we've only found about three thousand, out of the Solar System's four billion. It's no high percentage, but we think the ordinary rate of birth is enough to maintain our numbers.

"A few facts have come out: A large proportion of us are illegitimate children with mysterious fathers who have since disappeared; and there's excellent reason to suspect that even the married women who bore the rest did not have those children by their husbands. Illegitimacy is getting so common these days that we've never been able to track down any of these unknown men. Naturally, it would be wonderful to find a few fertile supermen, but I doubt that there are any. Our fathers, I think, carry some mutation, which combined with the normal human inheritance produces one of us, but their phenotype is probably quite human. It's well known that such crosses differ more radically from the norm than either parent; in fact, I think a good many defective births have the same fathers—unsuccessful crosses. At any rate, the hybrid human-semihuman is sterile like many other hybrids in the biological world.

"Sterile!" The bitterness was suddenly raw in his voice. "By all chaos, sterile! Our kind can reach the stars, but it can't do what the humblest plant can do; it can't maintain itself."

"Why?" she asked.

"WHY? WHO knows? Apart from the simple biology of it, I don't know of any deeper reason. Unless—well, other species have reached a peak and then suddenly declined and become extinct. It may be the same with man. There may be some basic reason why the ultimate development of a race must be sterile—an Indian summer before the long winter comes." He nodded. "Yes, I rather think it's something like that."

"But we aren't the end of evolution, Will. We know we could go higher. All those half-abilities we have—they must mean something."

"Uh-huh. But what? Humankind doesn't seem to have changed appreciably for the last half-million years—maybe million. Why is that? Why should it be static so long, when it had been one of Earth's most rapidly evolving lines before? And then why should we suddenly appear, all in one jump, which violates every law of biological probability? I don't know, Anna."

"I don't think we are the first," she said. "I think members of the race have been born for a long time, but they never knew who they were. There have been sterile geniuses in the past—at least, they never had children. Da Vinci, Roger Bacon—I wonder. I wonder how lonely they must have been."

"That sounds more reasonable," he admitted. "But even so, the birth of something so radically different from normal human stock—but no matter. We may find out someday. There's this problem here to solve first."

He got up and paced restlessly. "I thought maybe reviewing the facts would help me somehow with this," he said. "If there were a chance of a similar mutation, a third species of genus homo—but I can't see that. As you said, the thought just doesn't feel right."

His face was haggard as he looked out at the rain. "We've got to overcome them," he said between his teeth. "We have no choice, Anna. The need to control is in us. We can't fit into human society, it doesn't have goals or a structure suitable for us, so we have to dominate it. Not tyrannically, even though we can rule man better than he can rule himself. But the road humans take must be one that does not block ours. And if these aliens dispute our road—they have to go. For the sake of our sanity, they have to go."

The night brooded enormously over him, the dark was filled with the slow senseless power of rain spilling from the sky, mindless inorganic night of loneliness and despair. He stood waiting for the hours to end, sunk into the pit of the night.

Anna took up her violin and began to play again.

CHAPTER FOUR

AFTER THE rain, there was fog swirling through the hollow canyons of streets, blurring the lamps and the few shadowy vehicles which slipped by. Kennedy felt glad of the mist, though he knew it wouldn't hide him from the watchers of the enemy.

He stood in an alley across the street from the Terran Import Building, straining his perceptions into the wet gray dark. The building wasn't large as such structures went, but it loomed black and monstrous in the fog; it seemed a crouching beast waiting for him. He fought back the tension that thrummed along every nerve and groped for signs of life.

He had watched the place for several nights running. It seemed to be deserted after twelve or one, and it would be no trick to get inside. Only—was it really empty?

His sense of nervous energy reached out through the fog. He could feel the vibrations of the watchman, an ordinary untampered human making a sleepy round—no danger there. But what else was it that thrummed and pulsed in the building, just on the limits of his perception?

He strove to identify that deep steady wave, but it eluded him, maddeningly. It wasn't an electric or atomic machine of any sort, it wasn't—anything. He couldn't even be sure whether it really existed outside his own strained imagination.

But of course they would have unknown mechanisms operating, something subelectronic perhaps. It might be some sort of barrier, a death trap for the curious—worse yet, something that would seize control of a mind—but that was a chance he had to take.

If he could get in, if he could find *their* central offices and go through whatever files and apparatus there might be—even if no direct evidence of their origin and nature were present, he and Anna should easily be able to deduce enough from whatever they found to serve as a basis of action for the race.

The race, the race—the Councillors crouched over their receivers; the supermen waiting around the planet with their tremendous hidden weapons—the night was full of their tension. Strange struggle, beneath the surface of man's peaceful world! Briefly, Kennedy wondered what powers and intrigues might not make up the whole of reality, what hidden wars might be going on between beings whose existence even the supermen and their opponents did not suspect.

But no time for that, no time. He was going in.

He whispered into the communicator: "All clear, I think."

"Will—" Anna's anxious breath trembled in his ear. "Will— don't go in there."

"I have to, Anna."

"I—it isn't you alone, Will. It's all of us I have a feeling that we—we won't *like* what we find out tonight—"

He smiled wistfully in the dark and the drifting fog. "I don't like it now," he said. "But this is enough now. The next time I call, it will be with information of—some kind!" With a sudden tenderness he had never really felt before: "Goodbye, Anna."

Then quickly he walked across the street to the entrance of the building.

THE DOOR was locked, of course. That meant nothing, the tumblers clicked back from his magnetic controller and he stepped through into the lobby. It was in shadow, only a dim night-light burning—empty, empty.

He slipped over to the stairs and went up them at a rapid cat-footed pace. One hand lay in his pocket, the fingers wrapped about one of the supermen's small deadly energy guns. He knew how futile it was likely to be but the cold metal gave him animal comfort.

The vibrations of the machine were stronger now. It must lie somewhere near the top of the building, which was also the most logical place for the offices of the enemy. Probably no human was allowed up there.

Human! He felt the life-energy of the watchman, coming down the stairs, and flattened himself against the wall. It was best not to be too obtrusive physically, though—

It was easy. His mind seemed abnormally strong; it surged forth and gripped the old man's brain with impalpable fingers. It was just a matter of cutting off optical perception of that area where he stood. The watchman never saw him; he went on downstairs in his slow fashion, unknowing.

Kennedy stood looking after the retreating back. It wasn't often that he could control any portion of a human's brain that directly, but the tension that keyed him now had sharpened and strengthened all his faculties to a terrific pitch. If only he could rely on that ability, could have it all the time—

But he didn't. It was partial, sporadic, not really controllable. The physiologists said it was a new brain center, a mutation of the parapsychological powers possessed in very slight degree by humans; but superman didn't really have much more than *homo sapiens.*

Why not? Why are we incomplete? Why are we sterile, why has evolution come to a halt in us when there is so much left to do? How is it that we are born at all, who are our fathers, why should they have been mutated either? So many new abilities in one mutation just doesn't make biological sense.

But no time for that now, there's more urgent work at hand.

He went on up the stairs, flight after flight winding up into darkness. The building was silent, empty, but the monstrous nonauditory thrum of the machine filled his being now, shouted within him, raised shuddering echoes in the atoms of the walls.

Upward, upward. Now the top floor lay ahead, and it was closed off by a locked door. Kennedy opened it and stepped through into a corridor.

It lay blank and bare before him, lit by a couple of dull nightlights, full of shadows and silence. And the machine.

And the machine! The terrific pulsations shook his being now, quivered in every cell of him. Incredible that humans went blindly on their way, in and out of the building, and never sensed it, never dreamed of its existence or of the monstrous powers that laired in this hall. Fantastic, that the rulers of the world should be here.

No—not here. The floor was empty, there was no life anywhere in its stillness, only he had movement through the twilight. He breathed a shuddering sigh of relief. The enemy was gone. He was safe.

HE WENT down the corridor toward the ordinary glass-fronted door from behind which came the subliminal drone of the machine. His footsteps echoed hollowly between the walls; his shadow followed him, rippling over the bare polished stone. He could not shake off the irrational feeling that it was a fetch, a watchful ghost dogging him down a road along which there would be no return.

The vibrations of the machine must have affected his nerves. Grasping for sanity, he paused at a window to look over the city. Beyond the darkness of this area, it glowed and flamed with light; it was filled with the life of wakeful millions, the muted hum of traffic came faintly to his preternaturally sharpened hearing.

Mankind, unsuspecting mankind going about its ways while he stood in a tower of darkness, while the night was filled with a hidden struggle for the rule of those witless herds. Man, father to the superman, not knowing his sons for what they were.

But are we his sons? Is such a mutation even possible?

What, after all, was the most logical way for superman to evolve? Not in one fantastic mutation of unknown thousands of genes all working to produce the same result; the very formulation was an insult to the laws of probability. No, *homo superior* should have evolved from *homo sapiens* in the same way that other species had evolved from a parent stock—by isolation of a few not very different mutants, selection and intensification of the new traits, new mutations gradually appearing and being lost if they were unfavorable, being incorporated if they gave some advantage.

Like always tended to mate with like. Even in the earliest times, there must have been a strong tendency for the most intelligent people, or those differing from the norm in any fashion to get mates similar to themselves. If at an early stage such a kith had withdrawn from the mainstream of humanity—

And then as time went on and the differences became greater; the new stock would perhaps deliberately seek to incorporate such humans as showed similar traits into itself. Particularly if its high intelligence led it to early knowledge of the principles of inheritance. Thus, for a long time, the developing superman stock would be mingling unsuspected with *homo sapiens*, seeking out desirable humans for inclusion into the group—until finally the differences became so great that mating was no longer possible. Even then, *homo superior* could control *homo sapiens* whenever necessary, though probably the new species would hold itself aloof most of the time. It would have so little in common with the ancestral stock.

And that would also explain why the human genus, which had hither-to-been evolving at one of the highest speeds known to paleontology, should suddenly have become nearly static. There had been no appreciable change in man for the past half-million or even million years. Of course not—*homo superior* had been skimming off the cream of the crop!

It did not explain the fact that *homo superior* had *not* appeared in that fashion, that he was, instead, born to normal humans with all his alienage given him at one incredible step.

Nor did it say anything about the unknowns, except to suggest that perhaps they were another type of mutation. How unhuman could they be? *We're bad enough!*

But I'm wasting time.

The flashing thought, which had taken perhaps half a second, died within Kennedy. He threw back his shoulders, turned from the window, and walked up to the door.

It was locked with—something new. Something that held it shut but was not material, a binding force. Kennedy would have sworn if he had been human. As it was, he took out his energy gun and cut the door open. Let them realize that he had been here; it would be too late then.

THE ROOM beyond seemed strangely unreal. There was a cold white light streaming from walls and ceiling and floor, filling the very air. He had no way of gauging distances, the room might have been small or it might have reached out beyond the edge of the sky.

His eyes swung to the machine. It crouched low on the floor, a massive thing with angles and curves in its dark metal that did not seem to obey any sane geometrical laws. Multidimensional—what *were* the builders?

No time, no time. He looked about for other evidence, a filing cabinet, a desk drawer, anything. Yes, there was a strangely shimmering globe seeming to hang in midair. As he looked, the vague swirl of formlessness within it coalesced into symbols.

No language of Earth, that. He decided that it was somehow responsive to telepathic impulses, throwing the desired information onto a screen at the owner's mental command. He thought at it, *What is the origin and nature of your builders?* and his mind trembled as he did.

The symbols were meaningless, but he photographed them with a tiny microcamera. The superman philologists could, with the help of their electronic semantic analyzers, break down any rational language in short order. He flashed other questions: *What are their powers? What do they want on Earth? What do they know about us?,* and watched the symbols change.

His glee was boundless. Here was all the information that they needed. The supermen would know—and knowing, they could act, and—

And—

He turned at the sudden blaze within his nerves. His gun leaped into his hand. And then his fingers went limp, the weapon clattered to the floor and he was locked into physical paralysis.

The being that stepped from the machine looked manlike, but his magnificently domed head was bald and the great golden eyes held such a frightful intensity of power that Kennedy could not meet them, he cried out in terror.

The thoughts roared in his skull:

—It was about time you knew. Now that you have come this far, you may as well go back to your friends and warn them. They have their place in the— ?—plan, but it will be useless for them to oppose us. We can stop all their energies, freeze their minds, and cast them down to ruin. Accept the fact. Accept us as the rulers of Earth.

Grim amusement tinged the thought:—*The servant warned me and I came. But it was hardly necessary. The records would have told you the truth.*

Incredible that you did not suspect before. But you dared not realize the truth. It was staring you in the eyes, but your subconscious minds would not accept the conclusion.

—*You are essentially right about the origin of homo superior…Man and your breed have a place in our scheme, but you will never be able to understand its entirety.*

—*There are not many of us on Earth, and most of those are males. Others are on the great worlds of the Galaxy where proper—?—development is possible. Since we can easily disguise ourselves, and we are so made that human women are not repulsively alien, there are occasional hybrids.*

Hybrids, with only part of the powers of their fathers. Like most interspecies hybrids, sterile.

—*I pity you, half-brother. Go back to your kind now. Live your lives. As long as you do not trespass on forbidden ground, we will leave you alone. Goodbye.*

The steel grip on his mind was lifted. Kennedy stumbled, fell to the floor, looked numbly up at the figure that loomed over him against the blaze of energy from the machine.

"Father," he whispered. "Father."

THE END

If you've enjoyed this book, you will not want to miss these terrific titles…

ARMCHAIR SCI-FI & HORROR DOUBLE NOVELS, $12.95 each

D-71   **THE DEEP END** by Gregory Luce
            TO WATCH BY NIGHT by Robert Moore Williams

D-72   **SWORDSMAN OF LOST TERRA** by Poul Anderson
            PLANET OF GHOSTS by David V. Reed

D-73   **MOON OF BATTLE** by J. J. Allerton
            THE MUTANT WEAPON by Murray Leinster

D-74   **OLD SPACEMEN NEVER DIE!** John Jakes
            RETURN TO EARTH by Bryan Berry

D-75   **THE THING FROM UNDERNEATH** by Milton Lesser
            OPERATION INTERSTELLAR by George O. Smith

D-76   **THE BURNING WORLD** by Algis Budrys
            FOREVER IS TOO LONG by Chester S. Geier

D-77   **THE COSMIC JUNKMAN** by Rog Phillips
            THE ULTIMATE WEAPON by John W. Campbell

D-78   **THE TIES OF EARTH** by James H. Schmitz
            CUE FOR QUIET by Thomas L. Sherred

D-79   **SECRET OF THE MARTIANS** by Paul W. Fairman
            THE VARIABLE MAN by Philip K. Dick

D-80   **THE GREEN GIRL** by Jack Williamson
            THE ROBOT PERIL by Don Wilcox

ARMCHAIR SCIENCE FICTION CLASSICS, $12.95 each

C-25   **THE STAR KINGS**
            by Edmond Hamilton

C-26   **NOT IN SOLITUDE**
            by Kenneth Gantz

C-32   **PROMETHEUS II**
            by S. J. Byrne

ARMCHAIR SCIENCE FICTION & HORROR GEMS SERIES, $12.95 each

G-7   **SCIENCE FICTION GEMS, Vol. Seven**
            Jack Sharkey and others

G-8   **HORROR GEMS, Vol. Eight**
            Seabury Quinn and others

www.ingramcontent.com/pod-product-compliance
Lightning Source LLC
Chambersburg PA
CBHW050324200626
46810CB00022B/1251